CANDLES

FOR

THE

DEAD

ALSO BY FRANK SMITH

CANDLES

FOR

THE

DEAD

FRANK SMITH

ST. MARTIN'S PRESS  NEW YORK

Library of Congress Cataloging-in-Publication Data

Smith, Frank, 1927–
    Candles for the dead / Frank Smith. — 1st U.S. ed.
        p. cm.
    ISBN 0-312-20771-9
    I. Title
PR9199.3.S55155C36   1999
813'.54—dc21

99-29773
CIP

First published in Great Britain by Constable & Company Ltd.

First U.S. Edition: August 1999

10   9   8   7   6   5   4   3   2   1

This one is for Christine and Daniel,
two of the best.

Chapter 1

Monday – 13 May

The woman looked ill. The bus driver had been watching her through the mirror. Her face was pale and she held herself stiffly, arms clasped tightly around herself as if she were cold. Hollow-eyed, staring blankly out of the window. She'd been like that ever since she got on outside the bank.

He slowed for the T-junction ahead, then wheeled the bus into Compton Road without stopping. There was never much traffic out here at this time of day.

He'd been surprised to see her after all this time. Surprised and pleased. He'd missed her these past few months. He thought she must have moved or gone away, but then he saw her coming out of the bank one day as he made his regular stop. But she didn't get on. She was with a man and they'd walked straight past.

This was her stop, opposite the church. He liked this part of the run. It was quiet out here on the edge of the town. Nice bit of country. Not that it would remain so for long with the new housing estates creeping closer every day. His eyes went to the mirror again.

Good-looking woman. He didn't know her name. Well, not her last name. Beth something-or-other. Sometimes, on the last leg the journey, she used to move up front and chat. He'd looked forward to that. Then she'd stopped coming and he'd missed her.

But she hadn't even noticed him tonight when she got on. Just shuffled past along with all the others to take a seat half-way down the bus. He sighed as he pulled into the stop and waited for her to get off. But she didn't move. Just sat there staring off into space as if she were miles away.

'Farrow Lane,' he called loudly, watching her through the mirror. There was no one else on the bus. The woman stirred and glanced around, then scrambled to her feet. Their eyes met in the mirror.

'Sorry. I . . . Sorry.' She moved swiftly to the door, stumbled, but recovered quickly as she grasped the rail and stepped down.

'You all right?' he called after her, but she was gone. He watched as she crossed the road and set off down Farrow Lane. He supposed she'd be all right...

He glanced at the time as he pulled away. Four minutes late. He'd have to put his foot down if he was to get back by half-past.

Farrow Lane was less than a quarter of a mile long, but tonight it seemed endless to Beth Smallwood. Her head ached, and her legs felt as if they would let her down at any moment. She just hoped she could get inside without meeting anyone, especially Mrs Turvey, her next-door neighbour.

There were no houses between the church and the bottom of Farrow Lane; just fields on either side and the four cottages at the far end. Farm cottages until they were taken over when Broadminster pushed its boundaries southward. Now they were council houses. Small and a bit cramped, but snug enough, and the rent was within Beth's means. Just.

The smell of rain was in the air. She shivered and drew her coat around her. It was cold for May – at least everybody said so. She had barely noticed, what with all the worry.

Beth reached the cottage, unlocked the door and slipped inside, then stood there panting as if she'd run the length of Farrow Lane. Her legs began to shake and she knew that if she didn't force herself to move she would collapse there on the floor.

A bath! A steaming hot bath. The thought had been uppermost in her mind ever since she'd left work. Please God don't let the immersion heater play up again tonight. Not tonight. She would use the crystals she'd had since Christmas, her 'gift' beneath the tree at work last year.

Beth pulled off her coat and hung it up behind the door. Wearily, she climbed the stairs, stripped off her clothes and dropped them in a heap beside the bed. The old grey dressing-gown was warm and prickly against her skin, and yet she shivered as she surveyed the clothing on the floor. The dress wasn't all that old, she thought sadly, but she could never wear it again. Abruptly, she bent and scooped up all the clothes and took them with her as she made her way downstairs to the tiny bathroom off the kitchen.

Steam rose from the water pouring from the old-fashioned spout, and Beth offered up a silent prayer of thanks as she waited impatiently for the old claw-footed tub to fill. It seemed to take forever. She poured in some crystals, but nothing seemed to be happening. Impulsively, she poured in half the box, and suddenly the bath was full of bubbles, and the smell of lavender rose with the steam to fill the tiny room. Beth shut off the tap, put on a shower cap, and climbed over the side.

The hot water stung as she eased herself down, but she didn't care. It felt good. She leaned back, resting her head against the rim, and let the heat soak into her tired limbs. The pain was so exquisite . . .

A choking sob escaped her lips, and tears rolled down her cheeks.

Her fingers remained poised above the keyboard as she stared at the screen. £5000. The cursor pulsed insistently, waiting for the next command. She felt hot; her mouth was dry, and yet her fingers felt like lumps of ice. It had been bad enough the first time, but this . . . A sheen of sweat glistened on her forehead and the figures blurred before her eyes. She breathed in deeply; forced herself to remain calm.

Oh, God! She'd forgotten about the change she'd meant to make to cover the initial payments. After that . . . ? She refused to think about what might happen then.

Better make it six thousand – no, seven, she thought recklessly. She could change the form and it would give her more time. That's all she really needed. Time. Once Lenny was on his feet again, she'd pay it back.

Pay it back? How? taunted the small voice that had been mocking her for days. You can't manage now. Where are you going to get £12,000 – plus interest? Lenny spent the last lot on that motorbike, remember?

'But I need it, Mam,' he'd explained. 'How can I get work if I haven't got transport?'

Beth sighed. Lenny was right, of course. Not that he'd found work yet, but he would, she assured herself; he would in time. Once he was completely off the drugs. And he was trying. Still, she wished he'd saved at least something to pay off that awful man who'd got him into drugs in the first place. It was wicked the way he'd taken advantage. And yet, she thought guiltily, perhaps she was the one to blame for not noticing that something was wrong.

'I was feeling sort of down, Mam,' Lenny had explained. 'You know, not being in work, like, and tramping round every day, looking. I just needed something to pick me up a bit, that's all. This bloke I know swore the stuff

was harmless and I believed him.' Later, Lenny said, when he realized what was happening to him, the man had shown his true colours and demanded payment for the drugs. When Lenny couldn't pay, the man said he'd have to work off the debt by supplying others.

'But I won't do it, Mam,' he'd told her fervently. 'I won't do what he did to me. It's hard, but I'll kick the habit and I'll pay him off. It's the only way. But I have to have at least five thousand quid. You've got to help me, Mam.'

£5000! He might as well have said five million. 'But can't the police . . .?'

'The police?' Lenny scoffed. 'They can't touch him. He's got them in his pocket, and like as not they'd have me fitted up instead. Not that it would ever come to trial if I grassed because I'd be dead.'

Beth felt the chill of a deeper fear as Lenny's words echoed inside her head. She knew she had to help him no matter what the cost.

He'll do it! she said fiercely beneath her breath. He just needs a chance, that's all.

The figure on the screen changed, her fingers moving as if by their own volition. All she had to do now was touch one key. Still she hesitated. It was not too late.

Oh, God! she prayed silently, help me. Please help me. She closed her eyes and held her breath as if waiting for an answer, but all she could hear was a pounding in her ears like waves crashing on the shore.

A hand descended on her shoulder and she screamed. At least it sounded like a scream inside her head. In fact it was little more than a startled squeak that passed unnoticed by those around her. But the thudding of her heart was real. The noise inside her head was real, and the beads of sweat that seemed to burst from every pore were very real indeed. Her finger brushed a key. The figures vanished. Had he noticed?

'Sorry if I startled you, Beth.' The words were spoken softly, but he might as well have shouted. She felt the rush of colour to her face, and sat there frozen like a rabbit in a headlight's glare.

Arthur Gresham remained behind her, both hands now resting lightly on her shoulders. She could smell his after-shave; smell the nicotine on his fingers. Broad fingers that moved gently, stroking her shoulders as he felt her tremble.

'When you have a moment, Beth. I'd like to see you in my office.'

Oh, God! He'd been watching her. So intent had she been on what she was doing that she hadn't heard or seen him approach. But then, she thought bitterly, that's how he was. Silent as a cat and just as predatory. He'd been standing there behind her, waiting for her to commit herself.

10

Had she cleared the screen in time? A cold, hard knot gripped her stomach and she wanted to be sick.

She tried to speak, but no sound came out. She swallowed hard and tried again. 'Yes, Mr Gresham,' she whispered. His hands lingered on her shoulders, and then he was gone.

Beth shivered. Without thinking, she shut the computer down – something she never did until she'd finished for the day. But then, she supposed she was finished for the day: the day, the week, the year, forever. She rose unsteadily to her feet, tugged at her dress with nervous fingers, and pushed her chair beneath the desk.

There, all neat and tidy. She retrieved her handbag from the bottom drawer and opened it. The compact was in her hand before she realized what she was doing. She put it back. After all, what was the point?

Her soft dark eyes swept the office. It seemed as if there should be something more than this to mark the end of a career, she thought sadly, but no one so much as glanced at her as she moved toward the door.

Rachel Fairmont, Gresham's secretary, kept her eyes fixed firmly on her typing as Beth went past her desk. She knew, Beth thought. And yet how could she? How could anybody know?

Arthur Gresham was waiting for her, standing behind his desk with his back toward her when she entered. Feet spread slightly apart, he stood looking out of the window, hands behind his back like a captain on the bridge in full command.

'Close the door and sit down, Beth,' he said briskly.

Beth crossed the floor and sat down in one of the deep, upholstered chairs facing the desk. The chairs, like Arthur Gresham's massive desk, were symbols, not so much of his status in the banking hierarchy, but of the way he saw his own position there. He'd bought and paid for all the furniture himself.

Beth sank into the chair's depths and felt trapped by its warm embrace. Blood pounded in her ears with every heartbeat, and she felt as if she were going to faint. She wanted to get up and run from this place, but her legs had turned to water and she couldn't move. Sweat trickled down between her breasts and she was sure there must be dark patches on her dress. She folded her arms, not daring to look down.

Gresham turned and stood behind his chair, hands resting lightly on the padded back as he looked down at her. In his younger days, Arthur Gresham had been considered a handsome man; handsome and – although the term had not yet been coined – upwardly mobile. But years of self-indulgence had blurred his features and made them coarse. Receding hair

11

and a double chin combined to make his face more round, while his fondness for fine food and wine had transformed a once-trim waistline into a not inconsiderable paunch.

By the time he was thirty, it had become apparent to both him and the world of banking that he lacked the drive and initiative to climb the corporate ladder, although Gresham himself never quite gave up hope that things would change. But being a practical man, he set out to woo and win Lilian Cavendish, a rather plain woman whose personal fortune and social connections more than made up for her lack of physical charms. Since Lilian's only passion was breeding and raising Shetland Sheepdogs, and Arthur's main aims in life were self-indulgence and an entrée into Lilian's social circle, they'd rubbed along quite amicably over the years.

But, while Gresham grudgingly acknowledged his limitations in the business world, he still considered himself to be irresistible to women. The fact that his advances were, more often than not, rebuffed bothered him not a whit.

Beth cringed beneath his gaze. Gresham had the irritating habit of pursing his lips in a judicial way before almost every utterance, and he did that now. They were moist lips, pink and soft, and he spoke with just the faintest hint of a lisp. He took off his glasses, flicked out a handkerchief, and began to polish them.

'I've been keeping my eye on you for quite some time, Beth,' he said sternly. He breathed on the lenses and polished them again.

Oh, God. He was going to drag it out. Get every last bit of pleasure out of it. But then, what else could she have expected from Arthur Gresham? She didn't have to take this. She could simply get up and leave ...

Suddenly, the enormity of what she'd done hit her like a landslide. It wasn't just a matter of dismissal, was it? She had committed a crime. It was a matter for the police. Panic seized her. Perhaps they were already there, waiting for his signal to come in. She found herself bathed in sweat once more as she imagined two burly men in uniform marching her through the office in full view of everyone. She felt her senses slipping, and forced herself to breathe deeply. Keep calm. Keep calm, she told herself. Don't give him the satisfaction of seeing you're afraid.

He was speaking again.

'... choice was between you and Harry Beecham, and it hasn't been an easy one. After all, Harry has been with us a long time, but we do have to be realistic in these changing times. Your position will be that of "acting" manager of small business loans for the first six months, of course. That, as you know, is standard bank policy, but I have every confidence in you,

12

Beth, and I'm sure that the board will confirm the position at the end of that time.'

Gresham put the handkerchief away, slipped his glasses back in place, and smiled beningly. 'With my recommendation, of course,' he added almost as an afterthought.

He moved out from behind the desk and began to wander about the room. 'It will mean a rise, of course. I might even say a substantial one, although I should warn you that, due to constraints on our budget this year, we will not be getting a replacement to fill your old job. In other words, Beth, we're combining Harry's old job with yours, so you'll have to learn to delegate more.'

This couldn't be happening. What kind of sadistic game was Gresham playing? Harry Beecham wasn't . . . Suddenly it became clear. Harry's strange behaviour this morning. She'd thought at the time that it must have something to do with his wife; that something had happened to Helen and he'd had to rush home. He'd been in such a state when he emerged from Gresham's office. He'd looked positively grey.

She'd tried to ask him what was wrong, but he'd walked right past her; cut her dead. She'd thought it must be because he was so worried about Helen, but now . . . Her hands flew to her mouth. Gresham must have told him that she would be taking his job, and he'd thought she knew!

Arthur Gresham came to a halt in front of her. He leaned back against the desk and regarded her quizzically. He seemed amused by her continued silence. 'Surprised, Beth?' he asked softly. 'Cat got your tongue?'

Her mind was racing. She hadn't been discovered. It was like a gift from heaven. She would be in charge. No one would question her now. Not even Gresham. A loan could be extended almost indefinitely at the discretion of the loans manager as long as the interest was paid. It would give her the one thing she needed most, time to find a way to pay back what she'd st – borrowed. Perhaps her prayers had been answered after all. Something had stayed her hand today, and she realized now that it would have been madness to proceed. She could never have paid that much money back. Lenny would just have to . . .

But what about Harry? The thought came unbidden, and Beth was filled with shame. Here she was congratulating herself on her good fortune, while poor Harry had lost his job. It must have come like a thunderbolt to him. He hadn't a hope of getting similar work in today's market, not at his age.

'Beth?' Gresham reached out and cupped a hand beneath her chin. She found herself responding to the pressure and rose to her feet.

13

He was very close. The chair behind her prevented her from moving away. 'I – I don't know what to say,' she stammered. 'I mean, I didn't expect...I'm not sure I'm...' She floundered helplessly.

'Up to it?' he said. 'I wouldn't have recommended promoting you if I had any doubts about your ability, Beth. And I shall be here to help you.'

She tried to draw away, but his hands caught her by the shoulders. The edge of the chair pressed hard against the back of her legs.

Gresham was looking at her, frowning. 'Well?' he said impatiently. 'I thought you'd be pleased.'

'Oh, I am pleased,' she said hastily. 'I just don't know what to say, that's all. It was so – so unexpected, Mr Gresham.' Sweat prickled on her skin. Don't let me do anything to make him change his mind, she pleaded silently. Gresham had thrown her a lifeline, and she must grasp it with both hands. 'Believe me, I am grateful, Mr Gresham.'

Arthur Gresham gripped her shoulders tighter. 'I was sure you would be, Beth,' he said softly. His small pink tongue moistened his lips. 'We'll be working closer together, you and I, much closer, and I can't tell you how much I look forward to that. I'm sure you must feel the same.' His hands slid down her arms and his fingers brushed her breasts.

She closed her eyes. She should have known, she told herself bitterly. There was always a price. Arthur Gresham was known throughout the office as a man with roving hands, but so far she'd been able to avoid the worst of his casual explorations. She felt his hands slip round her waist; felt him pull her toward him; felt his hardness press against her body. Faintly, through the roar inside her head, she heard his voice again, soft, insistent against her ear.

'You do want the job, don't you, Beth? I mean, if I thought...'

She forced herself to speak. 'Oh, yes, Mr Gresham,' she said hoarsely, loathing herself as she did so. 'I do want the job.'

Abruptly, he let her go, and she stood there like a statue, immobile, eyes still closed, hardly daring to breathe as he moved away from her.

Reprieve! She opened her eyes; forced herself to move. 'I think I'd better be going...' The words died on her lips as she saw him at the door; watched him turn the key, then take it from the lock and put it in his pocket. He smiled and moved toward her. 'No one will disturb us now,' he said.

'Mr Gresham,' she gasped feebly. 'I...'

His hot hands slid over her body, drawing her dress up over her hips as he pulled her to him. 'Call me Arthur,' he murmured as his mouth came down hard on hers.

14

Beth sat there in the half-light in the tiny cubicle, head pounding, every limb quivering as she tried to erase the last half-hour from her memory. She felt sick; she felt soiled, but somewhere inside her head a small voice kept saying: It was your choice, Beth. It's your fault. You could have said no.

How could I? she thought despairingly. There was no choice if she wished to keep her job and avoid discovery. How she had managed to walk through the outer office past the girls without collapsing she did not know. Tears rolled slowly down her cheeks and she tasted salt. She must look a mess. She took a tissue from her handbag and scrubbed furiously at her face.

The door of the Ladies opened and someone came in.

'Beth? Beth, you in there? Are you all right?' Rachel Fairmont sounded hesitant, as if she were not quite sure whether she should be asking.

Beth forced herself to speak. 'I'm fine. Really, I'm fine, Rachel. Just came over a little faint, that's all. I'll be all right in a minute.'

'Mr Gresham told me. Congratulations.'

Beth couldn't decide whether or not the words were meant. She and Rachel had worked in the same office for several years, but even though they were of a similar age, Beth didn't think she would ever really know the woman. Rachel was friendly enough in a way, but she didn't encourage familiarity. She kept very much to herself, and she never mixed with the younger girls. Some of the girls had taken to calling her the 'old maid' behind her back, especially Ginny Holbrook.

'Bet she's never had a man,' Ginny had observed dismissively. 'You can always tell. She wouldn't know what to do with it if it was offered on a plate.' Ginny Holbrook was nineteen; Rachel Fairmont was thirty-five, two years younger than Beth herself, and Beth sometimes wondered what was being said about her behind her back.

She became aware that Rachel was talking to her again. 'Sorry. What was that, Rachel?'

'I said it's a shame about Harry. I've always rather liked him. But then, we've all known for months that there would be redundancies. I wonder what he'll do now? Did you know you were being considered for his job?'

'No. No, I didn't. Not until Mr Gresham had me in his office.' Beth caught her breath. What a stupid thing to say! She hurried on. 'It came as a complete surprise. I never expected it at all.'

'Are you quite sure you're all right?' asked Rachel sharply. 'You don't sound it.'

'I'm fine. Really, Rachel, I'm fine.' Beth dabbed at her face again. She couldn't put it off any longer. Rachel wasn't going to go away. Beth stood up, straightened her clothing and flushed the toilet. The latch of the door was stiff and she had to push hard to get it open. She kept her head down as she made for the wash-basin and turned on both taps at once.

'See? I'm fine,' she said over her shoulder. 'It's just that I wasn't expecting it, that's all, and I came over a bit faint.' She glanced into the mirror and wished she hadn't. Her lips were swollen, her face shone like a beacon, and her hair was a mess. She caught a glimpse of Rachel's critical eyes upon her, and ducked her head quickly. 'Silly, of course, but when I came in here I burst out crying.' She splashed water on her face, then turned swiftly to bury her face in the roller-towel, knocking her handbag over in the process.

Rachel darted forwrad, but was too late to save it. Several items spilled across the floor. She knelt and scooped them back in the bag and set it back in place beside the basin.

'Sorry,' said Beth, not quite knowing why she was apologizing, except she felt she should. 'I must look awful.' Reluctantly, she let go of the towel and turned to face Rachel's inquisitive eyes. Rachel dropped her gaze as if embarrassed, and Beth sighed heavily as she turned back to the mirror. She opened her handbag and began the tedious business of trying to repair the damage.

Behind her, Rachel moved toward the door. 'If you're quite sure you're all right, then, I have to go,' she said. 'I promised Mother I'd pick up her magazine and take it to her on my way home, so I'd better go before the shop closes. You will be sure to lock up, won't you, Beth? Goodnight.'

CHAPTER 2

Beth woke with a start and shivered violently. The water was cold; the bubbles were gone and she felt stiff and sore all over. She pulled herself upright and climbed out of the bath. Her teeth chattered as she pulled a towel around her and began to dry herself.

She jumped and almost fell over as someone pounded on the bathroom door. 'Mam? You in there? Mam?' The pounding began again.

Lenny! 'Oh, no,' she groaned beneath her breath. 'Not now. Not yet.' She needed time; time to gather her wits and decide just how to break the news to him. She tried to speak; cleared her throat and tried again. 'Yes, I'm in here,' she called. 'No need to knock the door down, Lenny. I'll be out in a minute.'

Beth pulled the plug and let the water drain away. Time enough to clean the bath later, she thought as she put on her dressing-gown. Not that she wanted to go out there and face Lenny, but she didn't have much choice, did she?

Lenny stood there facing her as she opened the door, garbed as usual in faded jeans and jacket and heavy boots. He was a full six inches taller than his mother, thin, lean-faced, hair lank, shoulder-length, and he looked as if he needed a shave. Where, she wondered, was that fresh-faced child with the halo of golden hair who lived so vividly in her memory?

'Hello, dear,' she said, dabbing at her face with a towel to avoid looking at him directly. He said nothing as she moved to go around him, but she could feel his eyes boring into her. What was she going to say? What *could* she say? Her legs trembled beneath her. She walked unsteadily to the table and sat down.

'Well, what are you waiting for? You going to ask her or not?'

Beth's head snapped up. She hadn't even seen the girl. Tania whatever her name was. She lounged against the wall, hands stuffed into the pockets of jeans that barely covered her hips. She wore a T-shirt, but she might as well have not bothered for all it covered. Beth looked with distaste at the expanse of pale young flesh. The girl stared back, eyes insolent, mocking. Beth looked away. Tania was nothing but trouble. Not the sort Lenny should be taking up with at all.

'Well?' Lenny demanded. 'Did you do it? When can I get the money?'

Beth looked up at him and slowly shook her head. 'I'm sorry, Lenny, but I can't do it,' she said quietly. Her lips trembled. 'I was almost caught today by Mr Gresham. I – I'm not sure, but I think he suspects. I daren't try again. It's too dangerous. You'll have to find another way. I've done all I can.'

'You didn't . . .' Lenny stared in disbelief. 'For Christ's sake, Mam, what do you mean, you didn't do it? I *need* the friggin' money. I need it now! You know what will happen if I don't get it. You *have* to get it. There *is* no other way.'

'I can't. I'm sorry, Lenny, but I just can't.'

'But – but you said you would,' the boy said desperately. 'You did it once and it was all right.' His brow darkened. 'You did

17

something stupid, didn't you? Christ! I should have known you'd blow it. Where do you think that leaves me?'

'Up shit creek without a paddle,' the girl broke in contemptuously. 'I told you she'd screw it up, Lenny. I told you she was scared. She doesn't *really* care about you at all.'

'But I do!' Beth said, reaching out to touch her son. 'I've tried my best. I've always tried my best for you, Lenny.'

Angrily, he pulled away. 'Your best?' he sneered. 'Christ! Look around you. Is this your best? You're pushing bloody forty and this is all you've got to show for your life? Jesus Christ!'

Beth looked down at her hands. 'Please don't take His name in vain, Lenny,' she said softly. 'You know I don't like ...'

The boy rolled his eyes toward the heavens. 'Jesus Christ. Jesus Christ. Jesus *Christ!*' he said deliberately. 'What do I have to say to get through to you?' He grabbed a chair and sat down in front of his mother. 'What happened?' he demanded roughly.

Beth avoided his eyes. 'I tried,' she said. 'I really did, but Mr Gresham came up behind me just as I was about to enter the loan, and I had to cancel.' She was on the point of telling him about the promotion, but the shame of the price she'd paid stopped her. Besides, Lenny would only see it as another opportunity for her to continue supplying him with money. 'I'm sorry, Lenny.'

'Sorry?' Lenny's fist hit the table like a sledge-hammer. 'You stupid cow!' His voice rose to a scream. 'I need that money. I need it now! Don't you understand what they'll do to me if I don't get it?'

'They'll kick the shit out of him,' said the girl dispassionately. 'Then they'll carve his face.'

'Shut up, Tan. Just bloody shut up,' Lenny snarled. He ran grubby fingers through his hair as he turned back to face his mother. 'Look, Mam,' he pleaded, 'Tan's right. I have to have that money. You have to try again tomorrow. It was probably just coincidence that the manager happened to be there today. He didn't *say* anything, did he? He can't have done or you'd have been sacked. So he can't know, can he? You can do it, Mam. You did it before.'

Lenny's voice dropped, coaxing, adopting the wheedling tone he'd used so successfully for years. Stupid cow. She never did catch on. All he had to do was coax her along. She'd come through. She always did in the end. He reached out and touched her hand. 'You just had a bit of bad luck, today,' he said soothingly. 'Shook

18

you up a bit, but it will be all right tomorrow. You'll see. You do it right and we could be rolling in it.'

Tomorrow. The thought of walking into the bank tomorrow morning sickened her, and she knew she couldn't do it. Beth raised her eyes and looked at Lenny, ready to plead with him – to *beg* if necessary – but the words died on her lips.

The face across the table bore no resemblance to the image of the little boy Beth had carried in her heart for so many years. It was the face of a man; a cruel and vicious man behind whose eyes lay nothing but contempt.

She had always been so afraid of losing him, she thought bitterly; of losing his love. Sadly, she realized now that she had never had his love, nor anything remotely like it, and certainly not his respect. How he must despise her; despise her weakness; despise her pitiful efforts to earn his affection. He'd used her. He'd always used her and always would. Beth's mind flashed to the scene in Gresham's office that afternoon, and she shuddered with revulsion at what she'd done for Lenny's sake.

It was as if she'd been asleep and had suddenly come awake. The person sitting across from her was *not* her son. Her son was gone. He'd been gone for years. How could she have been so blind? How could he have turned out like this when she'd tried so hard?

He's like his father! The thought chilled her to the bone and took her breath away. She tried to force it from her mind, but it refused to leave, clinging like some earth-bound spectre to her consciousness.

Guilt whispered in her ear: *Perhaps it's your fault. Perhaps this is your punishment. Perhaps . . .* Angrily, Beth pushed the thought away. Guilt had crushed her in the past, but she wasn't going to let it lay the blame on her again.

'It's finished, Lenny,' she said quietly. 'I'm finished. I can't go on like this. You are going to have to stand on your own feet from now on. I can't help you. You got yourself into this mess, and you'll have to find your own way out.'

Her voice began to break, but now that she'd started, she willed herself to go on. She might never find the courage again. 'I want you out of the house by the end of the week. I don't care where you go, but you can't stay here.'

He stared at her. 'You don't mean that, Mam,' he said. 'You're just upset. You know what will happen if I don't get that money, don't you? And you wouldn't let that happen to me, now would you, Mam?' He reached for her hand but she drew it away.

'I mean it, Lenny,' she said firmly. She began to rise and turn away.

The room exploded and she was on the floor. For a moment she didn't know what had happened or where she was. Her face was on fire and her eyes refused to focus. She struggled to sit up, but Lenny was there beside her, one knee across her stomach, a hand around her throat, choking her. His fist was raised to strike again. She struggled feebly, but she knew she was no match for him.

'Now you listen to me,' he hissed. 'You're going back to that sodding bank tomorrow and you're going to put that sodding loan through. Do you understand? I'm not asking you this time, Mam. I'm bloody telling you.' He bent over her until his face almost touched her own. 'And if you don't, I'll do you like I did that bloke in Buckland Road.'

Beth felt as if her heart had stopped. She'd lied for Lenny under oath. Lied before God, refusing to believe that her son was capable of the crime of which he was accused. He'd sworn that he was innocent, and she'd believed him. She felt the rush of blood to her face as a small voice mocked her from within. *But you knew*, it whispered. *Deep in your heart, you knew!*

He seemed to guess what was going through her mind. 'That's right,' he said, smirking. 'The coppers had it right all along, didn't they? But you did so well on the stand that the old fart of a magistrate bought it, didn't he?' Beth flinched as he put out his hand and patted her cheek. 'And you'll get that money for me tomorrow, won't you, Mam?' he went on softly. 'Right? No more screw-ups. Got it, Mam?'

Suddenly he was on his feet. 'Come on, Tan,' he said to the girl. 'Let's get out of here. This place stinks.' He made for the door and went out. The girl followed more slowly. She paused beside Beth and stood looking down at her. 'You'd better do as he says,' she told Beth softly, 'because you don't know the half of it. He's a rough bastard, your son, and he'd slice you as soon as look at you. You got off lucky this time.'

Beth sat at the table. She couldn't stop shaking. She touched her face, probing gently. It felt as if it were on fire, and there was a smear of blood on her fingers. She should put a cold cloth on it, but that could wait.

First, she had to make things right. The thought kept running through her head like an endless tape. Lenny had to be stopped. God knows why it had taken her so long to admit that he was using her; had used her ever since he was a child. But it was over now. Finished.

He was violent. She had seen the look in his eyes after he hit her, and she knew he could have killed her. It was only because he thought he needed her that he'd held himself in check.

She'd been terrified there on the floor, but she was determined not to be intimidated by her son's threats. Rather they strengthened her resolve. She would go to the police. She had to make things right. Beth trembled at the thought, but it had to be done. And it had to be done now.

But who...?

Nancy! The name popped into her mind seemingly from nowhere. That was the name of the young policewoman who had been so kind at the trial. The one who had brought her a cup of tea while she waited, terrified of what might come. Nancy had been there all three days, and she'd been very kind. Beth had been so upset that Nancy had written down her home telephone number and told Beth to ring if she had any more questions. She wasn't supposed to, she said, but she understood what Beth was going through. She had two boys herself.

Beth rose slowly to her feet. Where had she put that number? She rummaged through the drawer beneath the telephone. It was on the back of a card...Ah! there it was. Nancy King. That was it.

Beth closed her eyes and breathed deeply, then dialled the number.

'Yes?' The answer was curt. A man.

'Could I speak to Nancy, please?' She could hear sirens in the background. He was probably watching TV.

'Hang on a minute.'

Beth gripped the phone. Please! Please hurry, Nancy, before I lose my nerve.

'Hello?'

Her hands were ice cold. 'Hello, Nancy,' she said hesitantly. 'You probably don't remember me, but my name is Beth Smallwood. You helped me when Lenny was in court, and you told me that...'

21

'Beth? Of course I remember you. How are you?'

Beth felt tired. Almost too tired to go on, but the throbbing pain reminded her of what she must do. 'I need your help,' she said simply. 'I lied in court and I have to tell someone.'

Beth lowered herself into a chair. She was exhausted. Tomorrow, Nancy had said. 'Nine o'clock. You know where we are in Charter Lane? Right. I'll be in the office. Ask for me and I'll take you to someone who will take your statement.'

She'd done it! A tear slid down Beth's cheek as she thought what it might mean. She could go to prison, but that didn't seem to matter now. Nothing mattered any more. She had to make things right. She'd tell them everything. About Lenny; about the drugs; about embezzling the money.

She gasped as the silence of the room was shattered by the shrill ringing of the phone. Was there to be no end to the assault upon her senses? She clutched her head, covered her ears to shut out the sound, but it went on and on. She felt as if her head would burst.

Beth could stand the sound no longer. She rose and crossed the room to snatch the phone from its rest.

'Hello!' she answered angrily.

There was silence at the other end, and for a moment she thought the caller must have hung up. Then, 'Is this Mrs Smallwood?' a voice asked hesitantly.

'Yes, it is,' she snapped, and instantly regretted it. The side of her face pulsed with pain, her tongue was swollen and she felt as if her mouth were full of cotton wool.

'I'm sorry if I've caught you at a bad time,' the voice went on. 'This is the Reverend Parslow, Mrs Smallwood. I wondered if . . .'

'Oh! Oh, dear. I am sorry, Reverend.' Beth stopped. She didn't know what to say.

'Are you all right, Mrs Smallwood? You sound, well, muffled.'

'Sorry. I – I was eating something.'

'Ah.' Then in a puzzled voice: 'You're not having your tea, are you? It's almost eight o'clock.' Parslow spoke as if he thought no one should be eating at that time in the evening.

'No. It's just . . .' Beth felt very tired and it was hard to talk with this great lump in her mouth. 'What do you want?' she asked wearily.

'It's about the wedding at St Justin's,' he said. 'I'm afraid I made a mistake about the date. It's tomorrow, Tuesday, not Friday, and wondered if you could see to things this evening? I realize it's short notice, but since you live so close I didn't think you'd mind.'

Beth leaned her head against the wall. She couldn't. She just couldn't do it. Not tonight. 'I'm sorry, Vicar...' she began, but he cut in before she could finish.

'There's not a lot needs doing,' he said. 'Just the altar brasses and the candles. I don't know when they were last replaced, but the candles were quite low when I was in the other week. We should have new ones for the wedding, don't you think? You do have some, don't you?'

'Yes, I have some here, but...'

'Good! Good. That's all right, then. I do appreciate it so much. I don't know what we'd do without people like you, Mrs Smallwood. Sorry if I interrupted your tea.'

Beth put the phone down. What was the use?

She looked toward the mantel clock. Dear God, would this day never end? The last thing she wanted to do was go out again, but she supposed she must. She went into the kitchen and splashed water on her face, then dabbed it gently with a towel. There was blood on the towel. She moved to the mirror beside the door, peered into it and groaned.

Her face was a mess! Thank goodness she was only going up the lane to the church. The swelling covered one side of her face, half closing one eye, and there was a small cut above the eyebrow. She'd meant to put a cold compress on it but there wasn't time to stop for that now. Besides, it had stopped bleeding.

Getting dressed was painful, and when she heard the rain against the window, Beth felt like giving up. She sighed heavily. Better put her wellies on just in case.

Beth went to the sideboard and took out a pair of tapered candles. They were longer and heavier than most, and still sealed in their Cellophane wrapper. She thought of the young couple getting married tomorrow in the old church. She'd never met them, but she wished them well. At least she could start them off with fresh candles on the altar.

She was on the point of leaving when a thought occurred to her. She must phone and let them know she wouldn't be in tomorrow.

Not Gresham, though. Her face burned at the very thought. She looked down the list of numbers on the pad beneath the phone, and began to dial.

'I'd like a word with you, Beth Smallwood.'

Startled, Beth almost dropped the bag she was carrying. She turned to face the speaker. 'Lord! but you gave me a fright, Mrs Turvey,' she said, clutching her chest. 'What...?'

'As if you didn't know,' the woman sniffed. 'That boy...' She stopped abruptly. 'Here, what happened to your face? Did he do that?'

'Who? Lenny? Oh, good gracious, no, Mrs Turvey. I – I fell getting off the bus.'

The woman eyed Beth suspiciously. 'He did, you know,' she said. 'I heard it through the wall. Shouting and carrying on. He beat you up, didn't he?' Mrs Turvey peered closely at Beth's face. 'You're a fool, Beth Smallwood,' she said not unkindly. 'He may be your son, but he'll be the death of you if you let it go on.'

She sighed heavily. 'I'm sorry, Beth, but I've had enough. What with that bike coming and going at all hours, and that rock music in the middle of the day, it's more than I can stand. I'm going to ring the police and let them sort him out. He's a danger to us all.' She turned and made as if to go back inside the house, but Beth caught her arm.

'No! No, please, Mrs Turvey,' she pleaded. 'I *have* been on to the police – not twenty minutes ago. You're quite right, I can't let it go on. I realized that tonight. I've told Lenny he must leave, and I have an appointment to see the police first thing tomorrow morning. Really.'

Doris Turvey eyed Beth uncertainly. 'You just see that you do, then,' she said sternly. Her voice softened. 'I know it must be hard, but you have to do it, Beth, or you'll end up being one of them statistics they keep on about. I don't know how you've stood it for so long.'

A gust of wind drove a spattering of rain beneath the eaves, and Beth fumbled with her umbrella. The bag she'd been carrying fell to the ground, and the candles slid out. She bent to pick it up, but gasped as a sharp pain shot through her hip. She must have hurt it when she fell, but she hadn't noticed it until now.

Doris Turvey pursed her lips. 'You ought to have that looked at,' she said as she bent to pick up the candles and put them back in the bag. 'And that mouth of yours. I can hardly understand you. You shouldn't be going out at all.'

'I – I'm quite all right, thank you,' Beth said shakily. The pain was subsiding and she just wanted to get away. 'It's nothing, really.' She took the bag and glanced at the sky. 'I have to get these candles to the church. There's a wedding there tomorrow, and they need new candles for the altar.' She opened the umbrella and stepped out into the rain.

Doris Turvey watched as Beth set off up the lane. She shook her head and sighed. 'I hope you're telling me the truth, my girl,' she muttered softly. 'For my sake as well as yours. I can't take much more of this.'

CHAPTER 3

The sound of the lich-gate banging shut brought Tony Rudge to his feet. He moved swiftly to the window and lifted a corner of the piece of sacking covering the window. He leaned into the embrasure and pressed his face against the glass in order to see who was entering the churchyard. It had been raining, and a woman was shaking out an umbrella as she walked up the gravelled path. She had a scarf over her head and he couldn't see her face. Probably someone wanting to look round the old church, he decided, but she'd soon leave when she found the door was locked.

He visualized her mounting the church steps and trying the door. He listened but could hear no sound. She'd soon be gone. He turned from the window and drew deeply on his cigarette.

The girl sitting on the floor with the open sleeping bag draped around her shoulders watched him through half-closed eyes. She, too, was smoking, but in the manner of someone newly introduced to it, filling her mouth with smoke, then tossing her head back and exhaling quickly. Trying to show him how grown up she was, he thought. Silly little cow.

The sleeping bag slipped from her shoulders as she reached out and butted the cigarette in the makeshift ashtray, a blue-edged saucer stolen from the guest house where she worked. The guest house owned by Tony's father. She put her hands behind her head and arched her back. Her full, young, hard-nippled breasts thrust upward, her eyes inviting him to touch, to feel the creamy texture of her lissom body, and Tony felt a stirring in his loins again.

'Come back to bed,' she coaxed. 'I'm getting cold.'

He shook his head, listening, but heard nothing. He turned back to the window and peered out. No sign of anyone down there now. The woman must have gone.

'Bet you can't,' the girl teased.

Tony butted his own cigarette and moved toward her. 'I bet I can,' he said, standing over her.

Her eyes grew round as they travelled up his naked body. 'I'll bet you can, too,' she breathed, and reached for him.

Tony felt the tremor in the floor beneath him before he heard the sound. Half dozing with his face buried in Amy's neck, he was instantly alert. Someone was in the church. The sound could only have come from the heavy studded door below. He rolled off the sleeping bag, groping for his underpants and jeans. Amy stirred, burrowed deeper into the sleeping bag and went back to sleep.

Tony pulled on his trainers and moved swiftly to the corner of the room. He paused, watching the girl; making sure she was asleep before stepping through an opening to the stone steps leading down.

Someone was shaking her. Violently. Amy felt as if her neck would snap. She tried to speak but she couldn't get her breath. 'For Christ's sake wake up!' she heard as through a fog. She opened her eyes and tried to focus on the face in front of her.

'Tony! What the...?'

'Get dressed,' he ordered, stripping away the sleeping bag. 'We've got to get out of here. And make sure you take everything with you. We don't want anyone to know we've been here.'

Amy scrambled to her feet. 'Why? What's wrong?' she asked as she began throwing on her clothes.

Tony snatched the sleeping bag from the floor and began to roll it up. 'There's been an accident,' he said. 'We have to get out of here. Fast!'

'Accident? What sort of accident? What happened?' Amy stopped what she was doing. Her eyes narrowed. 'Here, you're having me on, aren't you? Tony? Stop a minute.'

Tony dropped the sleeping bag and grabbed her by the shoulders. 'For Christ's sake, *move*, you stupid little cow,' he snarled. 'There's a dead woman down there, and I don't intend to hang about here to be accused of having something to do with it.'

'Dead? Who's dead? You said it was an accident. What happened? Why should anyone...?' She gasped as his fingers dug into her shoulders. His eyes blazed and he raised his hand as if to strike her. He was shaking, and his face was white. She cringed and closed her eyes, waiting for the blow to fall. Abruptly, he turned away. 'Do what you bloody well like,' he muttered peevishly, 'but I'm getting out of here.' He began picking up the remains of the meal they'd had, sweeping the cartons from the take-away into a pile. He looked around for something to put them in, then unrolled the sleeping bag and dumped everything into it: cartons, cigarette butts, a couple of tattered cushions, a paperback book, and a broken candle. Last of all, he picked up the saucer with the lighted candle on it.

'Get your coat,' he told her roughly.

Amy snatched up her coat. She was frightened, now. Tony's actions scared her. 'The sack,' she cried, and Tony paused. 'Get it,' he told her, and smiled grimly to himself as she dashed to the window and pulled the sacking down. That was a bit more like it.

He shielded the candle. It was almost completely dark outside, and he didn't want anyone wondering why there was a light coming from the belfry.

She handed him the sacking and he dumped it in with everything else. He pulled the lighted candle from the bed of wax in the saucer and handed it to Amy. 'Hold on to that,' he instructed, 'and don't let it go out. I don't want to break my neck on those stairs.' He dumped the saucer into the sleeping bag, then twisted the corners together to form a pack.

Amy led the way down the worn stone steps, holding the candle high. Tony put a hand on her shoulder as she reached the bottom step. 'Open the door carefully,' he whispered. 'No, wait!' He reached over and doused the candle. 'Now open it,' he said.

The girl frowned in the darkness. What was he afraid of? Even now she only half believed there was a dead woman in the church. But he was scared shitless about something.

'What the hell are you waiting for?'

'All right! Keep your hair on.' Amy opened the door and stepped out into the porch. Tony followed, setting the sleeping bag down as he transferred the key from the inside of the door to the outside and locked it.

Suddenly, Amy clutched his arm. 'Tony! There's someone in the church!' she hissed. 'There's a light.'

He shook her off roughly. 'I know. I know,' he said irritably. 'The lights were on when I came down the first time.'

'What about the woman? I want to see . . . '

'There's nothing *to* see,' he growled. 'Now come on!'

'I don't believe you,' the girl said stubbornly. 'Nobody's *dead*. They can't be. I don't know what you're playing at, Tony, but I'm going to have a look.' She moved swiftly to the open doors leading into the nave.

'I don't give a shit what you believe,' he hissed. 'What the hell is the matter with you?'

But Amy was gone.

Three dust-encrusted bulbs hung on twisted flex from the vaulted ceiling, but the light they shed seemed to barely reach the floor. Two candles flickered dimly on the altar. Amy shivered. Their presence there seemed somehow sinister.

'There's no one . . . ' she began, then caught her breath. Was that a shadow on the steps?

'Oh, Jesus!'

She wanted to run, but her legs refused to move. As her eyes adjusted to the dim light, she could see the outline of a crumpled figure. Almost against her will, and certainly against her better judgement, she found herself tiptoeing down the aisle.

'Amy! For Christ's sake, what do you think you're doing? Come on! There's nothing you can do.' Tony hoisted the sleeping bag and its contents on to his shoulder.

But Amy barely heard him. It was as if some external force compelled her to go on.

'Look, I'm going. Are you coming?'

The girl ignored him. The aisle was short. An umbrella, partly open, was lodged on one of the pews to dry. Her mother had always said it was bad luck to open an umbrella in the house. Was it the same inside a church, she wondered?

The woman lay on her side as if she'd been kneeling and had fallen over. Her arms stretched out in front of her, and her pale hands lay like dead butterflies against the ancient stone. Two short candles lay just beyond the outstretched fingers, and beside them was a strip of crumpled Cellophane. Her open mac was pulled to one side, and the dress beneath had ridden up above her knees. A few feet away, as if thrown there, a handbag lay open, its contents scattered across the floor.

The woman's face was covered by her hair. Auburn hair. Amy reached out a timid hand to push the hair aside and touch the face. It was cold. Her exploring fingers moved the head, and it rolled over to reveal a dark, sticky mass of matted hair, its auburn strands stretched like cobwebs to the blood-soaked stone.

Amy almost fell over in her haste to pull away, and the candle she'd been holding slipped from her hand and rolled beneath a pew. For just a second there, she'd thought the woman was alive. But no one could live with their skull smashed in like that. Amy felt her stomach churn as she scrambled to her feet, and suddenly she was afraid. Wildly, she looked around for help, but only shadows moved as the candles on the altar flickered fitfully.

Tears spilled down her face. 'Tony!' she screamed as she ran back up the aisle. 'Tony, wait!'

The outer door stood open, but Tony was no longer there. Amy ran to the door, calling out again, but her cries were swallowed in the gathering darkness. From behind the church came the sound of a car being started. Lights flashed beyond the churchyard wall as the car shot into the lane. Tony! The bastard was going to leave her there. She ran down the steps as the car picked up speed.

The squeal of tyres drowned out her cries as the car slid to a halt beside the gate. 'For God's sake shut up!' he snarled as she scrambled in. He crashed the gears and the car leapt forward. Amy slid down in the seat and stole a glance at Tony. His face was set. Like stone. She shivered. He frightened her.

Wind whipped at her hair as the car gathered speed. 'What about that poor woman, Tony?' she ventured timidly. 'We can't just leave her.' Amy's voice trailed off as he looked at her.

'What woman?' His eyes bored into hers.

She frowned, confused. 'The woman in the church . . . ' She caught her breath. 'Please don't look at me like that, Tony. Tony!' Her voice rose. 'Don't look at me like that!' She began to whimper.

His mouth formed a thin line as he turned his attention back to the road. 'There was no woman,' he said so softly that Amy had to strain to hear him. 'Understand?'

Amy swallowed hard and nodded.

'Then say it!'

'Th-there was no woman,' she said, stumbling over the words.

His hand shot out and gripped her arm. 'I didn't hear you,' he shouted. 'I want to hear you say it, Amy. I want you to say it and *believe* it!' His fingers dug into her flesh.

Tears streamed down the girl's face. 'There was no woman!' she screamed at the top of her voice. 'There was no woman! There was . . . ' Her voice broke, and she fell back sobbing in her seat.

Tony Rudge stared into the night. His grip relaxed on her arm. He patted her shoulder lightly. 'Good girl,' he said. 'Now just remember that.'

CHAPTER 4

'Dead ugly' was the way one local resident had described St Justin's church, and no one had felt obliged to challenge the description. Utilitarian and unadorned, with its squat, square tower and foreshortened nave, it had neither grace nor beauty. Even the stonework, which should have mellowed with the passing years, had instead turned dark and sombre. But it was old, almost five hundred years old, and that, apparently, was sufficient reason for its continued preservation.

Once part of a large estate some distance from the town, St Justin's now found itself within Broadminister's boundaries, the rest of the estate having been sold off piecemeal long ago. The church was bordered on three sides by open farm land, but to the north only a thin strand of trees stood between St Justin's and a new development known as Broadmere. Once that was complete, the push would be on to tear the old church down.

And no doubt there would be others pushing just as hard to save it.

So thought Detective Chief Inspector Paget as he parked his car beside a forensic van. He got out and locked the door. A uniformed constable approached, recognized him, and stepped back quickly as Paget ducked beneath the yellow tape.

'They're all inside, sir,' the man said unnecessarily.

Paget entered the churchyard through the open lich-gate, now held back by yellow tape and draped with plastic sheeting. The grass was wet, the gravel soft beneath his feet, but at least the rain had stopped.

He mounted the steps and stood for a moment, surveying the scene.

Broad-shouldered and a couple of inches over six feet, his size was still impressive, but his old colleagues from the Met would certainly see a difference in him from the man they'd known three years ago. He was leaner now, his face was thinner, and his once brown hair was streaked with grey. His nose, always a prominent feature, had taken on a sharper thrust, and his eyes were more deep-set. His wife's untimely death had taken a heavy toll, and there was about the chief inspector an air of aloof detachment. It was as if he had withdrawn to some secret place inside himself, and that which he presented to the world was merely armour, sword, and shield.

Inside the church white-coated men and women performed their work in silence, while uniformed men stood about looking as if they wished they could be elsewhere. Below the chancel steps, two men stood talking while they watched a third man on his knees beside the body of a woman. The taller of the two men – the one who looked more like a doleful undertaker than a policeman – was Inspector Charlie Dobbs, the officer in charge of Scenes of Crime. The shorter, dark-haired man was Detective Sergeant John Tregalles, while the wheezing, rotund man on his knees was Dr Reg Starkie, the local pathologist. He talked softly as he worked, speaking into a lapel microphone.

Paget moved swiftly down the aisle, head thrust forward as if testing the air as he took in every detail of the scene. There was a chill about the place; an odour of decay and rising damp and sheer neglect. Not normally over-sensitive to atmosphere, he could not escape the feeling that in their quiet way the walls were crumbling, returning inexorably to the earth from whence they came.

31

'Charlie. Tregalles,' he greeted the two men cryptically. 'Sorry I'm late, but I was the other side of Bewdley when the call came through. What have we got?'

Tregalles consulted his notebook. He was some four inches shorter than Paget, a rubbery-faced, compact man with the strong upper body and tapering hips of a competitive swimmer. His dark hair and swarthy complexion bespoke his Cornish ancestry, although he himself had been born and raised in Bethnal Green and, despite his fifteen years in the border country, was still, like Paget, a Londoner at heart.

'The victim's name is Elizabeth Smallwood, according to the documents in her handbag,' he said. 'Late thirties. Lives close by at number 7 Farrow Lane. Found more or less as you see her now on the steps. Severe head injury. Looks as if someone hit her very hard with a not-so-blunt instrument. She also appears to have been beaten about the face.

'According to the two men first on the scene, she looked as if she might have been kneeling on the steps when she was struck. Handbag was rifled; contents scattered about the floor. Money and credit cards are gone, assuming she had some in the first place.'

'Married? Single? Next of kin?'

'Widow, according to a neighbour. She worked for Northern and West Counties Bank in Font Street.'

'Anyone been notified?'

'A constable has been to the house – it's just down the lane from here – but there was no one home. He spoke to a neighbour, a Mrs Turvey, and she said there's a son, Lenny, who lives there with his mother, but she had no idea where the son might be. But she did volunteer the information that wherever he was, he was probably up to no good.'

Paget raised an eyebrow at that, but made no comment. 'Who reported it?' he asked.

'Anonymous phone call from a box across the river in the Flats,' Tregalles told him. The Flats, as the area had come to be known locally, was originally a marsh, but developers had filled it in and built scores of terraced houses there. 'The call came in at nine forty-three. First uniform on the scene logged in at ten o'clock exactly. I haven't heard the tape, but I'm told it was a young woman or girl who made the report. She said there'd been an accident, and there was a dead woman in St Justin's church. Then she rang off without giving her name.'

'An accident?'

'That's what she said,' Tregalles closed the notebook. 'Looks more like a robbery gone wrong to me.'

Paget's answering grunt was non-committal. Tregalles was probably right, but he wondered why the call had come from across the river. 'Has the call-box been sealed off?'

Charlie Dobbs spoke up for the first time. 'Had that done first thing,' he said, 'but it's outside a pub, and someone was using it when my man got there, so I don't think we can rely on it being much help.'

'Anything to indicate why Mrs Smallwood was here at this time of night?'

'She'd come to clean the brasses and put new candles on the altar. I rang the vicar – his name and number are on the board in the porch – and he told me he'd asked her to do that in preparation for a wedding tomorrow afternoon.'

Paget frowned. 'I didn't think this church was in use.'

'It isn't. That is to say they don't hold services here any longer, but it is an historic building, and it's open to the public from ten till three each day from May to September. And they do the odd wedding here, apparently. I've asked the vicar to come over.'

Paget remained silent for a moment as he surveyed the scene once more. 'You say she came to put new candles on the altar,' he said slowly. 'Are those the old candles or the new ones on there now?'

'The new ones, I should think,' said Charlie. 'We found what looked like the old ones close to the body, together with the Cellophane wrapper from the new candles.'

Paget edged his way around Starkie and walked across the chancel to the altar. 'Then why, if they were to be used for the wedding, were they lit?' he wondered aloud. He examined the wax at the base of the two candles closely. 'They must have been burning for some time. Were they alight when you arrived?'

'Yes. We put them out when we got our own lights going.'

Paget continued to stare at the candles. 'Heavy candlesticks,' he observed thoughtfully. 'No doubt you'll be checking those out. And it might not be a bad idea to find out how long it takes for these candles to burn down this far. Perhaps, too, you could find out exactly what time it was when they were put out.'

Starkie was starting to pack his instruments away. 'Want to take a look before I send her on her way?' he asked Paget.

The chief inspector knelt beside the body. Elizabeth Smallwood looked peaceful in death – except for the gaping wound just above the left ear. The auburn hair was glued to her head with matted blood, and the collar of her coat was soaked in it. Paget looked away and breathed deeply several times before continuing his examination.

'This bruise on the cheek,' he said to Starkie. 'Could that have been done some time before she died?'

The pathologist nodded. 'At least an hour earlier, I'd say. Possibly more, as was the one above her eye and the bruise on her leg.'

'Time of death?'

Starkie pursed his lips as he looked at his watch. '*Estimated* time of death,' he emphasized, 'is somewhere between eight thirty and nine thirty. I may be able to narrow that down a bit tomorrow, but I doubt if it will be by much.'

Paget got to his feet and was dusting off his trousers when Charlie, accompanied by a thin, anaemic-looking man, approached him. 'Crawford tells me he thinks there is something interesting about the door leading to the belfry,' he said. 'Want to come along?'

'I don't know if it means anything,' the man said half apologetically as he led the way to the back of the church, 'but it seemed a bit odd to me. There's fresh oil on the hinges and the lock, but the door is not supposed to be opened according to the sign.' He pointed.

The sign read: TOWER STAIRS UNSAFE. THIS DOOR IS TO BE KEPT LOCKED AT ALL TIMES. A faded signature followed, and the condition of the notice suggested that it had been in place for a long time.

'What about the main door?' Paget asked. 'Have those hinges been oiled?'

'No, sir. I did check them.'

'Any sign of a key?'

'No, sir.' Crawford glanced at Charlie. 'But I could open it. It's a very simple lock.'

'Better wait for the vicar,' Charlie told him. 'He may have a key and an explanation.'

'Right.' Crawford sounded disappointed.

The Reverened Parslow arrived shortly after midnight. He was a small, pale, sharp-nosed man with thinning hair, and Paget took an instant dislike to him. Parslow's expressions of shock and horror sounded hollow to the chief inspector's ear. Indeed, the vicar's primary concern seemed to have less to do with Elizabeth Smallwood's untimely death than it did with the wedding scheduled for later in the day.

'It really is most inconvenient,' he said petulantly. 'The bride's parents will be most upset.'

Parslow could tell them little about Elizabeth Smallwood. He did know that she was a single mother, and that she lived with her teenage son at the bottom of Farrow Lane. He said he'd first met her one Saturday afternoon when he'd found her praying in the church. They had struck up a conversation, and she had said how sad it was that no one seemed to care for the church any more. 'I told her that we simply didn't have the money to keep things up,' Parslow said, 'and it was then that she volunteered to come in once a week and spruce the place up a bit. That was early last year, and she's been doing it ever since.'

When asked about a key to the belfry, he said it was kept in a cupboard in the vestry. He went off to get it for them, but returned within minutes looking annoyed.

'It's gone,' he said. 'The key's gone. Someone has forced the lock on the cupboard.'

'When was the last time you saw the key?' Paget asked him.

Parslow scratched his head. 'I really can't recall. You see, there's no need to go into that cupboard in the ordinary way. There's nothing in there but a few old hymn books and odds and ends. And the key, of course. So I am afraid I can't help you. It's the only key to that door as far as I know.'

'Mrs Smallwood didn't have a key, then?' Tregalles asked.

'No, but she did have a key to the main door.'

'That must be the key we found in her handbag,' Tregalles said. 'Any others, apart from your own?'

'None that I know of. In fact I had to have one made for Mrs Smallwood. Before that there was only the one.'

'Not to worry,' Charlie said. 'I'm sure my man can open it.'

'Really?' Parslow seemed intrigued. 'You do understand, of course, that the church cannot be responsible for your safety if you go up into the belfry. I mean, it has been declared unsafe, although to be quite honest, I've been up there myself and I couldn't see the reason for the notice. But it was inspected by engineers, I'm told, so I expect they knew what they were doing.'

Crawford had the door open in less than a minute. It swung outward noiselessly to reveal stone steps ascending into the darkness. The steps were badly worn and the edges were beginning to crumble, but they appeared to be solid enough. Charlie led the way, using a powerful torch to guide them.

The stairs took them to a small room. 'It's the old bell-ringers' room,' Parslow explained. 'Hasn't been used in years.'

Charlie moved slowly around the room. He bent to examine something on the floor. 'Candle wax,' he said. 'I'd say somebody has been up here, and not too long ago at that.' He straightened up and moved to the far end of the room, the harsh light of the torch probing ahead of him. He stopped before a dark recess. 'Something in here,' he muttered as he squatted down. He reached in and gingerly pulled out a cardboard box. 'Looks like rubbish,' he said over his shoulder. He probed the contents with his gloved hands.

'Bloody hell!' he exploded softly, and Paget heard the sharp intake of breath from Parslow as he craned to see.

'Condoms!' he announced disgustedly. 'And used ones at that!'

CHAPTER 5

The cottage was in darkness, and there was no answer to their continued knocking. 'Try the keys from Mrs Smallwood's bag,' Paget said. 'One of them should fit.'

'Here! What do you think you're up to, then?'

The two men turned to face a large, sharp-featured woman wrapped in a dressing-gown. She stood outside the open door of the cottage next to number 7. Her feet were clad in trainers without laces, and her hair was stiff with curlers.

'Police,' Tregalles said, introducing himself and Paget. He produced his warrant card. 'Would you be Mrs Turvey?'

'I would,' said the woman. 'What's young Lenny done this time, then? This is the second time someone's been round tonight.'

'You must be chilly,' Paget said. 'Perhaps we can talk inside.'

Doris Turvey eyed him critically. 'Chief Inspector, eh?' she mused. 'He must have done something serious to bring you out this time of a night.' She motioned them to follow her inside. 'I'll switch the fire on,' she said. 'It's that cold for May. Sit yourselves down, then. Would you like some tea?'

'Thank you, but we won't be staying long,' Paget told her.

The room was small and cluttered with furniture, and an astonishing number of knick-knacks of the seaside holiday variety occupied almost every square inch of space. Wisely, the two men chose to remain standing just inside the door while Mrs Turvey knelt beside a chair to switch on the electric fire.

'Funny, there being no one home next door,' the woman said. 'Can't say I've ever known Beth Smallwood to be out this late.' She glanced at the clock on the mantel. 'It's after twelve. That's not like her. She said she was just going up to the church.'

'What time was that?' Paget asked.

The woman thought for a moment. 'Must have been after eight o'clock,' she said at last. 'Yes, it was, because *Coronation Street* was finished and I'd made a cup of tea. Say ten past.'

'Where was she when you spoke to her?'

'Right outside that door. We had a few words, and . . .'

'What about?' Paget asked.

Doris Turvey squinted at him. 'What do you want to know that for?' she demanded. 'What's this all about? Something's happened, hasn't it? It's young Lenny, isn't it?'

'Why do you say that?' Tregalles asked.

Doris Turvey grimaced. 'I should have thought you'd know more about that than me,' she said. 'I mean, he *is* out on licence.'

Paget loosened his coat. The room was becoming warm. 'Could we go back to your conversation with Mrs Smallwood?' he said. 'You say she told you she was going to the church. Did she say if she was meeting anyone there? Anything like that?'

Mrs Turvey shook her head. 'She just said she was going up to the church to tidy up like she usually does. Oh, yes, and to take some candles. She had them in her bag. For a wedding there tomorrow.' She glanced at the time. 'Well, today, now, I suppose,' she amended.

'Did you talk about anything else?'

'Just young Lenny, like always. Never a moment's peace when he and that girl of his are about. Playing that rock music while his

37

mum's at work. Comes right through the wall, it does, and with my Fred on nights he can't sleep, you know.'

'Did you notice anything different about Mrs Smallwood when you were speaking to her?' Paget broke in. 'Did she seem all right?'

Doris Turvey looked at him. 'Ah, so that's it, is it?' she said, nodding sagely. 'No, she wasn't all right. Her face was all swollen, and she'd hurt her leg.'

'Did she offer any explanation for the swollen face?'

'Tried to tell me it was an accident,' the woman scoffed. 'Fell of the bus, she says, but I wasn't born yesterday. After all that shouting and carry-on when Lenny came home? That boy will be the death of her, and I told her so.'

Paget and Tregalles exchanged glances. 'Are you saying it was Lenny who did that to his mother?' Tregalles said.

'Like I said, she tried to say it wasn't, but that's Beth for you. Keeps a tight rein on her feelings, does that one. But I heard them going at it,' she said. 'Lenny shouting, and then there's this sort of crash, and I heard Beth, well, sort of cry out. I tell you, it gave me the shivers.'

'Then what happened?'

'Lenny and that girl of his came out of the house and went off on the motorbike. Glad to see the back of 'em, I was, I can tell you.'

'What time would that be?'

Mrs Turvey thought about that. 'Can't say I noticed the time,' she said. 'But it would be a good half-hour before Beth came out of the house.'

'Between seven thirty and quarter to eight, then,' Tregalles said. 'Would that be about right?'

The woman began to nod, then paused. 'No, I tell a lie,' she said. 'It was a bit before half-past seven. He always revs that bike up so loud you can't hear yourself think, and I was thankful that he did it before I sat down to watch the telly.'

Tregalles made a discreet note. 'You say Mrs Smallwood mentioned falling as she got off the bus. What bus would that be?'

The woman shrugged. 'The one from town, I expect. Not that I believed her. Funny, though, it was the first time I've known her come home on the bus for months. Late, she was, too.'

'I don't suppose you know what time that was,' Tregalles ventured hopefully. It wasn't entirely a vain hope; Mrs Turvey seemed to keep a sharp eye on the comings and goings of her neighbour.

The woman thought. 'It must have been around six,' she said slowly. 'Yes, that's right, because she was later than usual and I remember wondering why she hadn't been brought home by that Mr Beecham.'

'Mr Beecham?' Paget raised an enquiring brow.

'He's Beth's boss. At the bank. Brings Beth home in his car.' Mrs Turvey gave Paget a knowing look. 'Stops there a good long time, too, some evenings. But he didn't bring her home tonight. Came round later, though, in ever such a state. Banging on the door and calling out, so I went to see what *that* was all about. He wanted to know where Beth was, so I told him she was up at the church. Ever so short with me, he was. Not like him at all.' She lowered her voice. 'To tell you the truth, I think he'd been drinking.'

'And what time was that, Mrs Turvey?'

'Must have been going on for nine, I should think. It was beginning to get dark.'

'Do you know where Mr Beecham lives?'

Mrs Turvey didn't know, but she had the impression it wasn't far away. Paget questioned her closely, but there was little the woman could add to what she'd already told them. Paget switched direction. 'How old is Lenny Smallwood, Mrs Turvey?'

'Nineteen.'

'And he lives at home?'

'That's right. Except Beth did say something that made me think he might not be living there much longer. Talked about going to see the police tomorrow. And not before time, neither, as far as I'm concerned. Sounded like she meant it, too. He's a nasty bit of goods, is Lenny, and that's a fact. Not that I've ever known him to hit Beth before, but then, you never know what goes on behind closed doors, do you?'

Paget was about to ask another question, but Mrs Turvey held up her hand. 'Now, fair's fair,' she told him. 'I've answered all your questions; now you answer mine. I want to know what's happened. I know we don't always get on, especially when it comes to the way Lenny carries on, but I like Beth Smallwood. She's a good soul if only she wouldn't let that son of hers walk all over her. I hope she does throw him out, then we can all have some peace. Now, what's this all about, eh?'

Tregalles looked at Paget, and the chief inspector nodded. 'I'm afraid I have to tell you that Mrs Smallwood is dead,' he said. 'I'm sorry.'

The woman stared at him. 'Dead? Beth? You can't ... How? What happened?'

'We don't know ourselves at this point,' Tregalles told her. 'It appears that she may have been attacked while she was working in the church.'

'Oh, my God!' The woman shook her head in disbelief. 'But why? Who'd want to do such a thing?' She paused and her expression changed. 'He must have come back,' she said softly as if to herself. 'Beth told him he'd have to leave and he wouldn't like that, would he?' Mrs Turvey looked at Paget. 'It *was* Lenny, wasn't it?' she said. 'I was right. I knew it! I knew there'd be trouble one day. You ask my Fred. I always said ...'

'Mrs Turvey,' said Paget sternly, 'I must caution you not to jump to conclusions. We don't know who is responsible, and until we do it would be most unwise to indulge in speculation. Now, perhaps you can help us further. Do you know if Mrs Smallwood had any other close relatives?'

Doris Turvey shook her head. 'If she had any, I never heard her speak of them.'

'I see.' Paget stopped, head on one side, listening. The deep-throated sound of a motorbike could be heard coming down the lane. 'Is that ...?'

'That's Lenny, now,' Mrs Turvey said. 'I'd know that bike anywhere.'

There was a burst of sound, then silence. Paget opened the door and stepped outside, followed closely by Tregalles. It was very dark, but light from the open doorway outlined the bike. A helmeted rider was in the act of dismounting when Paget called out to him: 'Mr Smallwood? Leonard Smallwood?'

The figure paused, then in one swift motion remounted the bike and kicked it into life. Both policemen started forward, but they were too late. The bike leapt forward, almost unseating the rider before he brought it under control, and roared off into the night.

It was two o'clock by the time Paget let himself into the silent house. He scooped up a fistful of handbills that had been shoved through the letter-box, and walked through to the kitchen. He tossed them on the table. More rubbish for the recycling bin.

He yawned and stretched. He was tired but his mind refused to let him rest. He kept picturing the face of the woman on the chancel steps. Was Tregalles right? Was it simply a case of a robbery that had gone terribly wrong? Or was there more to it than that? Certainly the son's behaviour was suspicious, taking off like that when they approached him. But had it anything to do with the murder?

He filled the electric kettle and plugged it in, then slumped down in a chair to wait for it to boil.

Idly, he began to sort through the handbills and found an official-looking letter mixed in with them. Personnel Department, Metropolitan Police. What was that all about after all this time?

Curious, he tore open the envelope. Inside was another envelope, this one addressed to him at his old office in Victoria Street, and it bore a Canadian stamp.

He opened the envelope, took out the letter and read:

Dear Neil, Abject apologies for not writing before, but you know what it's like when you're settling in. Can't believe that it's almost five years since I left, but I suppose it must be. I always meant to write, but the first two years were a bit hectic, and well, you know I've never been much good at that sort of thing, so all I can do is say sorry again.

But I must tell you why I'm writing now. You'll never believe this but I'm getting married!!! Knew that would knock you over, but it's true!

Patrick Truscott, the perennial bachelor, was getting married. Paget shook his head and smiled.

Patrick had been best man at his wedding, but they had lost touch with each other after Patrick went to Canada to join a communications company as a security adviser. There had been a couple of Christmas cards, but then nothing. Their last Christmas card to him had been returned stamped 'Not known at this address', and there had been nothing since.

Then Jill had died.

Paget closed his eyes. He didn't have to look at the calendar to be reminded of the date. It would live forever in his brain. Three more days. He'd been aware of the date for weeks, yet, perversely, he'd tried to put it out of his mind. Three years ago this Friday was the day Jill died. God! it was hard to believe that she'd been gone for three years. He could see her now in his mind's eye as clearly as if she were there in front of him: dark hair, dark eyes, vivacious, with

41

that peculiar lop-sided grin of hers. So short a time together. Four years. If only...

The shrill whistle of the kettle interrupted his thoughts. He unplugged it without being conscious that he'd done so, his mind still full of memories. He picked up the letter and began to read again.

He stopped. He felt as if he'd been kicked. His hand closed on the letter and slowly crushed it. 'Damn you, Patrick!' he said fiercely. 'Why now? Why did it have to be now?'

CHAPTER 6

Tuesday – 14 May
'Leonard Ronald Smallwood. Nineteen. Charged last year with possession of stolen goods. First offence. One year probation.' Tregalles dropped the sheet in front of Paget, and moved back to prop himself against the wall, careful not to spill his mug of coffee. 'Word is that Smallwood was lucky to get off so lightly. He's well known as a tearaway, and there's more than a suspicion that he's into drugs in a small way. Selling coke to kids, mostly. Nothing they can prove so far, but the locals reckon it's only matter of time before they have him.'

Paget picked up the sheet and stared at it. His mind, usually so orderly and focused, was still preoccupied with the contents of Patrick's letter. He forced himself to concentrate. 'No word on his whereabouts, then?' he said.

'No. I shouldn't think it will be long, though.' Tregalles eyed Paget over the rim of the mug. 'Problems, sir?' he asked.

'What?' Paget seemed startled by the question. 'Oh. No. Just thinking. Nothing to do with the case,' he said brusquely. 'What about other relatives? Any luck there?'

'Nothing so far. Charlie's people are in the Smallwood house this morning, and I told him we'd be along shortly.'

Paget glanced at the time. Using the dead woman's key to gain access, he and Tregalles had taken a brief look round the cottage before leaving Farrow Lane earlier that morning, but a thorough search was best left to Charlie's team. 'You go ahead,' he said. 'I think I'll go over to the bank to have a word with this chap, Beecham. He should have a file on Mrs Smallwood, and I'd like to know why he went round to see her last night. Has Charlie finished in the church?'

'Just finishing up when I spoke to him this morning.'

'Anything of consequence to report so far?'

'He said they had more fingerprints than they knew what to do with, and it would take time to sort them out. Trouble is, they could belong to almost anyone; the church is open to the public. But he did say that one print they found on a candle under one of the pews near the body matches several found in the belfry.'

The sergeant finished his coffee. 'I'll be off, then,' he said, 'unless you have anything else in mind?'

'No. No, you go ahead,' Paget said absently.

'Right.' Tregalles paused at the door and looked back. There was a grim set to the chief inspector's face that hadn't been there last night, and the sergeant didn't think it was entirely due to lack of sleep. He closed the door quietly. Best not to ask, he decided.

It was quicker to walk to the Northern and West Counties Bank in Font Street than it was to take the car and try to find a parking space. Besides, Paget felt he needed the air to clear his head. He'd hardly slept at all last night after reading Patrick's letter. Even now, the words continued to echo inside his head.

It was the best move I've ever made, Patrick had written. *Things are so much different here, and to be honest, I've been very lucky. In more ways than one, as you will see by the pictures. I can't wait to see you two, and have you meet Louise. Isn't she a smasher? I still can't believe that I'm actually getting married at my age. Me, the confirmed bachelor.*

Louise is a nurse. She and a friend came out here from Coventry a year ago. Her friend went back, but Louise liked it so much (and she met me, which clinched it) that she wants to stay here. We still have to sort things out with Immigration, but we don't see any major difficulties.

The thing is, Louise's parents and her four brothers and their wives are all still in England, as are all her old friends, so we are coming over there to be married in June. As you know, I don't have any family left, but you two are as close to family as anyone could be, so I want you to be my best man, and Louise would like Jill to be a bridesmaid. Louise's best friend, a girl she

*trained with, is to be her maid-of-honour. And Louise says not to worry
about the dress; she'll sort that out with Jill when she sees her.*

*The wedding is set for June 29th, but we will be arriving in London June
15th, so perhaps we could all get together before Louise and I leave for
Coventry on the 17th. I know it's short notice, but I would like you both to
meet Louise as soon as we arrive. I know you'll love her . . .*

Already, Paget hated her. He knew he was being completely
unreasonable, but he couldn't help it. In fact, if the photographs
were anything to go by, Louise looked like a very nice girl. Well, not
a girl, exactly; she was probably close to his own age.

Paget ploughed his way across Bridge Street with a total disre-
gard for lights on amber. In fact, he admitted grudgingly, she
looked like just the right sort of woman Patrick needed. But to
stand by Patrick's side again as he had at his own wedding . . .
Without Jill? No, he couldn't do it. That was just too much to ask
of friendship.

'This gentleman is Detective Chief Inspector Paget, Miss Fairmont.'
The young woman who had taken him to the offices behind the
counter spoke in hushed tones as if afraid of being overheard. 'He
asked to see Mr Beecham, and I didn't know . . .' She trailed off into
an uneasy silence.

Rachel Fairmont looked over her glasses at Paget. A slight frown
puckered her brow, and Paget couldn't decide whether the woman
was annoyed or merely puzzled by his presence there.

'Thank you, Pauline,' she said crisply, her eyes still on Paget. 'I'll
take care of it.' She waited until the girl had gone, then rose to her
feet. A white cardigan hung loosely from her shoulders, and she
tugged it closer to her as if for protection as she came out from
behind the desk.

She was a tall woman, slim, fine-boned, neatly attired in what
struck Paget as an old-fashioned way: buttoned white blouse,
straight grey skirt that ended well below the knee, and neat black
shoes. She wore little make-up, and her only adornment consisted
of silver ear-rings in the shape of leaves. Her hands were long and
slender, and she wore no rings.

It was hard to tell her age. Mid-thirties he guessed, and not
unattractive if only she would get rid of those odd-shaped glasses
and the severe hair-style.

'I'm afraid Mr Beecham isn't available – that is – well, actually he's not here today,' she said, and it seemed to Paget that she was choosing her words very carefully. 'If you would care to tell me what you wished to see him about, perhaps I can direct you to someone else.'

Paget wondered why Beecham had chosen this particular morning to be absent, but that could wait. 'In that case,' he said, glancing at the brass plate on the door behind the secretary, 'I'd like to have a word with the manager. Mr Gresham, is it?'

'Yes, but...' The secretary looked at her watch and frowned. 'I'm afraid Mr Gresham isn't here either,' she said worriedly. 'It's most unusual for him to be late. He always lets me know if...Oh! Here he is now.' There was a note of relief in her voice as a heavy-set man entered the office.

'Mr Gresham, this is Detective Chief Inspector Paget,' she said breathlessly. 'He wanted to see Mr Beecham, but I told him Mr Beecham wasn't here today, so he said he'd like to talk to you.'

The manager stopped, set down his briefcase and held out his hand.

'Arthur Gresham,' he said, eyeing Paget speculatively. 'Chief Inspector, you say? Perhaps you'd better come through to my office.' His grasp was firm and brief.

Inside the office, Gresham took off his coat and waved Paget to a seat. He sat down behind his desk, took off his glasses and began to polish them. 'Now then, Chief Inspector, how can I help you?'

But Paget answered with a question of his own. 'Tell me, was it just my imagination or would I be right in thinking that your secretary was being somewhat evasive when I asked for Mr Beecham?'

Gresham slipped his glasses back in place and pursed his lips. 'Harry Beecham left us yesterday,' he said bluntly. 'In the light of what seems to be a continuing recession, we could no longer justify his position at Northern and West Counties. It's unfortunate, and it pains me deeply to have to resort to these measures, especially when it involves people who have been with us for so many years, but there it is. And, since that information won't be released – officially, that is – until later this morning, I can understand Miss Fairmont's reluctance to say more.'

'I see.' Was it just coincidence, he wondered, that Elizabeth Small-wood was murdered on the same day that her boss was dismissed, then later came pounding on her door? 'You have another employee, an Elizabeth Smallwood?' He paused, waiting for Gresham's reaction.

The manager leaned back in his chair, folded his hands across his bulging midriff, and began to rock gently. 'Yes,' he said cautiously. The slight lisp Paget had detected earlier had become more pronounced. 'Mrs Smallwood is one of our employees, but I'm afraid she is not here today either. She rang to say she'd had a bit of an accident.'

'When was that, Mr Gresham?'

'Last evening. She rang Miss Fairmont at home to say she wouldn't be in today. Said she'd taken a bad tumble as she was getting off the bus.'

'I see. So Mrs Smallwood was at work yesterday?'

'Oh, yes. As a matter of fact, she was promoted yesterday. She will be taking over Mr Beecham's duties.' Gresham unclasped his hands and leaned forward. 'In fact,' he said thoughtfully, 'that might have something to do with what happened. She was quite overcome when I told her the good news. She actually broke down and cried. She wasn't expecting it, you see.' He sat back. 'My fault, of course,' he went on. 'I should have given her more warning. Beth Smallwood is an excellent worker, but she is inclined to become emotional at times. Quite high strung. Probably still had her head in the clouds when she got off the bus and missed a step. But why do you ask? She is all right, isn't she?'

'I'm afraid I have to tell you that Mrs Smallwood died last night,' Paget said quietly.

'Died?' The surprise in Gresham's eyes appeared to be genuine, but it was the flicker of another emotion across the manager's face that interested Paget. Was it panic? Fear? Or had he imagined it? 'How? What happened? I mean, I had no idea her injuries were all that serious.'

'She was attacked and killed during an apparent robbery,' Paget told him.

'Good God!' Arthur Gresham appeared dazed. 'I don't know what to say,' he said at last. 'I find it hard to believe. It's...' He shrugged helplessly and fell silent.

'You say that Mrs Smallwood rang your secretary at home last night. Do you happen to know what time that was?'

'No, but I can call Miss Fairmont in and you can ask her if you think it's important.' Gresham reached for the phone.

Rachel Fairmont entered the room and closed the door carefully behind her. She seemed nervous, and kept glancing uncertainly at Gresham. He motioned impatiently for her to come forward. 'Sit down,' he told her brusquely. 'Chief Inspector Paget would like to know what time it was when Beth Smallwood rang you last night.'

The secretary took her seat, smoothed her skirt carefully and turned sideways to face Paget.

'It must have been about eight o'clock,' she said. She looked anxiously from one to the other. 'Why? Is there something wrong?'

Before Paget could reply, Gresham spoke. 'Beth was killed last night,' he said quickly. 'Apparently, someone tried to rob her.'

'Killed? Beth? Oh, no!' Rachel pressed her hands to her face, eyes wide in disbelief. 'What happened? Did someone break in?'

But Paget side-stepped the questions. 'Can you recall exactly what Mrs Smallwood said when she rang?'

Rachel Fairmont closed her eyes and breathed deeply. 'I didn't know it was Beth at first,' she said slowly. 'You see, she said she'd fallen getting off the bus, and she'd bitten her tongue, and it was quite swollen. She said she wouldn't be in this morning because she was going...' Her voice caught in her throat and died. 'I'm sorry,' she whispered. 'It's just that I still can't believe that Beth is dead.'

'Just take your time, Miss Fairmont,' Paget told her. 'Perhaps a glass of water...?'

'No, thank you. I shall be all right,' she assured him. A wan smile touched her face. 'I'm sorry, but I'm afraid I've forgotten what I was saying, Chief Inspector.'

'You said Beth Smallwood told you she was going somewhere.'

'Oh, yes. She said she was going to see the doctor this morning.'

'She rang you from home?'

'Yes.' Rachel hesitated. 'At least, I assumed she was at home.'

'Did she say anything about going out?'

'You mean last night? No.'

'Did she say anything else?'

'No. Well, actually she did but I'm afraid I had trouble understanding her. As I said, her tongue was swollen and it was hard for her to talk. It was all a bit muddled, I'm afraid.'

'I see. You and she were close friends, I take it?'

Rachel seemed surprised by the question. 'Well, no, not exactly. I mean, not *close* friends. We've worked together for several years, of course, but we rarely saw each other outside work, and to be honest, I know almost nothing of her private life.'

Paget regarded the woman quizzically. 'I'm wondering why it was that she rang you,' he said. 'I should have thought she would ring Mr Gresham, especially as she had just been promoted yesterday.'

'I expect she did try to get hold of me,' Gresham interjected, 'but I was out last night. I suppose she thought it best to ring Miss Fairmont, under the circumstances.'

He glanced at his watch, then turned to his secretary. 'Which reminds me: with both Beecham and Beth gone, we will have to make some adjustments in that department.' He pushed his moist lips out to the point of pouting and scowled. 'I suppose there's nothing for it but to have Ling take over pro tem.' The words were said so grudgingly that Paget wondered what it was that 'Ling' had done to earn the manager's displeasure.

Gresham turned back to Paget. 'I do apologize, Chief Inspector,' he said earnestly, 'but I'm sure you understand. In spite of what's happened, we still have clients to serve, and arrangements must be made.' He shook his head sadly.

'Have you noticed any change in Beth Smallwood's behaviour recently?' Paget asked him. 'Was she worried about anything? Or had she quarrelled with anyone, for example?'

Gresham and Rachel Fairmont exchanged mystified glances, and the manager slowly shook his head. 'Beth was such a quiet person,' he said. 'I can't imagine her quarrelling with anyone.' His voice hardened. 'And I really do not understand why you seem to be concentrating your efforts here, Chief Inspector. I can't see how there could possibly be a connection. You did say she was attacked and robbed, I believe?'

'I said the attack was made to *appear* that way,' Paget told him, 'but that may or may not prove to be the case. In the meantime, we have to explore every possibility. I'm simply looking to you for background information. Tell me,' he went on before Gresham could speak, 'how did Mrs Smallwood seem to you when she left here yesterday?'

48

Gresham glanced across at his secretary. 'Quite excited at the prospect of her new job, I'd say – wouldn't you say so, Miss Fairmont?'

'She was certainly excited when I saw her last,' Rachel agreed.

'And when was that?'

'It would be about a quarter past five. Beth was tidying herself up in the Ladies when I left.'

'So you didn't see her leave?'

'No, but I'm sure she would have left within minutes. Since Harry wasn't there to take her home, she would have to make sure she caught the bus at five thirty. After that they only run out her way every hour, I believe.'

Paget turned back to Gresham. 'I'd like to take a look at Mrs Smallwood's desk and her file,' he told him. 'I'm told she has a teenage son, but we haven't been able to contact him yet. Do you happen to know if she had any other relatives?'

Offhand, Gresham said he didn't know. Neither he nor his secretary could recall hearing Beth Smallwood mention anyone. Rachel left the room and returned with a file labelled 'Smallwood, E.', but apart from the usual standard forms and job history, there was little in the file of interest. The original application form showed mother and father as deceased, and Leonard Smallwood was named as next of kin. No other relatives were mentioned. Beth's annual ratings, signed by H. Beecham, had in the last two years moved from 'Satisfactory' to 'Very Satisfactory', and that was the reason, Gresham said, why he had given Beth the opportunity to prove herself as a manager.

Paget closed the file. 'What about Mr Beecham?' he said. 'How did he take the news that he was to be replaced by a subordinate?'

Gresham looked down at the desk. 'He was upset, of course, as you might expect, but on the other hand he had known for some time that someone in his department would have to go. It's unfortunate, but I didn't have a choice. My budget has been cut and I must take whatever steps I deem necessary to live with that. Believe me, Chief Inspector, I thought long and hard before I decided to let Harry go. Especially with his wife the way she is.'

'And what way is that, sir?'

Gresham looked uncomfortable. 'She's been ill for several years, I understand. Mentally ill, that is. Harry has always insisted on looking after her at home, but now...' He shrugged. 'I suppose it will depend on how soon he can get another job.'

'What do you think his chances are?'

Gresham took off his glasses and began to polish them. 'He's a good man,' he said carefully. 'Knows his job. Very reliable. I gave him a good reference.'

'But his chances can't be very good,' Paget persisted.

Gresham's fingers drummed on the desk. He wasn't used to being challenged. 'It all depends,' he said stubbornly. 'I'm sure he'll find something.'

Paget rose to his feet and thanked the manager and his secretary. 'And now, if I could have a look at Mrs Smallwood's desk, I won't take up any more of your time,' he continued. 'But I will need statements from your staff within the next day or two.' He shrugged apologetically. 'Routine stuff, of course, sir, but it has to be done. I'm sure you understand.'

'Yes, of course,' said Gresham curtly, but he looked less than happy at the prospect as Paget and Miss Fairmont left the room.

The cottage was small, a reverse plan of the one next door where Paget and Tregalles had spoken to Mrs Turvey the night before. Two rooms up and two rooms down. Plus a tiny bathroom off the kitchen.

Tregalles moved slowly through the rooms, not quite sure what he was looking for. The two people Charlie had assigned to the job, Rob North and Grace Lovett, had been through all the rooms on a preliminary search, and were now engaged in examining every scrap of paper: bills, bank-book, even notes on calendars. Oddly, there were no letters.

'Find something?' the sergeant asked, peering over Grace's shoulder. The young woman was looking thoughtful as she perused a set of legal documents.

'I think I have,' she said slowly. Tregalles waited. He had a lot of respect for Grace's work. Not only was she thorough, but she seemed to possess a sixth sense when it came to analysing evidence.

The sergeant, who had an eye for the ladies, thought Grace was beautiful. She was tall, slender, blonde, and her eyes were the most expressive Tregalles had ever seen. Blue – well, not exactly; perhaps more green than blue – it depended on the light, and when she looked at you...

He sighed inwardly. It was pleasant to fantasize, but that was as far as it went. Besides, if he'd read the signs correctly, she rather fancied Paget.

'Take a look at this,' Grace said, passing over the papers she'd been studying. 'I think our Mrs Smallwood has been fiddling the books.'

Tregalles scanned the papers. 'Looks like a lien against some property in Tenborough,' he said. 'What about it?'

'It is,' said Grace. 'Now take a look at this one.'

Tregalles studied the second document. 'They look the same to me,' he said.

'They are. Except for one thing. Look at the signatures.'

'J.L. Perriton,' Tregalles read out, then turned to the second set of papers. 'L. R. Smallwood.' He frowned. 'What are you saying, Grace?'

'The liens are against the same property, but a loan was made to two different people under two different account numbers,' Grace explained. 'Perriton is a small building contractor in Tenborough. I looked him up in the telephone book. He took out a loan amounting to £4300 in February of this year. A second loan of £5000 was paid out less than a month ago, using the same property as collateral. But it was paid to L. R. Smallwood.'

Tregalles scratched his head. 'But wouldn't the bank realize the two were the same? And Smallwood. I mean, it's a dead give-away.'

'Not necessarily. Once the originals were filed away – these are copies, of course, probably brought home to practise on – they would never be looked at together. And as long as regular payments were made on both accounts, no one would be the wiser. Presumably Perriton would pay off his loan in the usual manner, so that takes care of the original loan, but the one made out to Small-wood is different. All that's required here is that he pay the interest each month. The bank has the right to call for the principle at any time, but as long as the interest is paid and the rates don't rise significantly, why should they? And the "bank" in this case is, or was, since she was handling the account, Beth Smallwood. As for making the loan payable to her son, the name Smallwood is not uncommon in these parts. It was a calculated risk, but a necessary one if Lenny was using his own ID. Attempting to set up an account under a false name could be done but it's much more difficult.'

'But even paying the interest would use up the entire amount eventually,' Tregalles said, 'so I don't quite see the point.'

'Unless Beth Smallwood intended to float yet another loan to sustain the first one, and so on,' said Grace. 'What she was doing is a mug's game, but if she were desperate enough, who knows? By the look of things around here, I would say she's been living from hand to mouth, but Lenny's doing all right. Have you seen the load of high-tech gear he has upstairs? There must be a few thousand tied up in that. Unless, of course it fell off the back of a lorry.'

'That wouldn't surprise me,' Tregalles said. 'Which reminds me, have you come across anything that might give us a clue as to where he is?'

'You might try his girlfriend.'

'I would if I knew who she was,' Tregalles told her.

'Tania. Tania Costello,' Grace said with a grin. 'I'm surprised you didn't know that, *Detective* Tregalles.'

Tregalles sighed. 'Point to you,' he conceded. 'How did you find out?'

'I went through his tapes upstairs. Tania loaned him some and her name's on them.' Her grin grew wider. 'Dead easy, Tregalles, when you know what to look for.'

Rob North, who had been listening, came over and dropped two video cassettes on the table. 'You should have tried these,' he said laconically. 'They're empty now, but they've been used to hide cocaine.'

CHAPTER 7

Lenny Smallwood sat on the edge of the bed, knees pressed tightly together to make sure the magazine on them didn't move. He tapped the packet gently, carefully emptying the white powder into a tiny mound, then rolled a piece of paper into a thin tube and bent low over the magazine. With infinite care, he guided one end of the tube into his right nostril, closed the left with his finger, and sniffed. The powder vanished.

His eyes watered as he lay back on the bed and waited for the rush. Everything would be all right in a minute, he told himself. It would sort itself out. He'd just had a run of bad luck, that was all. He wouldn't be in this mess if his mother had done her job properly. It was all her fault. Christ! She'd got away with it once; what was to stop her from doing it again? But why bugger about with five thousand quid at a time when the bank had millions?

But no. She had to go and get cold feet. Stupid cow never did have any guts. Always giving in. Always trying to please. He'd played her like a bloody fiddle since he was four years old. Pitiful. Even when he'd banged up her car, she'd been so concerned about him that she hadn't even questioned his version of the crash. Not that it had been much of a car to begin with, but the insurance should have paid her *something* for it. Thieving sods. Which meant she couldn't afford another. And the way she was going on she never would have anything. And gullible! Christ, she'd even believed him when he'd insisted the accident wasn't his fault, despite what the police and the insurance company said.

Like she had in court last year. And that stupid magistrate had believed her! Lenny giggled, then laughed. He laughed so hard that he couldn't get his breath. He began to choke. He pulled himself upright, coughing and laughing; laughing and coughing, tears streaming down his face.

He wiped his eyes. He felt good! He wished Tan were here. He looked at his watch. It was time she was back. Job interview, she'd said. Yeah. Sure. She was probably being 'interviewed' all right. On some plush office carpet. She kept saying she was off the game, but she always had money.

Lenny got off the bed and moved restlessly around the room. Money. That's what it was all about. He fingered the remaining packets in his pocket. His supply had almost run out. The thought chilled him. How was he going to get more when he couldn't pay back what he'd taken? If only he hadn't blown that first £5000. But he'd been so sure there would be more. There *would* have been more if his mother hadn't been so bloody stupid.

Christ! he was thirsty. He flung open the door and clattered down the narrow stairs. Tania's mum was at work, so he didn't have to worry about her. He went to the fridge and looked inside. It was a mess. Bits of this and bits of that; open tins with God knows what inside. But no beer. He slammed the door shut.

The raspy doorbell rang. Twice. He stood there in the kitchen, irresolute. It wouldn't be Tania or her mum. They would have let themselves in. He'd just stay quiet and whoever it was would go away. The bell rang again. He waited, counting off the seconds in his head.

They should be gone by now. He turned back to the fridge. There had to be *something* in there.

A shadow passed the window. Lenny slid around the side of the fridge and pressed himself against the wall. Someone knocked on the back door. He held his breath. It might just be some neighbour. It might be all right, but he wasn't taking any chances.

Someone was peering in the window. He drew back. They wouldn't be able to see him through the lace curtain if he stayed absolutely still. The shadow disappeared, and he heard footsteps moving off. He listened intently. They were going back through the entryway to the street.

Lenny slipped out of the kitchen and into the front room. Moving cautiously, he approached the curtained window and looked out. A man was standing beside a car; a stocky, dark-haired man he'd seen before. The man paused to take one last sweeping look at the house, then got into the car and slowly drove away.

A cold, hard knot formed in Lenny's stomach, and he began to shake.

Hawthorn Drive was a long, curving street on the south side of Broadminster. Mrs Turvey had been right in her assumption that Harry Beecham lived not far from Farrow Lane. Five minutes by car at most.

Number 83 was a semi-detached house with a small patch of lawn and a few undernourished roses and hydrangeas separating it from the road. The house itself looked neat enough, but close inspection revealed a lack of care. As Paget walked up the path, he noted paint lifting from the window sills, brickwork that needed pointing, and moss well established in the cracks on the steps leading to the front door.

He rang the doorbell and waited. The morning paper was still in the letter-box, and it was almost noon. He was about to ring again when he heard someone coming to the door.

The man who opened the door was grey. Grey hair, grey moustache, grey pullover and trousers. Even his face was grey, and he looked as if he hadn't slept for a week.

'Mr Beecham? Harry Beecham?' enquired Paget.

The man blinked at him like some sort of automaton processing and digesting Paget's words. 'That's right,' he said at last.

'I'd like to talk to you. My name is Paget. Detective Chief Inspector Paget. May I come in?'

Beecham looked apprehensive. 'Police?' he said. 'What...? I don't understand. What do you want with me?'

'I'd prefer to discuss that inside, sir, if you don't mind.' Paget moved forward as he spoke, and Beecham automatically stepped back.

'What's this all about?' he asked. 'Has there been a – a robbery or something?' He looked up and down the street as if hoping to find the answer there.

Paget moved past him. 'In here, sir?' he enquired, pointing to a partly open door.

Beecham ran nervous fingers through his wiry hair, then shrugged resignedly. 'Yes. Yes, I suppose...' He closed the outer door and followed Paget into the front room.

The furniture, Paget noted, was old but nicely kept, as were the scattered carpets on the polished floor. Inexpensive pictures adorned the walls – pastoral scenes, for the most part, but Paget's eyes were drawn immediately to a charcoal sketch of a dancer. It was the only one of its kind in the room, and he felt the frame alone must be worth more than the rest of the pictures put together.

The artwork was magnificent. Paget was by no means a connoisseur, but he knew instinctively that everything about the drawing was superb. The flowing line of the body; the movement of the arms; the tilt of the head – he could *feel* the fluid motion and the freedom of the dance.

The chief inspector moved closer. 'H.B.,' he said aloud, turning to Beecham. 'Did you do this?'

Beecham shook his head. 'No,' he said curtly. 'That's Helen's work. My wife.'

'It's magnificent,' Paget said. 'But I don't recall seeing any of her work before. Does she exhibit locally?'

'No. That was done five years ago.' His words were clipped as if he didn't want to talk about it, but as Paget continued to look at the sketch, he offered a grudging explanation. 'Helen was just starting to exhibit when she became ill and had to give it up.'

'She's done nothing since?'

'No.'

'Pity. A great pity,' said Paget as he turned away. He indicated the chairs on either side of the fireplace. 'May we sit down?'

Beecham hesitated, then nodded. He waited until Paget was seated before lowering himself gingerly into a chair facing the chief inspector. 'What *is* this all about?' he asked again.

'I'm told you went round to Elizabeth Smallwood's house last night,' said Paget. 'Pounded on her door, in fact. Is that correct, sir?'

Beecham stared. 'Is *that* what this is about?' he asked. 'I mean, I know I was a bit short with Mrs Turvey, and I'm sorry, but did she actually report me to the police?'

'Do you mind telling me why it was so important that you find Mrs Smallwood?'

'No offence intended, Chief Inspector,' said Beecham stiffly, 'but I really don't see what business it is of yours.'

'Did you find Mrs Smallwood?' Paget persisted.

'No. And once again I don't see...'

'Mrs Turvey told you that Mrs Smallwood was in the church at the top end of Farrow Lane, did she not?'

'Yes, but I didn't go there.' Beecham sat forward and clasped his hands together like a supplicant. 'Look, I don't understand all this,' he said earnestly. 'Why do you want to know whether I saw Beth or not?'

Paget ignored the question. 'I find it strange that you should be so anxious to see Mrs Smallwood one minute, then not go to the church when you were told that she was there,' he said. 'Where *did* you go, sir?'

'I came home,' Beecham said tersely, 'and that's all I'm going to say until you tell me what this is all about.' The man looked exhausted, but Paget had caught a whiff of his breath as he entered the house, and suspected that what Harry Beecham was suffering from was a hangover. The question was: had he been drinking because he'd lost his job, or to blot out the memory of killing the woman who'd replaced him?

'Beth Smallwood was killed last night,' he said, watching Beecham closely.

Beecham sat up straighter in his chair and blinked rapidly. 'Killed? he repeated shakily. 'How? Where? What happened?'

'She was beaten to death in St Justin's church by someone who wanted us to believe she died while being robbed.'

Beecham stared slack-jawed. 'Oh, God,' he said weakly. 'Poor Beth.' He rubbed his face with his hands as if trying to stir some life into the putty-coloured flesh. 'But you can't think that I...? I mean, I went round to the house, yes, but...'

'Mrs Smallwood had just taken over your job,' Paget interjected. 'A job from which you had been dismissed after many years of service.'

Beecham's mouth set in a thin, hard line, and for the first time since he had opened the door his eyes became alive. 'You've been speaking to Gresham,' he accused.

'According to my information,' Paget continued as if Beecham hadn't spoken, 'you arrived at Mrs Smallwood's house about eight thirty last night, and began hammering on her door. When Mrs Turvey came out to see what was going on, you demanded to know where Beth Smallwood was, and when she told you she was at the church, you went up there to find her. What happened when you got there, Mr Beecham? Did all that pent-up rage and resentment at losing your job suddenly boil over?'

Beecham's head was shaking violently. 'No, no, no! You've got it all wrong!' he protested weakly. 'I never saw Beth. I told you I came straight home.'

Paget's eyes showed disbelief.

'It's true! Honest to God; I swear it. Mrs Turvey did tell me that Beth was at the church. She said something about preparing for a wedding, so I thought there would be someone else there as well, and I wanted to talk to Beth alone. So I came straight home.'

'What did you want to talk to Mrs Smallwood about?'

Beecham looked away and did not answer immediately. 'I wanted her to tell me herself why she had given in to Gresham,' he said bitterly. 'I wanted Beth to tell me to my face that she hadn't agreed to sleep with that slimy bastard in order to get the job.' He looked down at his hands. 'Not that I would have believed her if she had denied it,' he ended, speaking more to himself than to Paget.

'Sleep with Gresham? Come now, Mr Beecham. That is a very serious allegation.'

'That would be his price,' said Beecham flatly. 'Just ask any of the girls. Gresham can't go near a woman without trying it on.' He sighed. 'The only reason Gresham would promote Beth is if she agreed to sleep with him. She'd have never got the job otherwise. Beth is a good worker – or was – and I liked her, but she wasn't management material by a long shot, and Gresham knows it.

'But he's a canny bastard. He knew that Beth was desperate for money. She simply couldn't afford to turn down a promotion, even if it meant taking it on Gresham's terms.' Beecham shook his head sadly. 'As for the job, she'd muddle through with Gresham's help, but there would be a price to pay, and Gresham would take great delight in exacting it. But I doubt if it would have lasted long. Once Gresham tired of her, he'd find some excuse to get rid of her.'

Suddenly Beecham's face broke into a crooked smile. 'But now he'll have no option but to put Terry Ling in there,' he said softly, 'and he won't like that!'

Paget remembered the name. 'Who is Terry Ling? And why doesn't Gresham like him?'

'He's a management trainee. Came over from Hong Kong three years ago. He's been at our branch for about six months, now. He's young, he's intelligent, and he's ambitious. And he's had excellent training in Hong Kong. My old job would be a doddle for him.'

'So, what's the problem?'

'First of all, Terry was sent here by head office and Gresham didn't have any say in the matter. And Terry's being Chinese made it even less palatable. Gresham is not known for his tolerant nature, believe me. On top of that, Terry probably knows more about banking that Gresham ever did, and he sees him as a threat. Oh, no,' concluded Beecham, 'Gresham won't be happy about this at all.'

'Tell me about your relationship with Beth Smallwood outside the office,' said Paget. 'I'm told you were in the habit of taking her home.'

Beecham sighed. 'Mrs Turvey, again, no doubt,' he said wearily. 'Beth was a friend. That's all. There was nothing between us. I love my wife dearly, Chief Inspector, but I cannot talk to her.'

Beecham leaned his head back and stared at the ceiling. 'My wife suffers from long bouts of black depression,' he went on. 'She also suffers from agoraphobia. She never goes out. We have no social life at all. It's not the sort of thing one discusses over coffee at work, but I could talk to Beth. I used to drive her home after work, and we would talk. Sometimes I would stop there for tea.'

He raised his head and looked directly at Paget. 'I wouldn't hurt Helen for the world, so I never told her. I lied. I said I was working. It seemed so much simpler that way.'

'I see. Did Mrs Smallwood ever mention any relatives, other than her son, I mean?'

'She said something once that made me think she had a sister, but she would never talk about her family. I don't think she'd had a very happy time of it when she was young, so I stayed away from the subject.'

'Any idea where this sister might live? Or her name?'

Again Beecham shook his head. 'Sorry. It was some time ago, and as I said, it was only an impression. I could be wrong.'

'What can you tell me about Mrs Smallwood's son, Leonard?'

'Lenny?' Beecham grimaced. 'I can tell you he made her life a misery,' he said sourly. 'Should have had a damned good hiding years ago, but Beth wouldn't hear a word against him. The kid was always in some sort of scrape, but it was never his fault. He was in court, you know. Stealing or receiving stolen goods or some such thing. I remember Beth went to court with him and he was put on probation. But she would never talk about it.'

'Was Beth Smallwood in any kind of trouble?'

Beecham frowned. 'What kind of trouble?'

'Was she worried about anything? Was she frightened of anyone? Did she ever mention anything like that?'

'No.' Beecham scoffed at the idea. 'She was always worried about Lenny, of course, but that was normal. She was hardly the sort to make enemies.'

But she probably made one of you by taking your job, thought Paget. He rose to his feet and Beecham followed suit.

'Thank you for your time, sir,' he said as he made his way to the door. He paused. 'There is just one more thing, though. What were you doing between the time you left the bank yesterday and when you arrived on Mrs Smallwood's doorstep last evening?'

'Driving around, mostly. Still in a state of shock. One minute I was doing my job; the next I was out on the street, literally. I didn't know what to do, so I just drove. I stopped several times, but I couldn't tell you where.'

'Had you been drinking when you arrived at Mrs Smallwood's house?'

Colour flooded into Beecham's face. 'I – I may have had the odd drink,' he said nervously.

Paget raised an eyebrow. 'The odd drink, Mr Beecham? Yet you say you drove around all day but can't remember where you stopped?'

Beecham's face grew darker. 'All right, so, I did have more than a few. If you must know, I had a damned sight more than a few. God knows I had good reason, and you can do what you like about that! And, yes, I was upset; yes, I wanted to talk to Beth, but when Mrs Turvey said she was at the church I assumed there would be others there as well, so I came straight home. You have to believe that.'

'Can anyone confirm what time it was when you came home? Your wife, perhaps?'

Beecham sighed heavily and shook his head. 'Helen was sleeping when I got in last night and I didn't wake her. You see, as I explained, my wife never goes out; I have to bring the world to her, and the last thing I wanted to do was talk about my day.'

CHAPTER 8

'Officially, between eight thirty and nine fifteen last evening is the best I can do,' said Starkie. 'Unofficially, if you put the time of death at around ten to nine, you won't be far wrong. Getting to her so soon after she died, and the stable temperature in the church, helped narrow it down.'

'Can't ask more than that,' said Paget. 'What about cause of death?'

'Confirmed,' said Starkie. 'In non-technical terms, it was a vicious blow to the side of the head. The victim must have died instantly. But she wasn't kneeling. In my opinion she was standing when she was hit, and went down heavily on her knees when she fell. There was also a scrape on her left arm, which I believe happened when she tried to ward off the first blow. Which also means she was facing her attacker. It was the second blow that got through.'

'And the weapon?'

'Ah! I was coming to that. Forensic found traces of blood in the grooves in the base of one of the candle holders on the altar, and it fits the injury. More tests have to be done, but I'd say it's a safe bet. But she'd been in the wars even before that. Those injuries to her face and the bruises on her body were caused by someone punching her in the face and knocking her down at least an hour – possibly more – before she died. But there's more. I found evidence to suggest she'd been raped. Or, if it wasn't rape, it was certainly rough sex. Her lips were swollen, bite marks on the breasts, and there was heavy bruising around the vaginal area as well as on her back and buttocks. Finger marks can be seen quite plainly on her back.'

'You're saying she was attacked and raped an hour or two *before* she was assaulted in the church?' said Paget incredulously.

'No, that's *not* what I'm saying,' said Starkie. 'Unless I'm very much mistaken, the physical evidence suggests that Mrs Smallwood was raped several hours before she died. Say in the middle of the afternoon or thereabouts. Then, about an hour or so before she died, she was punched in the face and knocked down. The bruises were made at different times.'

'Good God!' Three separate assaults in so short a space of time? What had the poor woman done?

'I also found several fibres under the nails of her left hand, none of which matched her own clothing, so I sent them on to the lab. I suspect they came from the killer's clothes when she tried to ward off the blow.'

'On the other hand, they could have come from something with which she came in contact before she was killed,' Paget suggested.

'No. I don't think so. There were too many of them and the fibres were quite long. They would have been a nuisance. She would have pulled them off immediately.'

'Thanks, Reg. Appreciate your call. You'll let me have the full report as soon as possible?'

'First thing tomorrow morning,' Starkie assured him.

Tregalles, who had been hovering in the doorway for the last couple of minutes, entered the office. 'Nancy King – you know, the tall brunette who works in the office downstairs – was just in to see Len Ormside,' he told Paget. 'She says that Mrs Smallwood rang her at home last night to ask her advice. It seems that Nancy met Mrs Smallwood when Lenny appeared in court, and when she rang last night, she told Nancy that she'd lied at the trial and she wanted to set things right. Nancy told her to come in this morning, and she would make sure she was looked after.'

'And now she's dead,' said Paget slowly. 'I wonder if young Lenny knew his mum was about to shop him?'

Grace Lovett sat in Paget's office, one slender, nylon-clad leg draped over the other knee, foot swinging slightly as she watched him peruse the papers in front of them.

'Good of you to bring these over yourself, Grace,' Paget said without looking up, 'but Tregalles could have brought them.'

'It was no trouble. I came myself in case you had any questions.'

Paget continued to study the papers while Grace studied Paget. She could have sent the papers over with Tregalles, but she'd wanted to see the chief inspector again. She was probably being silly, she told herself, but she was fascinated by the man. He was so – unreachable; so remote. Not that he hadn't always treated her with courtesy and the utmost respect, but, dammit, she'd like something *more* than respect from him. She'd like to be noticed for herself.

He looked tired; in fact his face was drawn. He works too hard, she thought, and he could do with a few home-cooked meals. She wished she had the nerve to invite him to dinner.

Grace had rarely seen him smile. All business; everyone who knew him said so; a workaholic in fact. Still not entirely over the loss of his wife. He must have loved her very much, she thought, and felt a twinge of jealousy.

'Very good, Grace,' said Paget, looking up. 'You did well to spot it. I'll take this round to the bank manager tomorrow morning and see what he has to say about it. There will have to be an audit, of course.'

'I'm sure there will,' she said. 'Would you like me to come along?'

'No. Thank you, Grace. I can take it from here.' He stood up. 'And thanks again for coming in.'

Grace scrambled to her feet and smoothed her skirt. 'No trouble,' she said again. She paused at the door. 'Perhaps you would let me know how it turns out at the bank?' she ventured. 'I'd rather like to know.'

'Of course,' he said. 'I'll be talking to Charlie, and he can fill you in.'

She smiled her thanks. That hadn't been exactly what she'd meant.

Lenny Smallwood didn't dare go back to Tania's house. Not that her mother wanted him there in any case, but she didn't have much say in it. Tania would soon put her in her place. Perhaps, he thought, it had been Tania's mum who'd shopped him. Maybe that's why that bloke had come snooping round. He wouldn't put it past her. Bloody old slag!

The question still remained: where to go? He'd spent the afternoon riding round the countryside, considering it to be safer than staying in Broadminster where he might be spotted. But now it was getting dark and he needed a bed for the night, and he daren't go back to his own house where they might be watching for him.

Bernie's. That was it. Bernie would put him up. He could sleep in the back of the shop where Bernie rebuilt bikes. He'd bought the bike from Bernie; the least Bernie could do was put him up for a night or two until he could work out what to do. Maybe, if he was lucky, he could hit Bernie up for a snort. Just to tide him over.

It was almost dark by the time Lenny rolled the bike into the yard. The shop was in darkness but there was a light on upstairs. Lenny propped the bike on its stand, went over to the door and pressed the bell. The bell rang in the shop, but Lenny knew it could be heard upstairs. He rang again, and heard a window raised above him.

'Whadyawant?' growled a voice.

He stepped back and looked up. 'It's me, Bernie,' Lenny called, trying to keep his voice down. 'Lenny Smallwood.'

'So?'

'I – I could use some help. Can you come down?'

There was no reply, but the window went down. Lenny waited nervously. Suddenly a bolt slid back, a key turned in the lock and the door opened.

Bernie Striker was a big man. Heavy. Round face, small eyes, and a crinkly beard that began at his ears and finished somewhere in the middle of his massive chest. Silhouetted against a feeble light, he looked enormous.

'Smashed up the bike, I suppose?' he said, glancing around. 'Can't say I'm surprised.' He caught sight of the bike and scowled. 'What's this?' he demanded, fixing his eyes on Lenny.

'It's n-not the bike, Bernie,' Lenny stammered. 'It's me. I need a place to kip for the night. Any old place. The back of the shop. I can sleep on the floor.'

Bernie shook his head. 'Bugger off home,' he said, and began to shut the door.

Lenny's hand shot out to hold the door. 'Please, Bernie,' he pleaded. 'Just for tonight. I – I'll be gone early in the morning. Before you open the shop, I swear. Please, Bernie.'

The big man sighed heavily and shook his head as if to say he was acting against his better judgement. 'Better come in, then,' he told Lenny. 'You in trouble?' he demanded as he rebolted the door.

'Not with the police,' said Lenny quickly.

'Who, then?'

Lenny avoided the big man's eyes, but Bernie was waiting for an answer, and you didn't keep Bernie waiting. 'It's a misunderstanding, that's all,' he said. 'It's not my fault. Over a bit of money. Like I said, it's not my fault.'

Bernie's eyes narrowed. 'Who?'

Lenny shrugged and tried to smile to show he wasn't worried. 'Archie Stern,' he said weakly. 'He...'

'Stern?' Bernie fairly bellowed the name. 'Jesus Christ!'

'It – it's nothing, really,' Lenny stammered. 'Honest, Bernie. He's going to get his money. It's just that...'

'I don't want to know,' the big man said. He eyed Lenny for a long moment. 'You can kip down over there,' he said, indicating a corner of the shop behind some half-assembled bikes. 'But I want you out of here come morning. Understand?'

'Yeah, Bernie, I understand. And thanks. I won't forget...'

But Bernie had turned his back, and moments later Lenny heard his heavy tread retreating up the stairs. He looked round the shop. There wasn't much with which to make a bed. Two pairs of overalls hung behind a door, and there was a bin half full of oily rags.

Lenny ignored the rags. He spread one pair of overalls on the floor and rolled up the other pair to make a pillow. The floor was cold and very hard. He whimpered as he tried to sleep.

He was falling! Where from he did not know. He just knew that when he landed it would all be over. He smashed into something on his way down, but it was dark and he couldn't see what it was. Pain shot through his belly and he vomited into the void. Still falling. He fought for breath. Bang!

Another jolting hit, this time in his chest. Light! He peered into the darkness, straining to see. Blazing light! He tried to cover his eyes with his arms but they wouldn't move.

He woke up retching. His whole body was consumed by fire. He couldn't see.

'On your feet, Lenny, boy.' The voice came from behind the light. 'We've got a message for you.'

Lenny groaned. He couldn't move.

'Don't think he heard you,' said a second voice. 'Trouble with his ears, I shouldn't wonder. Need cleaning out.'

A boot crashed into the side of Lenny's head. For one split second he was grateful, because now he could die and there would be no more pain. Darkness engulfed him. He began the long slide down; to where he did not know, but neither did he care.

He screamed, writhing, choking, gasping for breath as pain such as he'd never known exploded in his head. He screamed again when they pulled him to his feet, then choked as someone stuffed an oily rag half-way down his throat and bundled him through the door.

Upstairs, Bernie watched from behind the curtain as they frog-marched Lenny into the yard and threw him into the back of a waiting car. The two men climbed in after him, and the car pulled out of the yard with hardly a sound. Bernie went downstairs. Cautiously, he opened the double doors at the back of the shop and slipped outside. He moved quietly for such a big man.

He closed the gates, then wheeled Lenny's bike inside the shop, closing and locking the double doors behind him.

He stood there for a moment, just looking at the bike. It was a nice machine. A few years old, but in good nick. Lenny had looked after it; he'd give the kid that. Stupid little git. Skimming from someone like Archie Stern was just asking for trouble.

Bernie sighed as he picked up a spanner. It seemed a shame, but it had to be done. And the sooner the better. It was too dangerous to leave the bike as it was. He grunted heavily as he squatted down beside the bike and began to strip it down.

Paget finished the washing up and put everything away. He could have left it for Mrs Wentworth in the morning, but he had little else to do, and he was restless. He wandered through the house. There was nothing worth watching on TV, and he didn't feel like reading. He felt irritable and ill at ease for no reason.

He dropped into a chair and closed his eyes. But there *was* a reason, he thought guiltily, and it was right there in his pocket. Patrick's letter. He would like to see Patrick again. They had shared digs together in the early days, and they had remained friends even after they had gone their separate ways. Not that they had seen a lot of each other after he and Jill were married. But every few months or so, Patrick would come to dinner or they would meet somewhere for a meal. Patrick always had a girl in tow, but he'd made it clear that he was not the marrying kind.

'A policeman's wife is not a happy one,' he used to paraphrase, and Jill would thump him and tell him it was time he settled down.

So now, after all these years, he was getting married. It would be nice to see Patrick again – find out about his job in Canada; talk about old times? But be his best man? There was no way. Not without Jill.

CHAPTER 9

Wednesday – 15 May

'It's possible, of course, that Beth Smallwood was killed by a stranger,' said Paget. 'But considering what this woman went through that day, I think it is much more likely that she was killed by someone she knew.'

Paget was in Detective Superintendent Thomas Alcott's office. The chief inspector had spent a restless night, and his face looked pale beneath the fluorescent lights. Outside, the rain bounced off the window sill. The forecast said it would last all day.

Alcott dragged heavily on his cigarette. 'What about the son? Could he have killed his mother?'

'He's certainly well up on the list,' said Paget. 'He did run when he saw us and we haven't been able to find him. Tregalles tracked down the girl, but she claims she hasn't seen Lenny since yesterday morning.'

Alcott leaned back in his chair and regarded Paget through a veil of smoke. 'What about this rape?' he said. 'Do you think the boy did that as well?'

'No. Not if Mrs Turvey's interpretation of events is anything to go by. And the timing's wrong. Lenny and the girl weren't in the house that long, and what Mrs Turvey described was an argument that ended when Lenny hit his mother. He and the girl left very soon after that. She could be wrong, of course, but she keeps a pretty close eye on what goes on, so I'm inclined to believe her version of what happened.

'But Harry Beecham said something interesting. He said that Gresham would never have given his old job to Beth Smallwood unless she agreed to sleep with him. And in view of Starkie's findings...'

Alcott shook his head impatiently. 'He's hardly likely to say anything good about the man who'd just sacked him, is he?' he said. 'Beecham had just lost his job, and it's been given to a junior. He thought she was his friend and now he believes she stabbed him in the back. He's lashing out.'

'That's not quite the way it came across to me,' said Paget. 'According to Starkie, someone had sex with Beth Smallwood, and not all that long before she was killed. And Rachel Fairmont said Beth didn't leave work until everyone else had gone, which was after five. Mrs Turvey estimated that Beth Smallwood arrived home around six, which is consistent with the bus schedules. I have someone checking with the driver who was on that run that day to see if we can confirm that. Lenny didn't arrive until around seven, and he was only in the house some fifteen or twenty minutes, again according to Mrs Turvey.'

Paget hitched his chair closer to Alcott's desk as he made his next point. 'The Reverend Parslow says he rang Mrs Smallwood just before eight, and he seemed to think she was having her tea when he called. But Starkie says her stomach was virtually empty. In his opinion she hadn't eaten for some time, possibly since breakfast. So when did this sexual attack, encounter, or whatever it was, take place? Starkie believes it occurred during the afternoon. And where was she in the afternoon? At work.'

He sat back and waited while Alcott stubbed out the cigarette. The superintendent's face was deeply lined, and his skin was sallow. His eyes, deep-set astride a narrow nose, moved constantly as if afraid of missing something. And in repose, the corners of his mouth turned down, giving the impression that he was perpetually dissatisfied.

'That's a very tenuous connection,' he said brusquely, 'and it may or may not have anything to do with the murder. We know nothing of this woman's sex life; she may have been having it off with almost anyone.'

'We've turned up nothing either at her house or at the bank to suggest that she had a social life of any sort, let alone a sex life,' said Paget, but Alcott brushed that aside.

'Arthur Gresham is a respected member of the community,' he said firmly. 'His wife is the niece of an earl, and quite wealthy in her own right. I happened to meet her some years ago when my youngest daughter wanted a dog. Lilian Gresham breeds Shetland Sheepdogs, and she judges at county dog shows.

'On the other hand, it looks to me as if you need to find the son. The fact that this Lenny took off like greased lightning when he saw you suggests guilt. Perhaps he went into the church to carry on his argument with his mother, and things got out of hand.'

'That, too, is possible,' Paget said carefully, 'but from what I've heard about the boy, something doesn't add up. He doesn't strike me as the type to go fiddling around with candlesticks after he'd used one of them to kill his mother. My impression of him is that he might know enough to wipe his prints off, but after that he'd drop the candlestick and run. The same reasoning applies if it was a simple case of robbery by someone as yet unknown.'

Alcott lit another cigarette. 'Beecham had a motive,' he pointed out. 'You said he claimed he didn't go to the church, but that seems unlikely, considering the state he was in, especially when he had to pass it on his way home.'

'It seems unlikely to me, too,' Paget agreed, 'but I have no proof he's lying.'

The phone on Alcott's desk rang. He reached out for it but held his hand in check. 'Anything else?' he enquired. Paget shook his head. 'Right. Keep me informed, then. And don't waste your time on Gresham. Concentrate on Beecham and Lenny Smallwood. Chances are it's one of them.'

The incident room that had been set up first thing Tuesday morning was on the ground floor directly below Paget's own office, and he made his way there now.

Sergeant Ormside was the man in charge, and Paget found him sorting through a stack of paper several inches thick. Len Ormside had a talent for gathering and co-ordinating information. He knew the name of every copper from the highest to the low, but his greatest strength lay in his knowledge of the local district and its people.

The sergeant was a thin, sharp-featured man with ginger hair. His movements were slow and measured, but his mind was quick, and he took no guff from anyone no matter what their rank.

'Morning, Mr Paget,' he greeted the chief inspector as he pulled a sheet of paper from the pile in front of him. 'We've got some good news and some bad news on Lenny Smallwood. The good news is that we've found him; the bad news is that he's in hospital. Somebody did a very professional job on him: concussion; fractured wrist; internal injuries, as yet undetermined; fractured jaw; and multiple lacerations. He's in the operating room now, and it seems unlikely that we'll be able to talk to him for some time.'

Paget sat down beside the desk. 'Where was he found?'

'A farmer found him in a lane about five miles up the Clunbridge road shortly before six this morning. He told the ambulance people he thought the boy had been run over, but the doctor who examined Lenny when he was brought into Casualty said he was certain he'd been beaten. He reckoned Lenny had been thrown out of a car when they were finished with him.'

'We have someone with him at the hospital?'

'Yes.'

'Good. Anything else?'

'We're trying to trace the sister, assuming she exists, but no luck so far. I've got a list of telephone numbers and addresses Charlie's people took from Mrs Smallwood's house – address book, numbers scribbled on calendars and suchlike. They are all being checked out. Starkie was asking about formal identification of the body for the records, but I told him it might take a while, what with young Lenny out of the picture. I suppose we could get the manager of the bank to do it.'

'No.' Somehow the thought of Arthur Gresham identifying the body of Beth Smallwood went against the grain. Perhaps it wasn't rational, but Paget rebelled at the idea. 'At least, not at this time,' he went on, seeing the question in the sergent's eyes. 'Let's try to find a relative. Anything else?'

'Not really. Forensic say they are swamped with work, but they'll let us know as soon as they have anything.'

'Right. Now, I'd like you to find out what you can about Beecham and his wife. Beecham claims they've had no social life whatsoever since his wife's been ill, but someone must know something about them. Helen Beecham used to be a pretty good artist. Some of her artist friends may have kept in touch, so you might try that line of enquiry.'

Paget put on his coat. 'I'm going back to the bank with the material Grace Lovett found at the house yesterday, and to see if I can get more background on Beecham and Mrs Smallwood. And I'll call in at the hospital on my way back to find out how Lenny Smallwood's doing.

'Oh, yes. One other thing. Have Tregalles bring in Lenny's girl-friend, Tania Costello. Now that Lenny is in a critical condition, she might be a bit more helpful. Chances are she knows who did this to him. Tell Tregalles to lean on her if he has to. Does she have any form?'

'Soliciting,' Ormside said. 'Started when she was thirteen. Nothing in the past six months. Either she's off the game or she's learned to keep her head down.'

'How old is she now?'

'Seventeen.'

There were so many like her out there, thought Paget, and not a hope in hell of ever getting them off the streets. But that particular problem, as always, would have to wait; he had more pressing matters to attend to at the moment.

Tony Rudge slipped into the room and closed the door behind him. He moved swiftly to the old-fashioned desk and sat down behind it. This was his father's office, and even though he knew his father was in town this morning, Tony's palms were sweaty as he began to rummage through the pigeon-holes.

He was nervous and excited. Not just because he was going through his father's records, but because he knew who had killed Lenny Smallwood's mum. He *knew*! – and he could hardly contain himself.

And now he was going to do something about it. This was his big chance, and by God he was going to take it.

He'd hung around the office yesterday, hoping his father would leave, but all he'd managed to do was make his father angry. 'Got nothing better to do than hang about the place, have you, lad? Bone bloody idle, you are. That back lawn needs cutting, and the potting shed needs clearing, so go on, get on with it. You are in my care, remember.'

As if he were likely to forget. That was one of the conditions of his release: that he work for his father at the guest house until his time was up. Cheap labour – that suited his father very well, Tony thought bitterly. And he still had months to go before he'd be free. After that, he'd be off to London; look up Chalky White. Chalky should be out by then, and he'd told Tony to come and see him. Things would be different then.

They could be different after tonight, as well, he thought, if only he could find what he was looking for. A lot different. This time he would do it on his own. No partners. No one to let him down. No one like Lenny Smallwood. It had been a sad day when he'd teamed up with Lenny, although they'd done all right at first, breaking into houses. Small stuff, easy to carry, easy to unload. There was this bloke who came in from Wolverhampton with his van once a week. He'd give them a list of things he needed next time round and they'd steal to order.

But that wasn't good enough for Lenny because by then he was snorting coke and he needed more and more money just to buy the stuff. He became careless, and that's when things went wrong.

On this particular day, Lenny was supposed to be keeping watch, but when Tony went upstairs Lenny plunked himself down in a big armchair, took a snort of coke, and sat watching telly. Unaware that Lenny wasn't keeping watch, Tony was on his way downstairs, arms full of loot, when the owner walked in and saw him. He was a big man, and there was nowhere for Tony to go. They both just stood there, each as startled as the other. The man didn't notice Lenny slumped in the chair behind him.

Tony was rooted to the spot, waiting for the inevitable to happen. He'd never been caught before, so chances were he'd get off with nothing more than a slap on the wrist. It wouldn't be that bad, he told himself. But he'd reckoned without Lenny. The idiot had snatched up a heavy ornament and hit the man on the head with it. The man went down like a stone, and Tony was too paralysed with fear to run.

But Lenny wasn't. He was already on his way out the back when a second man entered the house. He grabbed Tony and slammed him down so hard he'd broken three ribs, then held him while he telephoned the police.

Fortunately, the owner of the house recovered, but it was touch and go for a few days. The police made it very clear to Tony that if he didn't give them the name of his accomplice, he could be gone for a very long time indeed. Tony had no qualms about grassing on his partner. Lenny was a nutter; he deserved to be locked up.

But Lenny got off with probation. Even thinking about it now made Tony angry. The bastard had got off, thanks to his mum lying her head off about where he was that night. And since neither man had actually seen Lenny, the only thing the police could charge him with was receiving stolen goods – goods from other robberies he'd been foolish enough to keep at home.

Tony scowled. Well, Lenny's mum had copped it good and proper. Serve her right. He felt no pity for her.

But what he needed now was a name. He knew the face. Knew where he'd seen it before, but he needed a name, and it should be here somewhere.

Bills, receipts, bookings, letters. Angrily, Tony shoved them back again. He looked down. The filing drawers. Probably in there. He tried the right-hand drawer and found it full of odds and ends: a stapler, three-hole punch, books, a tube of glue, and a batch of empty file-holders. The left-hand drawer was locked, but Tony remembered seeing keys in the shallow middle drawer.

The first one he tried opened the drawer. He found what he was looking for in a file three-quarters of the way back. The document was stapled together with half a dozen others, and the name he wanted was there at the bottom of the page. And legible, thank God! Tony could hardly contain himself as he put the file back in the drawer.

The telephone directory was on the top of the desk. Tony opened it and searched through the pages. Yes! There it was. He closed the book with shaking fingers. Now, all he had to do was set his plan in motion.

CHAPTER 10

Arthur Gresham stared at the documents, then slowly shook his head. 'I can't believe it,' he said. 'Beth Smallwood, of all people.' He directed a sharp look over the top of his glasses at Paget. 'This one is dated the twentieth,' he said. 'The day she was promoted! My God! She sat there in that chair, and . . .' He broke off, removed his glasses and began to polish them. 'She betrayed me,' he ended petulantly.

Oh, how she must have been chuckling up her sleeve when he told her she was to be in charge. The thought of what might have happened made Gresham's blood run cold. Thank God it hadn't gone any further. As it was, there would be an audit, but at least nothing concerning Beth Smallwood's promotion had been committed to paper. There would be enough questions asked by head office as it was without his having to explain *that* decision.

'Speaking of that day,' said Paget, 'would you mind telling me where *you* were on Monday evening, sir?'

Gresham looked startled by the question and colour began to rise around his collar. 'Where I . . . ? Really, Chief Inspector! I hardly think that has any bearing on your investigation,' he said coldly.

'Please don't misunderstand me, sir,' said Paget smoothly. 'No one is suggesting that you had anything to do with Mrs Smallwood's death. But if she was killed by someone she knew – and we think she was – then the more people we can eliminate from our list, the easier it is for us to concentrate on those who may have been involved. Most people are only too happy to tell us where they were so they can be crossed off the list, as it were.' He smiled to soften what he was about to say. 'Unless, of course, they have something to hide.'

Gresham didn't seem to know quite how to react. 'I still don't see the need,' he huffed, 'but I suppose there's no harm in telling you where I was. As it happens, I was visiting my father. He is in Golden Meadows. He had a stroke two years ago, and needs constant supervision. I try to get over there to see him at least once a week.'

'I see. Do you happen to recall what time that was?'

'I must have arrived there about seven or just after,' he said. 'I wasn't paying much attention to the time.'

'And you left when?'

A frown of annoyance crossed Gresham's face. 'Shortly before nine. I had an appointment at nine.'

'With...?' Paget prompted.

'Ivor Trent,' said Gresham irritably. 'Town Planning. I'd arranged to meet him in the Three Crowns. A business matter.'

'Thank you, sir.' Paget changed the subject, and asked to see Beth Smallwood's bank account. Gresham produced a record of a current account that was barely afloat. It peaked on pay-days, Paget noticed, and dwindled to almost nothing by the time the next pay-day came round. It confirmed the conclusion Paget had come to much earlier: Beth Smallwood had been living hand to mouth in spite of the money she'd stolen from the bank.

There was no record of Lenny Smallwood ever having had an account at the local branch, but a computer search by Rachel Fairmont produced the information that he had one in the Shrewsbury branch, and indeed, the sum of £5000 had passed through the account less than a month ago.

Paget thanked Gresham for his help. 'And now,' he said, 'I'd like to have a word with members of your staff. I'll take them one at a time, and I shan't keep them long. Perhaps there's a room where I could speak to them in private?'

'I really don't know what they can tell you that I haven't told you already,' Gresham objected. 'This is all very disruptive, you know. Very unsettling, and we're short-handed as it is.'

'I do appreciate that, sir, but I thought it would be preferable to asking everyone to come down to the station to be interviewed.'

The thought of having members of his staff parading one by one down to the police station made Gresham shudder. God knows what sort of rumours would be flying around town by the end of the day, and he had enough explaining to do to head office as it was. 'Very well,' he said. 'Take Harry beecham's old office. Miss Fairmont will show you where it is.'

'But Mr Ling is using the office...' the secretary began, only to be cut off sharply by Gresham. 'Then he can go back to his own desk until this is over,' he snapped. 'It isn't as if he's the actual manager, is it?' He turned back to Paget. 'And I'd be obliged if you could conclude your business here as soon as possible, Chief Inspector.'

Beecham's old office was small and cramped. The top of the desk contained the usual telephone and in- and out-trays, and in the very centre of the desk, placed there with precision, was a name-plate made of polished brass. Dark letters stood out boldly: TERRENCE LING. It was the first thing one noticed upon entering the office.

'Where is Mr Ling?' Paget asked.

'I'm not quite sure where he is,' Rachel confessed, 'but I expect he will be back shortly.'

'In that case, please sit down, Miss Fairmont. There are one or two questions I'd like to ask you.'

Rachel sat gingerly on the edge of the chair, hands folded in her lap, and looked expectantly at Paget.

'Tell me about Mrs Smallwood,' he said. 'What sort of person was she?'

Rachel looked thoughtful. 'Quiet, I suppose,' she said tentatively. 'She's been with the bank for almost eight years, and the last three were spent here in SBLs – Small Business Loans, that is – under Mr Beecham. She was always a very private person. She never talked about herself.'

'I believe you said Beth Smallwood was still here when you left on Monday afternoon. How did she seem to you at that time?'

'I think she was probably a bit overwhelmed,' the woman said slowly. 'She'd been crying, but then, Beth was always a bit emotional. Actually, I didn't realize she was still here until one of the girls asked me what was wrong with Beth. So I went into the Ladies to see if she was all right.'

Paget waited expectantly. The silence lengthened between them. 'What did she say?' he prompted

Rachel moved uncomfortably in her chair. 'It was a bit embarrassing, actually,' she said. 'I mean, she kept apologizing for the way she looked and for being so silly. She dropped her handbag; spilled everything on the floor and I had to help gather things up for her, and it was at that point I felt it would be better to leave and let her get on with it. It was just reaction, I'm sure.'

Paget made a mental note to have a set of Rachel's prints forwarded to Forensic, together with a note of explanation regarding any prints they might find on Beth Smallwood's handbag or its contents. He explained the process carefully to Rachel. 'You've no objection, I trust?' he ended.

The secretary looked down at her fingers and wrinkled her nose. 'I suppose not, if it's really necessary,' she said, and it occurred to Paget that Rachel was more concerned about ink on her immaculate fingers than she was with the actual surrender of her prints.

'Were you present when Mr Beecham was dismissed on Monday?'

'Yes.'

'How did he take it?'

Rachel looked troubled. 'Not very well, I'm afraid. To tell you the truth, I think he was still in a state of shock when he left the bank. Mr Gresham and I escorted him to his office – this office – to make sure that he took only his personal belongings with him when he left, then Mr Gresham took his keys and saw him out.'

'And Beecham had no warning that he was to be let go?'

The secretary shook her head. 'I know it sounds harsh,' she said defensively, 'but it *is* standard bank policy. Once an employee has been notified that he or she is being – umm – terminated, they must be escorted off the premises immediately. Otherwise they could do enormous damage to the bank if, for example, they decided to change or destroy records in the computer. The computer access codes are changed immediately, of course.'

Paget knew that similar rules applied to anyone dismissed for cause from the Force, but it must have been a hell of a jolt for Beecham, coming as it had straight out of the blue. No warning at all, and a subordinate he considered poor management material taking over his job.

'Why Beecham? Why not Beth Smallwood, for example?'

Rachel's slim fingers moved restlessly across her skirt, smoothing imaginary creases. 'You'll have to ask Mr Gresham,' she said primly. 'I'm sure he had his reasons.'

'How would you describe the relationship between Mr Beecham and Mrs Smallwood?' Paget asked.

Rachel considered. 'They seemed to get along well in the office, and Mr Beecham used to drive Beth home at night. It was on his way, I believe.'

'Is it possible that they were more than friends?'

Rachel avoided Paget's eyes. 'I'm not sure that I . . . I mean, I don't *know* if they were, and now that she's dead . . .' Rachel stumbled to a halt and looked anxiously at Paget. 'I wouldn't want you to get the wrong impression, Chief Inspector. I mean, it was just a *feeling*. Not that you could really *blame* Harry if there was. It must have been very hard for him all these years with his wife the way she is.'

The secretary moved restlessly in her chair. 'If there's nothing else, sir, I should be getting back to my desk.'

'I won't keep you long, but tell me again exactly what Beth Smallwood said when she rang you at home on Monday night.'

'She said she had fallen and hurt herself and she wouldn't be in the next morning, and she asked me to let Mr Gresham know.'

'And did you tell Mr Gresham?'

'Well, no. I didn't have a chance, did I?' she said defensively. 'If you remember, he came in a few minutes late yesterday morning while you were there, and you both went straight into his office.'

'Ah, yes, of course. Did Beth Smallwood say anything else that you remember?'

'No, I don't think so. She was a bit hard to understand. She had trouble talking. She said she'd bitten her tongue when she fell.'

A short, chunky, round-faced man with black hair brushed straight back appeared in the office doorway. He stopped abruptly when he saw Paget sitting there. But it was Rachel Fairmont he addressed.

'What is this, Miss Fairmont?' he enquired. 'Who is this gentleman?'

Paget had no doubt that Terrence Ling knew exactly who he was.

He rose to his feet. 'Mr Ling?' he said, and introduced himself. 'Sorry to be such a nuisance, but with the death of Mrs Smallwood, I know you'll understand the need. Mr Gresham did say he was sure you wouldn't mind if I used your office – just for a short time, of course.'

'Of course.' That Terrence Ling wasn't pleased was obvious, but it seemed he was prepared to be courteous. 'Please continue.' He began to withdraw, but Paget stopped him.

'Miss Fairmont is just leaving,' he said, 'and I would like to talk to you, if you have a moment? Thank you, Miss Fairmont.'

The man stood aside as Rachel made her escape. 'Please, come and sit down, Mr Ling. I'm sure you would prefer your own chair.' Paget began to move out from behind the desk, but Ling insisted that he stay there, and sat down firmly in the seat vacated by Rachel.

Paget returned to his seat. 'I suppose this unfortunate business has left you with a lot on your plate,' he said conversationally. 'It must be difficult to step in at such short notice.'

'It is not difficult if one is organized and prepared,' said Ling. He spoke with the precision of one for whom English was not his first language.

'I'm sure Mr Gresham will be pleased about that,' said Paget, deliberately probing.

He waited, but Ling remained silent. 'Well, perhaps we should get to the matter at hand,' he said. 'Tell me what you can about Beth Smallwood. I imagine you and she must have worked quite closely together. What sort of person was she?'

Ling seemed puzzled by the question. 'Why do you ask me?' he wanted to know. 'What has it got to do with her murder?'

'To be honest, I'm not sure,' said Paget. 'But we think it is possible that Mrs Smallwood knew her attacker, so the more we can learn about her, the better. Anything you can tell me may prove useful.'

Terrence Ling thought about that for a moment. 'She was a nice lady,' he said, 'but she was not very good at her job. I would not have had her working for me.'

Paget sat back in the chair. It wasn't often that people were as forthright as Ling. 'Go on,' he said quietly.

Ling shrugged. 'I assume you wish me to be honest,' he said. 'Otherwise, you will have a false picture.' His tone softened slightly. 'I am sorry she is dead, but she was not organized in her work. That is not good for business. Not efficient.'

'And yet she was to have taken over Mr Beecham's job.'

Ling's face was impassive. 'Yes.'

'So why would Mr Gresham promote someone who, you say, would not do a good job?'

Ling eyed Paget steadily. 'Because she was a woman,' he said flatly. 'And she would do what he wanted.'

Paget was deliberately obtuse. 'You mean she would toe the line. Follow previous policy. Is that it? Perhaps not be quite as innovative as you might be?'

Ling started to say something, then apparently thought better of it. 'Yes,' he said. 'That's what I mean.'

That was *not* what Ling meant, thought Paget, but he let it go. 'Did you see Beth Smallwood leave Mr Gresham's office Monday afternoon? That is, after she'd been told of her promotion.'

'No.'

Paget tried another tack. 'Did Mrs Smallwood have any particular friends here at the bank?'

According to Ling, Beth Smallwood was not close to anyone at the bank, except, perhaps, Harry Beecham. But when Paget asked if Ling thought there might be more to their relationship than friendship, the man said he did not know, and refused to be drawn beyond that.

'And what about you, Mr Ling? How did you get along with Beth Smallwood?'

Ling didn't answer at once. It was as if he sensed it was time to be cautious. 'All right,' he said carefully.

'But?' Paget prompted. 'Come along, Mr Ling; you said you wished to be honest.'

Ling scowled. 'It was frustrating for me,' he burst out. 'She was not organized. She worked hard but not smart, but it was not my place to say anything. It was not right,' he went on heatedly. 'That job should have been mine! I have more experience. I know how to organize my work. In Hong Kong I worked in every department of three big banks for five years. Three banks, Chief Inspector. Much bigger than this. Yet I have not been given any real responsibility since coming to this country.'

'So you resented the fact that Mrs Smallwood would be your new boss?'

'Wouldn't you under the same circumstances?' Ling countered.

'But now that Beth Smallwood has gone, you are the new manager,' Paget pointed out.

'*Temporary* manager,' Ling reminded him. 'Mr Gresham made that very clear.'

'But if you perform well, wouldn't this prove to be the chance you have been looking for?'

Terry Ling shook his head and smiled sadly. 'You think I killed Beth for *this* job?' he said softly. His voice rose. 'This job?' That's utterly ridiculous!'

'That suggestion was yours, not mine,' said Paget. 'But since you've brought it up, where were you on Monday evening? Let's say between eight and ten o'clock.'

Ling regarded him stonily. 'I was at home,' he said.

'You're married?'

'Yes.'

'Was your wife at home that evening?'

'No. My wife was at work.'

'Is there anyone who can verify that you were at home during the hours I mentioned?'

'You question my word, Chief Inspector?'

Paget shook his head. 'Not at all,' he said. 'But it makes things so much simpler if we can verify where everyone was at the critical time.'

'There is no one,' Ling said tonelessly.

'Very well. In that case, I think that will be all for now, Mr Ling, but if you should remember anything that might help, please ring me at my office.'

When Ling had gone, the chief inspector sat quietly trying to sort out his impressions of the man. On the one hand, he felt some sympathy for him. He didn't doubt for a moment that it would be hard, if not impossible, for Ling to get ahead while Gresham was in charge. But it must have been a terrible blow to his ego when he learned that he had been passed over in favour of Beth Smallwood.

How angry would he be? Very angry, Paget thought. But angry enough to track her down and kill her? Possibly – in the heat of the moment.

CHAPTER 11

Tania Costello stared defiantly at Tregalles. She was scared but determined not to show it. 'Like I've told you a dozen times already, I don't know!' she said. 'Could have been anybody. Somebody who wanted his bike. There are a lot of nutters out there.'

'Whoever it was came within an inch of killing him,' Tregalles said. 'Don't you want to see them caught?'

"Course I do, but I can't tell you what I don't know, can I?'

'Oh, I think you know all right,' the sergeant said quietly. He turned to the uniformed woman seated at the end of the table, and nodded. The WPC opened a brown paper bag and produced a clear plastic envelope containing a video cassette which she handed to Tregalles.

'Ever seen this before?' he asked the girl.

Tania shrugged. 'Seen lots of 'em.'

'Like this, have you? With no tape inside?'

The girl studied her chipped nails. They were bitten down to the quick, and it was all she could do to stop herself from nibbling on them now. God! but Lenny was stupid. She'd *told* him to get rid of the stuff, and he'd said he had.

The sergeant was waiting, and the lengthening silence was getting on her nerves.

'I want a cigarette,' she said.

Tregalles shook his head and pointed to the sign on the wall. 'Sorry,' he said as if he meant it, 'but smoking's not allowed. And you haven't answered my question.'

'I don't have to, do I?' Tania retorted. 'You can't keep me here.'

'Tell me about this,' Tregalles persisted, tapping the cassette.

'I've never seen it before. All right? Now can I go?'

Tregalles sighed. 'Not yet, I'm afraid,' he said. 'In fact, I think you might be with us for quite a long time. You see, I don't believe you, Tania. You say you've never seen this cassette before, and yet your prints are all over it. Along with Lenny's of course.'

The girl gnawed on her lower lip. She vowed to kill Lenny if she ever got out of there. 'So?' she said defiantly.

'Trafficking in drugs is a serious charge, Tania.'

'I don't see any drugs,' the girl retorted. 'You can't prove anything just because my fingerprints are on there. How do I know what somebody might have used it for? You've got nothing!'

Unfortunately, the girl was right. They couldn't prove that she'd known the cassette was being used as a container for cocaine or anything else for that matter. She was a tough little nut, and quite obviously more frightened of whoever had beaten up her boyfriend than she was of anything the police could do to her.

Tregalles shrugged as if it were of little consequence. 'Then I suppose we'll just have to go back to your house and turn the place over, won't we?' he said pleasantly.

Tania's heart sank. Bloody Lenny. 'Just hang on to this for a while, Tan,' he'd said. 'It's not safe at my place. If me mam finds it I'm dead. She'll know I've been lying. I swore to her I was off the stuff. That's the only way I could persuade her to get the money to pay Archie back.'

Pay Archie back – that was a laugh. Look what he'd done to Lenny, poor sod!

She shuddered inwardly. How could Lenny have been so stupid as to think that Archie wouldn't notice he was being ripped off? Lenny just *might* have squared things if he'd had enough sense to make up what he'd skimmed before Archie discovered the loss. He'd had the money; his mum had arranged that, believing he was going to use it to get treatment to help him get off drugs, but the stupid sod had used the five thou as a down payment on the bike.

And God alone knew what Lenny might have left behind in her room.

All this flashed through her mind in an instant. If she told the police what they wanted to know, they might not search the house. But she couldn't, could she? Not unless she wanted to end up like Lenny.

'Do what you like,' she shrugged, 'but it'll be a waste of time. There's nothing there.'

Tregalles sighed. 'I hope for your sake you're right,' he said quietly, 'because if you're not, you could be in a lot of trouble, Tania, and I don't see Lenny sticking his neck out to help you.'

The girl tilted her head defiantly. 'That's my problem, then, isn't it?' she said.

Tregalles exchanged glances with the WPC. 'Right,' he said. 'So let's get on with it. Tell me what happened at Lenny's house on Monday night.'

The girl who faced Paget across the desk was very young. Ginny Holbrook was a pretty girl, and she knew it. Red hair; big blue eyes that looked innocent but were far from it; pale, delicate face sprinkled with freckles; slim, and neatly dressed.

Ginny was the last one on the list supplied by Rachel Fairmont, and Paget had gained the impression that this young woman was not one of Miss Fairmont's favourite people. He had wondered why at the time, and now he hoped to find out. Once more, he explained why he was there.

Ginny leaned back in her chair, crossed her legs and made herself comfortable. This was better than standing at the counter dealing with an endless line of people, smiling sweetly and saying the same thing over and over again until she could scream.

She smiled now at Paget. He wasn't half bad looking, in a craggy sort of way. Getting on a bit, but he looked as if he'd know his way around.

'You don't mind if I smoke?' she said brightly as she took out a cigarette.

'I'm afraid I do,' said Paget pleasantly. 'Tell me, Miss Holbrook, when was the last time you saw Beth Smallwood?'

Ginny's lips drew together in a moue of displeasure as she dropped the cigarettes back into her handbag. 'Just before I left work on Monday,' she said. 'She was in the loo when I went in to, well, you know.'

'Did you speak to her?'

'Not really,' the girl said.

Paget frowned. 'What do you mean by that?'

'Well, we didn't actually speak,' said Ginny, 'because when I went in she was at the mirror doing something to her face, and as soon as she saw me she ducked into the toilet.'

'Did you see her face?'

'Just for a second or two in the mirror.'

'And?'

The girl grimaced. 'It was all puffy and white and she was crying. I thought she was ill at first, and I was going to ask if there was anything I could do, but it was obvious from the look she gave me in the mirror – like it was my fault for coming in – and the way she ducked out of sight, that she didn't want me there, so I didn't hang about. But I did tell Miss Fairmont, and she went in to see if Beth was all right.'

'I see. How well did you know Beth Smallwood?'

Ginny wrinkled her nose. 'I can't say I knew her well at all,' she said. 'She was, well, quite a bit older than most of us. And she was in the office, of course, so we didn't see much of each other. She and Miss Fairmont didn't really mix with the rest of the staff. They were more of an age if you know what I mean.'

'But you must have formed some opinion of Mrs Smallwood,' Paget insisted.

Ginny thought about that for a moment or two. 'I think she was a bit of a dark horse,' she said. 'I think there was more to Beth Smallwood than met the eye.'

'Oh? How so, Miss Holbrook?'

'You can call me Ginny, if you like,' the girl told him.

'If you wish,' said Paget. 'You were saying?'

Ginny uncrossed her legs and sat forward in her seat. 'Well, for a start, she wasn't all that bad looking – for an older woman, I mean, *and* it didn't go unnoticed.' She sat back and looked at Paget for a reaction.

'Didn't go unnoticed by whom?' he said.

The girl drew in a long breath and compressed her lips. 'By Mr Beecham for one,' she said. 'He used to take her home in his car every night, and well... you know.'

'No. I'm afraid I don't know,' said Paget. 'Why don't you tell me?'

Ginny Holbrook hesitated. She wasn't quite sure whether Paget was having her on or not. He couldn't be *that* thick. He must *know* what she meant. But his eyes were still upon her, and she found his steady gaze unnerving.

She shifted uncomfortably in her chair. 'Well, what with Mr Beecham's wife being ill all these years, and then the two of them, you know, he and Beth, working together all the time, and him taking her home every night...' She trailed off into silence. She wished he'd say something instead of just looking at her like that.

'You said "Mr Beecham for one,"' Paget prompted. 'Who else showed an interest?'

The girl fiddled with her handbag. She wished she could have a cigarette.

'Miss Holbrook?'

Ginny wriggled uncomfortably. She could feel the warmth rising in her face. 'I shouldn't have said that,' she told him. 'I didn't mean it.'

'I think you did mean it,' Paget said sternly. 'If this very brutal murder is to be resolved, I need to know as much as possible about Beth Smallwood's relationship with everyone. What you tell me here today remains confidential, so I would like you to be very frank with me. If you know something, please tell me. Now, you obviously had someone else in mind, and there aren't that many male members on staff, are there?'

In fact, there were only three; or there had been before Harry Beecham's abrupt departure on Monday. Now there were only two. He waited.

Ginny's face was burning. 'It's just that...' She bit her lip and looked down at her hands in her lap. 'I don't *know* anything,' she insisted.

Paget waited. His eyes never left her face.

Ginny squirmed. She'd gone too far this time, and she didn't know how to get back on safe ground. Her eyes pleaded with him. 'I could lose my job,' she said desperately.

'Then let me help you. Are you referring to Mr Ling?'

Ginny's eyes opened wide in surprise. 'Oh, no! Not...' Too late she saw the trap.

'Are you trying to tell me that Mr Gresham and Mrs Smallwood were having an affair?' asked Paget.

The girl shook her head violently. 'Oh, no! Nothing like that,' she burst out. 'At least, I don't think...' She stopped, frowning.

'Then what did you mean, Miss Holbrook?'

The girl refused to look at him. She clasped her hands together in her lap to stop them from shaking. She was very young and certainly foolish, but Paget had no intention of letting her off the hook.

'It's just that Mr Gresham seemed to take a fancy to her, sort of,' the girl stammered.

'In what way?' he asked blandly. 'How did this attraction manifest itself?'

Ginny Holbrook closed her eyes and stifled a groan. 'He – perhaps I'm wrong, but it was the way he used to...well, look at her, that's all. You could tell that he fancied her. I mean, we've all been...' Ginny's hands flew to her mouth and her eyes grew round. 'I didn't mean...'

'I believe what you are trying to avoid saying, Miss Holbrook,' said Paget deliberately, 'is that other female members of the staff have experienced a similar sort of thing at some time or other. Is that right?'

The girl didn't know where to look, but he could tell by her face that he wasn't far wrong. It seemed that Harry Beecham's assessment of Gresham had some foundation in fact.

'If that is the case, why hasn't someone done something about it?'

Ginny wrinkled her nose. 'That's what I asked them when I first started work here, but they're all scared of losing their jobs. Most of them have kids, so they put up with it.'

'And you?'

Ginny shrugged guiltily. 'I'm as bad as the rest,' she admitted. 'I thought if we all stuck together people would believe us, but no one would back me up, and being the newest here, I wouldn't stand a chance of being believed, would I?'

'And Beth Smallwood? What about her?'

The girl hesitated. 'It's funny you should ask,' she said slowly, 'because, come to think of it, he never *used* to bother her. It was only lately. But you could tell she didn't like it.' Ginny wrinkled her nose. 'Well, she wouldn't, would she? Not with him being so old and all. None of us did.' Ginny sat forward in her seat. Now that the hurdles were down, she seemed almost anxious to talk. 'It was sort of funny, sometimes. He'd come up behind her, and she'd suddenly take off through the filing cabinets. And then Harry, that is, Mr Beecham, would sort of wander over and ask Beth a question, like he was coming to her rescue. We could see it all through the glass in the office. We used to have a bit of a giggle about it at coffee time, and ...' She stopped abruptly and looked contrite. 'I'm sorry,' she said in a small voice. 'I didn't mean ... I mean, she *is* dead, isn't she?'

CHAPTER 12

As he left the bank and set off for the hospital in the car, Paget thought about what he had learned. Not everyone had been as forthcoming as Ginny Holbrook or Terry Ling, but he had sensed an uneasy reticence in the other female members of the staff. Understandable of course, if what Ginny had told him was true. Rachel Fairmont had been the most discreet, but then, she was Gresham's secretary, and no doubt she, too, wished to keep her job.

But he cautioned himself against accepting blindly Ginny Holbrook's word regarding Gresham's behaviour. The girl was young and impressionable, and it was possible that she had allowed her imagination to run away with her.

In Terry Ling's case, frustration had been the trigger for his candour. Indeed, if Ling was as clever as Harry Beecham had indicated, he had good cause to be resentful about Beth Smallwood's elevation to a position beyond her capabilities. Ling had made an oblique reference to Gresham preferring a woman in the job, but had backed away from explaining that when Paget had pressed him.

The late afternoon traffic was beginning to build as Paget turned into Edge Hill Road. Sunlight, pale but welcome, glinted on the river far below, perhaps heralding an end to a cold and dreary spring. He certainly hoped so. He was tired of the rain.

His thoughts returned to something that had been puzzling him since early afternoon. When he had spoken to Gresham in his office on Tuesday morning, the manager had told him that Beth Smallwood had telephoned Rachel Fairmont at home the night before to say she wouldn't be in the following day. Yet Rachel had said she hadn't had a chance to pass the information on to Gresham because he had come in late that morning, and had gone straight into his office.

So how had Gresham known? Had Rachel lied? Had she in fact been in contact with her boss? Or had Gresham learned of the call in some other way? And if so, how?

He turned left at the next corner, then swung across the road and entered the hospital grounds. He parked the car at the far end of the car park quite deliberately in order to enjoy the sun as he walked back to the entrance. Wisps of steam rose from the damp earth of the flower beds, and the air was soft and warm.

He took the lift to the fourth floor where he was directed to Lenny Smallwood's room at the far end of the corridor. The door was open and a uniformed WPC sat on a wooden chair just inside. She rose hurriedly to her feet as Paget entered.

'Afternoon, Constable,' said Paget affably. 'Liscombe, isn't it?'

'Yes, sir. Afternoon, sir.'

'How's the patient?'

'Still out of it. He's not been down long, sir, but one of the nurses was telling me that he's not quite as badly hurt as they first thought, so it might be possible to talk to him when he does come round.'

'Have you spoken to his doctor?'

The corners of Ann Liscombe's mouth turned down. 'I'm afraid he's not all that communicative,' she said carefully. 'Seems to think it's none of my business.'

Paget frowned. 'Does he understand how important it is that we talk to Smallwood?'

'Oh, I think he understands all right,' the girl said. 'It's just that he's not, well, very forthcoming, if you know what I mean, sir. I think it might be different if a man asked him.'

Paget's eyes grew cold. 'I see,' he said. 'Where can I find him?'

'I believe I heard him being called to Lansing ward a few minutes ago,' she said. 'That's down on three.'

'Thank you, Liscombe. And his name?'

'Trotter, sir.'

'Thanks. I'll get back to you.'

Paget took the stairs down to three and walked along the corridor to Lansing ward. Dr Trotter, he was told, was with a patient, but he would be out in a few minutes if Paget cared to wait.

Paget thanked the nurse and wandered over to a window overlooking Royal Park. It extended to the north of the hospital grounds and was bounded by a sweeping curve of the river. Dense clumps of willow, ash and sycamore ran down to the river's edge, while giant oaks stood guard above the paths that wound their way across the sloping parkland.

It struck him that in all the time he'd been in Broadminster he'd never once walked in the park. Nor had he found time to walk the hills and valleys that beckoned so invitingly. He and Jill used to enjoy walking, and when they were first married they would often go out on weekends and walk for miles.

But then the job . . . Paget sighed. They hadn't been out once in the year before Jill died, and now there didn't seem to be much point in going out alone.

'Chief Inspector Paget?'

Paget turned and found himself looking down at Dr Trotter. His name tag was pinned to his lapel. The doctor was a small, neat, thin-faced young man with pale blue eyes. His fair hair was brushed straight back, and he had a pencil-thin moustache. 'You wished to see me, I believe?'

'Yes. About Leonard Smallwood,' Paget said. 'I understand there is a possibility that we may be able to talk to him soon.'

Trotter's lips compressed into a thin line. 'I've no idea who told you that,' he said flatly. 'It's far too early to say.' He began to turn away but Paget stopped him.

'I'm sure you must realize how important it is that we talk to him,' he said. 'His mother was killed on Monday night, and we think he may be able to help us with our enquiries.'

A quick frown of annoyance crossed Trotter's face. 'That is of no concern to me,' he said primly. 'My concern is for my patient. His condition is serious, and I'll not have him badgered by the police or anyone else. And I must remind you, Chief Inspector, it *is* my decision.'

Paget was fast losing patience. 'No one is suggesting it isn't your decision, Doctor,' he said thinly, 'but I repeat: the sooner we can talk to Smallwood, the better. All I'm asking for is your co-operation. I would appreciate it if you would let the constable on duty know when you feel Smallwood can answer a few simple questions?'

Trotter's moustache quivered. 'I'm not in the habit of discussing my patients with constables, Chief Inspector,' he said brusquely. He turned and began to walk away.

Paget's anger boiled to the surface and spilled over. His hand shot out and grabbed the little man by the shoulder and spun him round. 'Now you listen to me,' he began, but stopped dead when a voice behind him said: 'Is there a problem here?'

It seemed to Paget as if every nerve-end in his body had suddenly gone cold. He thought his ears were playing tricks on him. It couldn't be. It wasn't possible. But even as he turned, he knew it was.

The woman who faced him was almost as tall as he was. Slim, dark hair, dark eyes in an oval face; finely chiselled features – perhaps a little fuller in the face than he remembered. She stood there with her hands thrust into the pockets of her white coat, eyes cool; quizzical; challenging.

He felt like a schoolboy caught smoking behind the bicycle shed as he removed his hand from Trotter's shoulder.

'Andr – Dr McMillan,' he said. 'How nice to see you again.' Even as he spoke the words, he thought how utterly banal they sounded. 'I had no idea you were back.'

'Chief Inspector,' said Andrea McMillan neutrally as she turned to Trotter. '*Is* there a problem, Doctor?' she asked again.

Trotter brushed angrily at his shoulder as if Paget's hand were still there. 'The chief inspector seems to think he knows more about the condition of my patient than I do,' he said spitefully. He lifted his chin. 'He can't wait, it seems, to interrogate a boy who is still unconscious.'

Andrea McMillan turned her gaze on Paget. Her face held no expression. 'Is this true, Chief Inspector? We are talking, I assume, about the boy under police guard?'

So formal. So cold!

'We are,' he said stiffly. 'Leonard Smallwood. I would like to *talk* to him as soon as possible. I am well aware that his condition is serious, and I have no wish to challenge Dr Trotter's authority, but I would like him to agree to let the constable on duty know as soon as he thinks Smallwood is fit enough to answer a few questions.'

Andrea turned a questioning eye on Trotter, who shrugged. 'I have no objection to *that* request,' he said, 'and if it had been phrased in that way in the first place, then...'

'Good. Then we can consider it settled,' said Andrea. 'I shan't detain you further, Doctor. I know you're busy.'

Trotter flashed a spiteful glance at Paget, then turned and walked away.

Paget searched for words. There had been no words left to say when they'd parted months before, and now it seemed that nothing had changed.

'I'm afraid you took me by surprise,' he confessed. 'I had no idea that you were back. You're looking well. The country life must have agreed with you.'

When she had made her decision to return to Broadminster, Andrea had known that there would come a day when she would come face to face with Neil Paget, and she had believed herself prepared for that moment. But this was not the way she had imagined their first encounter. Down there on the farm, working with Kate Ferris, she had come to terms with the fact that Neil had only been doing his job to the best of his ability. It was she who had lied to him. Not that she'd had any choice, but she could hardly blame him for his suspicions when every shred of evidence he had pointed to her. Yet, illogical as it might be, she *did* blame him for not trusting her. Perhaps if he hadn't been quite so much the policeman...

And now she'd come round the corner to find him manhandling one of the doctors, his face dark, his manner threatening. Not that Trotter was any prize, but still...

'Yes, I think it did,' she said. She began to move away. Seeing him again had stirred emotions she had thought were safely locked away, and all she could think of was that she must get away. She needed time. She was not ready for this.

'And Sarah? How is she?' He fell in step beside her.

'Sarah's fine. Just fine, thank you.' The door to one of the work stations was open, and she walked purposefully toward it, seeking an escape. 'I'm sorry, Neil,' she said abruptly, 'but I am rather busy, so unless there is anything else...?'

The hope that they might talk died within him. It was obvious by her tone, by her very manner, that Andrea wished him to be gone. 'No, I don't think there is, Andrea,' he said quietly. 'But it is nice to see you back here again.'

Andrea closed the door behind her and leaned against it. She could hear a drumming in her ears and realized she was listening to her own heart. How could she have cut him off like that? What must he think? If only... But it was too late, now.

Paget walked slowly down the corridor, his thoughts in turmoil. Andrea's abrupt departure had taken him as much by surprise as her unexpected appearance. Not that he could blame her. He must have looked every inch the bullying policeman as she came round the corner, no doubt confirming what she already thought of him. If only she could have heard that weasel, Trotter, a few seconds earlier...

But she hadn't, had she? Savagely, he punched the button for the lift.

But why had Andrea returned to work here at this very hospital where they had first met? He'd have thought that this would be the last place she would have chosen. But one thing was quite certain, he thought ruefully as he made his way out of the hospital: Andrea had not come back because of him! She'd made that absolutely clear by literally shutting the door in his face.

And that, he thought dispassionately, tells me exactly where I stand.

Yet he replayed the scene in the hospital corridor over and over again in his head as he made his way back to Charter Lane. If only he had said this; if only it hadn't been Trotter, perhaps...

He sighed heavily and pushed the turbulent thoughts firmly to the back of his mind, forcing himself to concentrate on his driving. Late afternoon traffic was beginning to build, and children on their way home from school clogged the narrow streets. It was like this every school day, but today it irritated him. And it did nothing to improve his temper when he arrived at headquarters to find his parking space occupied.

Annoyed, he drove round the back, and was only slightly mollified when he spotted a young WPC getting into her car. He pulled to one side to allow her room to back out, then fumed impatiently while she adjusted her seat belt, checked her lipstick in the mirror, then lit a cigarette before starting her car. She smiled disarmingly as she passed – and it was only then that he remembered he'd told Liscombe he'd get back to her.

CHAPTER 13

Tania Costello ignored the curious stares of passers-by as she, Tregalles, and a policewoman got out of the car outside the maison-ette in Burton Road. She led the way up the cracked flagstone path to the front door and was about to open it when she stopped. 'It's open,' she breathed softly. 'Mum never leaves it open.' She took a step backward, and the policewoman gripped her arm as if afraid the girl might try to run.

Tregalles moved forward and pushed the door open. The lock was broken, and the wood around it splintered. The hall and stairs were empty. He stepped inside. A faint sound came from some-where near the back of the house. A door to his right stood open and he looked in.

The room had been hit by a tornado by the look of it. Pictures hung awry, furniture had been overturned and ripped to shreds, and anything that would break was broken. Tregalles moved on to the door at the end of the short hall, and pushed it open. That room, too, had received the same treatment.

He heard the sound again, this time louder, and he saw a woman huddled in a corner behind an overturned table. She had blood on her face and she was whimpering.

'Mum!' Tania pushed past him and flew across the room. She knelt and put out her hand, but the woman flinched and pulled away. Her eyes focused on the girl, and her face became distorted.

'Get out!' she snarled. 'Get out!' Her voice rose to a thin scream. 'This is all your fault. You and that Lenny Smallwood.' Her hand shot out and strong fingers fastened in the girl's hair, twisting viciously.

Tania shrieked as she fought to free herself, and both Tregalles and the policewoman dropped to their knees as they tried to part mother and daughter. The woman on the floor kicked out savagely and caught Tregalles on the knee. He fell back against the girl. Tania wrenched herself free and in a second she was gone, down the hall and out into the street. The policewoman scrambled to her feet and started after her, but she was far too late. By the time she reached the door, the girl had vanished.

The policewoman returned to help Tregalles attend to Tania's mother, who, now the girl was gone, began to calm down. The sergeant had the feeling he'd seen the woman before, but he couldn't place her. Her ash blonde hair fell untidily across a face that was heavily made up, and he thought she must have been pretty once. But time had not dealt kindly with her. The once firm flesh sagged beneath the make-up, and the eyes had lost their lustre. She couldn't be more than forty at the outside, but she looked much older.

Between them they got her to a chair, but not before she'd made them find her cigarettes and light one for her. There was a nasty cut across her forehead where, she said, one of the two men who'd burst into the house had hit her. She'd fallen heavily, and her arm and hip were badly bruised. While Tregalles called for an ambulance, the policewoman bathed and bound the cut, then found a blanket and wrapped the woman in it.

As for the two men who had attacked her, she said everything had happened so fast that she couldn't begin to describe them. But she avoided their eyes, and it was evident to Tregalles that she had no intention of giving them an accurate description.

'What did they want?' he asked.

'Money,' she said. 'I told them they'd be lucky. I asked them if they thought I'd be living like this if I had any money. That's when one of them hit me.' The woman shivered and huddled down inside the blanket. 'They said Lenny told them the money was here. That I had it. The little swine!' She glanced around. 'Then they tore the place apart.'

'*Did* Lenny leave money here, Mrs Costello?'

The woman glance up sharply. 'That's *her* name,' she snapped. 'Kept her father's name, though God knows why. Mine's Price. Misty Price.'

Misty Price! Now Tregalles remembered. She used to work the strip at the bottom end of Bridge Street. He'd pulled her in more than once himself. Must be close to ten years ago. 'The money?' he reminded her.

Misty Price drew deeply on her cigarette. 'If that lying little git ever had any money, I never saw any of it,' she said. 'And I told 'em so. Sneaking in here of a night. I knew he was up there. I could hear them whispering and going at it. They think I don't know, but I do.'

The cigarette fell from her fingers, and she began to shake. Delayed shock took hold of her, and rasping sobs racked her body until it was all they could do to hold her in the chair.

Paget sat at his desk long after everyone else had gone. Seeing Andrea this afternoon had awakened feelings and emotions he'd thought were safely buried.

Two days from now would mark the anniversary of Jill's death, and he had been preoccupied for weeks with memories of their short time together. The letter from Patrick had sharpened those images, and now he felt guilty because his mind was filled with thoughts of Andrea.

Paget rubbed his face with his hands and yawned. Brooding over it wasn't going to get him anywhere. Time to pack it in for another day. He stood up, stretched, and made his way downstairs and out into the fresh air. The clouds were tinged with red, and he hoped that meant the weather might be changing for the better.

Dusk had settled over the valley by the time he arrived home. He walked through to the kitchen and put the light on, and the first thing he saw was Patrick's letter on the table where he'd left it that morning.

He tried to ignore it, but it was no use. He would have to write. Try to explain. He sat down at the table and read the letter again, then crushed it in his hand.

He didn't *have* to do it tonight. Tomorrow would be soon enough.

Tony Rudge gathered up the scraps of newspaper and stuffed them in a drawer. He pulled on the rubber gloves he'd taken from the cleaners' room earlier in the day, and picked up the sheet of A4 paper once again. It had taken him more than an hour to cut and paste the letters on, but it was time well spent, he told himself.

It had been hard deciding how much to ask for. He didn't want to be too greedy. That was where people made their mistake. Asking for too much. Five hundred. That would do for a start. There would be more later. Lots more.

He shivered with anticipation. He could hardly contain his excitement as he folded the paper carefully, then put it in an envelope and sealed it. Now, all he had to do was get it there, but he'd thought that out as well. His car was old, clapped out and noisy, so he'd parked it as far away from the house as possible so no one would be disturbed when he started up.

He'd thought of posting the letter, but he couldn't wait that long. Besides, something might happen to it along the way. No, he'd deliver it personally through the letter-box.

A tremor of excitement ran through him. The thought of slipping unseen through the night to push the letter through the slot brought a rush of adrenalin, and he could hardly keep his hands from shaking.

Now, the name. It mustn't fall into the wrong hands. Tony dragged out the old portable typewriter from under the bed. He hadn't used it in years; since he'd been at school, in fact. He blew the dust off it and tucked the envelope in behind the platen. The platen was small and hard to turn and he had to force the envelope through. He should have addressed the envelope before he put the letter in, but he supposed it wouldn't matter if it was a bit creased.

He typed the name. The print was small, and he felt disappointed. The letters should have been big and bold. He went back and underlined each word, then added 'Personal and Private' in the lower left-hand corner. That looked better.

Tony slipped the letter into his pocket and checked the time. Ten to twelve. Still a bit early. Best wait for half an hour; make sure that everyone was asleep.

CHAPTER 14

Thursday – 16 May
There was no stamp on the envelope, so it must have been hand delivered during the night. The name and address had been underlined, and it was marked 'Personal and Private' in the lower left-hand corner.

The message inside the envelope was made up of cuttings from a newspaper. The cuttings were glued to a standard size sheet of writing paper, and there could be little doubt about their meaning.

The reader's hand shook as the fingers smoothed the paper. £500? Why such a modest sum? Not that it would end there, of course.

It was short notice. The sender wanted the money tonight. The instructions were clear enough. Time, place, conditions, small notes, no police. Not that the police *could* be called in, of course; the blackmailer must know that.

The reader read the warning again. *We will be watching you. Don't try anything funny* suggested that more than one person was involved. And yet the whole tenor of the letter suggested the work of one person, and not a very bright person at that. The instructions were amateurish; the language dramatic. And how many ways could you split £500?

No, this whole thing was the work of an amateur, the reader decided. But amateur or not, it could not be ignored.

It was half-past ten before Paget was able to get away from New Street. Chief Superintendent Morgan Brock had been at his boring worst, plodding through endless charts and graphs as he made each pedantic point. Costs were rising; break-in figures were up; crimes of violence were on the increase; and the percentage of cases solved had dropped two months in a row. When reminded that a total of nine members of the CID, including two inspectors, had been seconded to a special task force introducing new procedures throughout the region, Brock dismissed it as irrelevant.

While Paget smouldered silently, Alcott chain-smoked. There was no point in trying to reason with Brock. It would have only prolonged the meeting and accomplished nothing.

On their return to Charter Lane, Alcott went with Paget to the incident room for a briefing from Len Ormside.

The sergeant pulled a pad toward him. 'We've found Mrs Smallwood's sister,' he said without preamble. 'Her telephone number was one of those found in the Smallwood house. I've spoken to her on the phone. A Mrs McLeish. Lives near Oban. Husband's a glass-blower. She's agreed to come down on the bus, but she won't be here until tomorrow. Apparently she hasn't seen her sister for years, nor spoken to her. She didn't come right out and say, but I gathered there may have been a bit of bad blood between them.'

Ormside flipped a page of the pad. 'Charlie rang to say he's had a report back from the lab regarding the candles in the church. The ones on the altar had burned down fifty-one millimetres, and the average rate of burn, according to the manufacturer, is twenty-seven millimetres an hour. Which means they were burning for 1.89 hours, or one hour and fifty-three minutes.'

Ormside looked at the two men to make sure they were following him, then consulted his notes once again.

'The candles were doused when the auxiliary lighting went on, which was at 22.40. That's an approximate time, but Charlie reckons it's pretty close. So, assuming the candles were new, that means they were lit at approximately 20.47, or thirteen minutes to nine. Which ties in very nicely with Dr Starkie's estimated time of death.'

'No prints on the candles, I suppose?'

'None. They'd been wiped with some sort of coarse cloth, according to the lab, which suggests that the murderer lit the candles since it seems hardly likely that Mrs Smallwood would do that.' Ormside scratched his head. 'But why go to the trouble?' he went on. 'I don't see the point.'

'Probably to add credence to the idea that Beth Smallwood was kneeling on the steps when she was attacked,' said Paget ruminatively. 'And to draw attention away from the candle holders as a weapon. Anything else, Len?'

'They have a match on a set of prints taken from the belfry in the church.' The sergeant looked askance at Paget. 'Charlie said they came off a used condom, but I reckon he was having me on. You know Charlie.'

Paget grinned crookedly. 'In this case, I think he was telling the truth,' he said. 'I was there when he found them.'

Ormside wrinkled his nose in disgust. 'Sooner him than me,' he muttered. 'Anyway, the prints belong to a young tearaway by the name of Rudge. Antony Rudge. Got eighteen months inside for thieving. The original charge included GBH, but it was dropped. He's out on licence now. Twenty-two years old, single, lives with his father, who owns Strathe House. It's a guest house overlooking the river on the old Ludlow road.'

97

Ormside rose and went to a map on the wall where he pointed out the location. 'Not far from the church,' Paget observed. 'I wonder if he was there on Monday night?'

'Ah!' said Ormside knowingly as he went back to the desk. 'There's something else that ties him in. Rudge said at his trial that it was Lenny Smallwood who was with him the night he got caught, and he claimed it was Lenny who bashed the owner of the house, Walter Latham, when he came in unexpectedly. But Smallwood got off with probation. Seems they couldn't prove that Lenny was ever actually on the premises, and his mother managed to convince the court that he'd been at home with her that night. But he was nicked for being in possession of stolen goods.'

'And we're told that Lenny's mother intended to come in on Tuesday morning to amend the evidence she gave in court,' said Paget. 'Interesting.'

Alcott, who had remained silent until now, said, 'Sounds to me as if Rudge might not be too happy with his mate's mother. And he'd be even less happy if she caught him in the church the other night while he was up to no good. Maybe she threatened to tell somebody. He grabs a candlestick and hits her.'

'That's certainly a possibility,' Paget agreed, 'provided we can put him there at the same time as Beth Smallwood. Right now, all we have are prints. We don't know when those prints were made.'

Alcott shrugged and lit a cigarette. 'That,' he said cheerfully, 'is your problem, Paget.' He glanced at the time. 'And my problem is I've got another meeting to attend.'

'Anything else?' Paget asked Ormside when Alcott had gone.

'As I said, there were no prints on the candle or the candlesticks, but there are partials on the inside of the Cellophane wrapper the candles were in, and they don't belong to the victim. They could belong to the killer, but the wrapper was so crumpled that they are having trouble getting enough of a print to work with.

'There were also prints on the candle they found beneath one of the pews near the body. They match several prints found in the belfry. Not Rudge's; someone else's. Possibly a woman's, but they can't be certain of that.' Ormside flipped through the notes before him. 'And I think that's the lot,' he concluded.

'Not bad to be going on with,' Paget observed. 'Any word from Tregalles?'

'He said he was going to see someone who knew Harry Beecham and his wife. I expect he'll be back shortly.'

'Right,' said Paget. 'No news from the hospital, I suppose?'

'Not yet.'

'Then let's pull Rudge in for questioning. See what kind of alibi he has for Monday evening. Meanwhile, I think I'll take a run out to Golden Meadows to see a man about his son.'

Golden Meadows lay across the river, not far from the railway station. Paget turned off the main road at a faded sign that read: 'Golden Meadows – a Home Away From Home'. The lane was narrow, bounded on one side by a sagging wire fence that marked the edge of the railway cutting, and on the other by brambles that reached out to brush the car.

The lane was short, abruptly ending in a circular driveway. Paget dutifully followed the sign directing visitors to the right, and parked the car.

The building was a long, low, brick structure punctuated at regular intervals by narrow windows. They were streaked and dirty, and the metal frames were rusted, staining the bricks below. It was not at all the sort of place Paget had envisioned. Surely Arthur Gresham could have done better than this for his own father, he thought as he mounted the steps leading up to the front door.

The foyer was dimly lit. A sign on one of the doors said: OFFICE, and beside it was a sliding glass panel, partly open. He looked inside, but there was no one there.

'There's no one about,' said a voice behind him. He turned to see a white-haired woman watching him from a wheelchair. She hadn't been there a moment ago, and he hadn't heard her approach. 'They're seeing to lunch,' she told him.

'I see. Thank you,' said Paget. 'Could you tell me where I might find Mr Gresham?'

The woman frowned in thought. 'Ah! You mean Claude,' she said. 'Oh, yes, he's down at the end.' She pointed down a passageway which led off to the right. 'Thirty-six or thirty-seven, I think it is. He doesn't come out much these days. You might as well go down. They'll be busy for a good half-hour yet. Not enough staff, you see.'

99

'Thank you again,' said Paget, glancing at the gold band on her finger. 'Mrs...?'

'Wickins,' the woman supplied. 'You a relative?'

'No.' The answer seemed inadequate. 'It's a business matter,' he explained.

The woman nodded. 'Not many visitors bother coming any more,' she said. 'Got two sons in Bridgnorth, but they don't come. Husband died eight years ago and I've been here for three.' She sighed. 'Mind you, I know they're busy, what with family and all, but still...'

Abruptly, she spun the wheelchair round and departed as silently as she had come.

Claude Gresham's name, together with three others, was on the door of number 36. The door was partly open, and Paget knocked and entered.

The room was fairly large, but four empty beds took up much of the space. At first, Paget thought the room was empty, but a slight noise drew his attention to a bald-headed man dozing in a chair beside one of the beds. He had slumped to one side, and a book he had been reading lay face down on the floor. Paget picked it up. It was a large print edition of Le Carre's *Tinker, Tailor, Soldier, Spy*. He set it on the bed. A name-plate on the footboard said: 'C. B. Gresham'.

Paget pulled up a chair and sat down carefully, but the chair creaked, protesting beneath his weight. The man stirred and opened his eyes. A thin stream of saliva dribbled from the corner of his mouth and dripped on his collar. He stared blankly at Paget, then slowly pulled himself upright.

'Arthur?' he enquired. The voice was thin and reedy, as was the man himself. His face was deeply lined, and his eyes were set deep within their sockets. He fumbled for his glasses, which were hanging by a cord around his neck, and put them on.

'You're not Arthur,' he said accusingly. His speech was slightly slurred, and Paget realized that one side of his face was paralysed. 'What time is it?' he demanded. 'Have I had my dinner?'

'I don't think so,' said Paget. He consulted his watch. 'It's ten minutes past twelve. Do they bring it to you here?'

'Molly does, if she's here.' The old man scowled. 'The others don't. They say if I'm hungry I'll go to the dining-room. So I say to hell with them and stay here. Food's not that good anyway. Who are you? Health visitor?'

'Policeman,' said Paget, and introduced himself. 'I'd like to ask you a few questions, if you don't mind, Mr Gresham.'

'And if I do?'

'That's entirely up to you, sir.'

'Hmph!' The old man looked disappointed. It was as if he were looking for an argument. 'What about?' he demanded. 'If it's about this place, then you'd better take off your coat and get out your notebook. Will I have to testify in court?'

Paget laughed. 'No, it has nothing to do with Golden Meadows,' he said. 'I'd like to talk to you about your son, Arthur.'

'Why? What's he done?'

'I don't know that he's done anything,' said Paget. 'But I do need to confirm something he told me. He said he came here to visit you last Monday. Do you remember that?'

'There's nothing wrong with my memory,' Claude Gresham snapped.

'I didn't mean to imply that there was, sir.'

'Yes you did. I could hear it in your voice. Just because I'm getting old and dribble down myself, it doesn't mean I've lost my senses. What do you want to know for?'

'One of the bank's employees was killed on Monday night,' Paget explained, 'and it makes our job much simpler if we can account for the movements of everyone who came in contact with her shortly before she died. It's a process of elimination,' he concluded, 'so if you can confirm what your son told us, you'd be doing him a favour. Was he here on Monday evening?'

'What day is it today?' Before Paget could reply, the old man leaned forward and tapped him on the knee. 'Now don't go getting the idea that I'm senile just because I asked you that,' he said sharply. 'It's just that every day's the same round here. I've not had the news on today, so I've lost track.'

'It's Thursday,' Paget told him.

'Ah!' The old man leaned back. 'Let's see, now,' he mused. 'It wasn't last night, and it wasn't the night before, so, yes, that's right, it was Monday.'

'I see.' Despite what Claude Gresham had said, Paget couldn't help wondering how reliable the old man's memory was. 'Do you happen to recall what time he came and what time he left?'

Gresham eyed him shrewdly. 'Who died?' he asked abruptly. 'You said it was a woman. Do I know her?'

'I don't know. Do you? Her name was Beth Smallwood.'

Claude Gresham shook his head. 'No, never heard of her,' he said. 'Do you think Arthur had something to do with her death? Is that why you're asking?'

Paget met the penetrating gaze head on. 'When it comes to murder, Mr Gresham, I suspect everyone until it can be proved that they couldn't possibly have done it,' he said quietly.

The old man remained silent for some time. 'He was here,' he said at last. 'Came about seven – something like that. Don't know what time he left, exactly.' He shrugged. It was almost an apology. 'See, sometimes I fall asleep, and I did that night. When I woke up Sylvia was in here making sure we were all tucked up for the night, and Arthur was gone.'

'Would Sylvia have seen your son leave?'

'You'd have to ask her, but she's not on today.' The old man sighed. 'We don't see that many visitors,' he said. 'There's some in here who never see their families. Stick us away and forget us, mostly. Not that Arthur is like that,' he added hastily. 'He's been very good lately.'

'How often does he come to see you?'

'Two or three times, some weeks,' said the old man. 'Doesn't stay long; just pops in. Brings me the odd book. I expect he'll be here again tonight.'

The answer surprised Paget. He hadn't thought of Arthur Gresham as a man who would go out of his way to visit his aged father.

The old man pursed his lips and paused before he spoke, and Paget was reminded forcibly of Arthur. 'Funny how he's changed,' he mused. 'Didn't use to come at all when I first came in here. Never used to see him from one month to the next. But now he comes regularly two or three times a week. I've told him he needn't, but he says it's no trouble.'

'And he's been doing this for some time?'

'Oh, yes. Been doing it for months, now. Took him a while to realize what it's like to be stuck in here, I suppose.'

A short, stout, matronly woman bustled into the room, carrying a tray. She stopped short when she saw Paget. 'I'm sorry, Claude,' she said. 'I didn't realize you had a visitor. I've brought your dinner.' She lowered her voice. 'Custard tart for afters,' she said. 'But don't tell the others. It's jelly in the dining-room.'

102

Paget got to his feet. 'I was just about to leave,' he said, 'so I'll let you get on with your dinner, Mr Gresham. And thank you for your help.'

But Claude Gresham had already dismissed his visitor from his mind as the woman set the tray before him. 'You're a good girl, Molly,' he said fondly, and reached out quite casually to run his hand up beneath the woman's skirt.

Just as casually, Molly smacked his hand away. 'You keep that up, my lad, and I'll give your custard tart to someone else,' Paget heard her say as he left the room. It seemed that Arthur Gresham had more than one thing in common with his father.

CHAPTER 15

Strathe House was tucked into the hillside above the river. Built originally in the 1920s as a small but exclusive hotel, it had fallen on hard times during the 'thirties, and had somehow missed the recovery enjoyed by others after the war. Now, its clientele consisted mainly of commercial and other itinerant travellers seeking relatively cheap lodgings for a night or two. Occasionally, an overseas visitor would turn up, lured by carefully worded advertisements, but they seldom stayed there long.

Viewed from the outside, the building still retained some of its old-world charm, but inside was another story. The carpets were frayed and threadbare; the floors squeaked abominably; the paintwork was cracked and chipped; the lighting was poor; and the plumbing was, to say the least, unreliable. But there was no money to put it right, nor was there likely to be in the foreseeable future.

As Jack Rudge saw it, it was a classic case of Catch 22. To make the place over in order to attract more people, he needed money, but in order to get the money, he needed more people. He'd cut costs to the bone as it was, using part-time workers and youngsters such as Amy, and doing as much as possible himself. There was Tony, of course, but he was next to useless. Always skiving off if he got half the chance. And Rudge was almost certain that it was Tony who was pinching cigarettes.

Jack Rudge was in this gloomy frame of mind when a car pulled up outside and a man got out. Two-piece suit; good quality; air of authority; no luggage. He groaned. Not another bloody inspector! He hadn't seen this one before, but he was quite certain that the man would not be asking for a room.

He put on a smile as the man entered and came to the reception desk. 'Good afternoon, sir. Lovely day after that bit of rain. What can we do for you?'

The man acknowledged the greeting with a nod and produced a card. 'Chief Inspector Paget, Westvale Police,' he said. 'Are you Mr Rudge?'

The smile faded. 'That's right,' he said cautiously.

'I'd like a word with your son, Tony, if he's about,' said Paget.

Rudge's expression became grim. 'What's he done now?' he demanded. 'Whatever it is, I didn't know about it. I've tried my best with that lad, but I haven't got eyes in the back of my head.'

'I'd just like to talk to him,' said Paget.

'What about?'

Paget remained silent.

Rudge sighed heavily. 'All right, don't tell me, then,' he said sullenly. 'I'm only his father!' He jerked his thumb in the direction of a narrow opening. 'He's out the back doing the flower beds – that is if he hasn't skived off by now.'

'Thanks,' said Paget as he moved toward the passageway.

Tony Rudge scrambled to his feet as he heard the sound of the back door opening. He dropped his cigarette and ground it beneath his heel, snatched up a spade and thrust it into the ground.

'Tony Rudge?'

Tony turned as if surprised. He didn't know the man coming toward him, but he suddenly felt uneasy. 'Who wants to know?' he asked.

The man approached and held out a card. 'I do,' he said quietly. Tony peered closely at the card, but he didn't need to read it to know that this man was a policeman.

He felt the prickle of sweat beneath his collar. He wanted to run. What had gone wrong? How could anybody know? Unless...

Unless they'd caught the killer. He shivered but covered the movement by picking up his jacket and slipping it on.

'Cool when you stop digging,' he remarked in what he hoped was a steady voice. He lit a cigarette.

104

Paget eyed him thoughtfully. 'We found a set of your fingerprints in a most unusual place,' he told the boy, 'so I thought I'd come round to see if you could offer an explanation.'

They couldn't have! He'd been careful. He'd used gloves; there wasn't any way he could have left prints on the paper or the envelope. He'd even used gloves when he'd shoved it through the letter-box.

'Don't know what you mean,' he said, frowning.

'I think you do. Where were you Monday night?'

'Monday?' Tony almost fainted with relief. He scratched his head. 'Dunno,' he said. 'Why?'

'Think harder,' Paget told him. 'And think about who was with you.'

Oh, shit! Amy. She'd told someone. But she couldn't prove it. He'd say she was lying. He'd say she had a crush on him and he'd told her to get lost, and this was her way of getting back at him.

Tony pretended to think. 'I was around here as far as I can remember,' he insisted. 'Why? What's all this about fingerprints? I haven't done anything.'

Paget sighed. 'You left your prints all over the belfry and the doors in St Justin's church the other night,' he said. 'Now don't mess me about, Tony. I want to know who you were with and what you were doing there.'

Frances Duncan was the owner of Creations, a small but exclusive art gallery in Bridge Street. She had a mannish, skeletal face whose outlines were made even sharper by the way her hair was pulled back and tied behind her head. Her skin was pale, almost translucent, and her neck seemed to be extraordinarily long. She wore a simple black dress with three-quarter length sleeves, and both wrists were adorned with several heavy bracelets. She would be about fifty, Tregalles judged.

They sat close together, knees almost touching in a tiny office at the back of the gallery. Ms Duncan, as she preferred to be called, sat sideways behind her desk in her tilted swivel chair, while Tregalles perched on a folding metal chair facing her.

Ms Duncan lit a cigarette, inhaled deeply and blew a stream of smoke toward the ceiling. 'Harry Beecham,' she said ruminatively.

'I haven't seen him for ages. Not that I ever knew him well. I knew Helen, of course. Helen Best, she was when I first met her. Such a pity. So much talent. What's this all about, Sergeant? Is Harry in some sort of trouble?'

Tregalles dismissed the suggestion with a wave of his hand. 'It's more of a background check, really. A woman who works at the same bank was killed the other night, and we have to do a routine check on everyone who knew her.' He went on quickly before Ms Duncan had a chance to speak. 'But you say you know Helen Beecham better than Harry?'

'Knew, Sergeant. Knew. I haven't seen her in years. But what prompted you to come to me for information?'

'I couldn't find anyone who knows much about the Beechams,' he told her. 'They don't seem to have any friends or relatives, and as far as I can tell, they have absolutely no social life at all. In fact, I can't find anyone who has seen more than a glimpse of Mrs Beecham in years. But someone did say they remembered that she used to exhibit paintings here.'

Frances Duncan nodded slowly. 'Yes, she did, and I wish I had some of her stuff now. She was just beginning to become known. She had a marvellous talent; fresh and clean and exciting. She was self-taught, you know. Never had the money to go to art school. Orphaned when she was just a child – two or three, I believe – and brought up by an aunt. Then the aunt died when Helen was still quite young. Left her nothing to speak of. Helen was working in a draper's shop at the time; pitiful wages, so she didn't have any money of her own.'

Ms Duncan fell silent. The cigarette smouldered between her fingers, and Tregalles's eyes began to water.

'I didn't know her then, of course,' the woman continued. 'I found out most of it later when she began bringing some of her sketches to me. Funny little thing. Timid, almost apologetic for troubling me. Quite frankly, I didn't believe the work she brought in could be hers, but it was. She had a marvellous eye for line.' Ms Duncan grimaced wryly. 'We could have made a lot of money between us if she'd carried on.'

'What happened?'

Frances Duncan shrugged. 'She just stopped coming in. To be honest, I thought she had decided to take her business elsewhere after that write-up in *Arts World*, and I was furious. But then I heard that she was ill, and I thought that once she was better she would come back again.

'But she didn't. The illness dragged on, and she began having these fits of depression, and as far as I know she's never touched a pen or brush since.'

Tregalles frowned. 'You say she was ill,' he said. 'Ill in what way? I mean did she go to hospital or what? Did you see her? Talk to her at that time?'

'I really don't know how it started. I spoke to her on the telephone several times. I had people asking for her work, but she seemed quite distant, indifferent. She sounded listless; as if even talking was too much trouble. So different from the way she was at the wedding. I felt sorry for Harry. Such a nice man. He was devastated. And so soon after they were married. He used to pop in from time to time to let me know how things were, but he stopped coming after a while.'

'When exactly did this happen?'

'Five years ago. I remember the wedding was in March. The fifteenth, as a matter of fact. I remember because we made a bit of a joke about it being unlucky. You know, the "Ides of March" and all that. Unfortunately, it turned out to be a very bad joke.'

'Five years ago,' Tregalles mused. 'How old is Helen Beecham?'

'She must be about thirty-six or seven by now. I know she was over thirty when she married Harry.'

'They married late.'

Ms Duncan nodded. 'This was Harry's second marriage. His first wife died a couple of years before he met Helen. It was her first, of course, and I was so happy for her. She was such a mouse before, but she seemed to blossom when she met Harry. And her work improved. It had been good before, but she seemed to catch fire then, and there was no stopping her.'

Frances Duncan lit another cigarette. Smoke trickled from her nostrils. 'It's a damned shame,' she said fiercely. 'She could have gone straight to the top.'

'I can't find anyone who has a bad word for Harry Beecham,' Tregalles said. 'The neighbours say you can set your watch by him each morning as he leaves for work – at least you could before Tuesday, but one woman did say she'd noticed that he'd been coming home later in the evening these past few months. He appears to be devoted to his wife; even does the shopping because she has this thing about not wanting to leave the house.'

'Doesn't Mrs Beecham *ever* go out?' Len Ormside asked. He, Tregalles, and Paget were seated around his desk in the incident room.

'The neighbours say she will only talk through the letter-box if anyone comes to the door, and she never asks anyone in. One or two say they have seen her in the garden in the summer, but they say she disappears if anyone speaks to her across the fence. It's almost as if she panics and runs for cover as soon as anyone comes near.'

'That certainly fits with what Beecham told me the other day,' said Paget, 'and I must say the man seems harmless enough. It's just that I have trouble believing that he would go right past the church without going in, especially when Mrs Turvey said he seemed so hell-bent on talking to Beth Smallwood. He said he didn't go because he thought there would be others at the church as well, but I have trouble with that.'

He turned to Ormside. 'Have someone make the rounds to see if we can find out where Beecham went after he left the bank that day,' he said. 'I suspect he spent a good part of the day drinking, so try the pubs. Someone should remember him. Find out if he talked to anyone, and what his mood was like.'

Ormside made a note.

'Right. Well now, Tony Rudge.' Paget hesitated. 'The boy admitted to having been in the belfry – not that he had much choice with his prints all over the place – but claimed they were there from the time when he and Lenny Smallwood used the place to store stolen goods. When I mentioned the condoms, he suddenly "remembered" that he'd taken a girl up there some weeks ago, but he claimed he met her in a pub and didn't know anything about her except she called herself Pat. He said that any other prints we'd found up there must be hers.

'He's lying, of course. Forensic says that at least two of the condoms were used as recently as Monday evening, which puts Rudge and his girlfriend in the belfry at or close to the time when Beth Smallwood was murdered.'

'And we know he had good reason to hate Beth Smallwood,' said Tregalles. 'What did he have to say about that?'

Paget shrugged. 'What could he say? He denied it; said that was all in the past, and continued to swear that he hadn't been near the church for weeks.'

'So what happens now?' asked Ormside.

'We find out who Rudge's girlfriend is, then bring them both in for questioning.' Paget glanced at the time and rose to his feet. He still had a report to prepare for Alcott before he went home.

Ormside and Tregalles exchanged glances. 'This girl called Pat,' Tregalles ventured. 'Did Rudge give you the name of the pub where he is supposed to have met her?'

'He claimed he couldn't remember. But don't waste your time on that. I'm quite sure Rudge made that up.'

'Then, who *are* we looking for, exactly?'

'His *real* girlfriend, of course,' said Paget as he made his way to the door. 'The one he was with on Monday night.'

CHAPTER 16

The view from room number 12 at the top of Strathe House was the best of all by far, but hardly anyone ever saw it because the room was small and cramped and seldom let.

Which was why Tony Rudge chose to meet Amy there. He wasn't taking much of a chance. The stairs leading up to the room were steep and narrow, and since only five of the twelve rooms were occupied, there was hardly anyone about.

He glanced at his watch. Where the hell was Amy? He'd told her to meet him here before she went home. Time was getting on, and his father would be shouting for him any minute to come and help with dinner. He was dying for a cigarette but he didn't dare light up. This was supposed to be a non-smoking room, and if his father ever came up and smelled smoke – and he would – he'd blame Tony.

Impatiently, he paced the floor. Of all the rotten luck! Why did Lenny's mum have to go and get herself killed in the church while he was there? Not that he was sorry she was dead; she bloody well deserved to be after the way she'd lied in court to get her precious Lenny off. But in his haste to get away that night, he'd quite forgotten fingerprints. But then, who the hell would think of lifting prints from condoms, for God's sake? Filthy bastards. You'd think they'd have better things to do.

But he'd have to watch his step. That chief inspector was no fool, and he'd be back to ask more questions. Tony paced up and down the tiny room. He daren't go through with his original plan for tonight; they might be watching him.

Thank God he'd been able to head Paget off about the girl. At least they didn't know about Amy. If they ever found out he'd been bonking a fifteen-year-old...

The door opened and Amy slipped through and closed it behind her.

'Took you bloody long enough,' Tony greeted her belligerently.

The girl looked hurt. 'I couldn't get away before,' she said. 'Your dad said...'

'I don't give a damn what my dad said,' he snapped irritably. 'I wanted you...' He stopped abruptly, remembering what it was he wanted the girl to do. He held his temper and forced a smile.

Amy's face lit up. 'You wanted me and you couldn't wait,' she said archly. She came to him and slid her arms around his waist. 'Love me, Tony,' she whispered.

He kissed her and caressed her body, then gently pulled away. 'Later,' he said gruffly. 'Sit down. We have to talk.'

They sat on the bed because there was nowhere else to sit. Amy slid her hand between his thighs, but he took hold of it and held it firmly. 'I said we have to talk! Don't you ever think of anything else?'

'Not when you're around, Tony,' the girl said dreamily.

She was becoming tiresome, but he needed her. Tony kissed her lightly. 'Just hold the thought for a bit,' he told her. 'Tonight it's business first.'

She giggled. 'Monkey business, I'll bet.'

Her childish mannerisms irritated him. He was beginning to wonder what he'd ever seen in her. True, she had a great little body, but there were plenty of other girls out there. He would have to put her off him somehow – but not yet.

He smiled down at her and stroked her hair. 'I want you to do me a favour,' he told her. 'There's twenty quid in it for you.'

'Twenty quid? You're joking!'

'I'm not.'

Amy pulled away and looked at him. 'You don't want me to do something weird, do you?' she said hesitantly. 'I mean, I like it the way we do it now, and I thought that you did too.'

'Good God, no.' He laughed. 'Silly girl,' he chided. He pulled her into his arms. 'It's nothing like that. I just want you to pick up a package for me. Well, an envelope, really. Will you do it?'

'Why can't you do it?'

'Because it would violate the conditions of my probation,' he told her glibly. He slid his hand beneath her blouse and began to stroke her breast. 'You see, there's this bloke I loaned some money to while I was in the nick, and he's out now and wants to pay it back. But we're both out on licence, so we can't meet. It's against the rules. Consorting with known criminals, it's called.' He was pleased with the explanation, and Amy wouldn't know enough to challenge it.

'Why can't he just send it through the post?'

Tony shook his head. 'You know what Dad's like. Even if it's addressed to me, he'd open it, and I don't want him to know about it. If he gets his hands on it, I'll never see a penny of it.'

Amy nuzzled contentedly against him and raised her lips to his. He kissed her tenderly. 'So what do you want me to do?' she asked.

'Well, he's got to leave tonight, so he said he'd hide the money in a safe place down at the old sheds beside the railway lines, and I could pick it up there. But I can't, you see, because of the police. That's why I want you to do it for me.' He began to undo her blouse.

'Let's not talk, Tony.' Amy caught his hand and tried to move it down, but Tony pulled away.

'In a *minute*, Amy,' he said, laughing gently. 'Don't be so damned impatient. I want it too, you know, but I have to get this sorted first.'

The girl wriggled impatiently. 'So tell me what you want me to do.'

'I want you to go down to the sheds and pick up the envelope for me, that's all. OK?'

'But *why* can't you do it? You wouldn't be meeting him, so they couldn't say you were consorting or whatever it is, could they?'

'Because I think the police are watching me. You saw that man who came round this afternoon?'

'Yeah. Who was he?'

'He's a chief inspector, and he's got it in for me. He's just waiting for me to make a slip, then bang! he'll have me back inside. You wouldn't like that, would you, Amy?'

The girl turned a troubled face toward him. 'He can't do that, can he, Tony? I mean, what's he got against you?'

Tony shrugged helplessly. 'They found out that I know Lenny Smallwood,' he said, 'and they seem to think that I might have had something to do with his mum's death.'

Amy's eyes opened wide. 'They don't know that we were there, do they?' she asked fearfully.

'Of course they don't,' he assured her. 'They know that I was in the church sometime or other because my prints were there. But I said that was from when I used to meet Lenny there. They don't know about you, and there's no way I'd ever let them know.'

Amy flung her arms around his neck and kissed him. 'I don't know what I'd do if you had to go away,' she said fiercely. 'You won't, will you, Tony? You won't ever leave me, will you?'

'Of course not, but I'm relying on you to help me,' he told her. 'You will pick up the money for me, won't you, Amy? I really need it.'

'Oh, yes, Tony. Yes. Just tell me what you want me to do.'

'It will mean you'll have to sneak out of the house after midnight and . . . ' He stopped abruptly and cupped her face in his hands. 'No. This is wrong,' he said firmly. 'It isn't fair on you. I keep forgetting that you're so young.' He pulled her to him. 'Forgive me, Amy. I'll just have to risk it myself. I just hope that . . . ' He broke off as he slipped the blouse from her shoulders and buried his face in her flesh.

Come on, Amy, say you'll do it. Now's your chance to prove you love me. Come on, you silly little cow! Say it!

Amy clutched him tightly and pulled him down on top of her. 'I can do it, Tony,' she breathed fiercely in his ear. 'Honest. I *want* to do it for you. You don't have to give me any money. I love you, Tony.'

Friday – 17 May

Amy eased the door shut and retrieved her bicycle from behind the house where she'd left it when she came home last night. Normally, she wouldn't have risked leaving it outside; bikes and anything else not nailed down had a habit of disappearing from the Flats. She made her way swiftly down the narrow passage between the houses and out into the street.

The old railway sheds were less than a mile away, and it was an easy ride once she reached Tavistock Road at the top of the hill. She ignored the turning that would take her down to the sheds. It was a narrow road, and steep, and she didn't fancy chancing it in the dark. Besides, the area at the bottom was littered with old cable reels, sleepers, and rusting lengths of track. It would be much easier and a lot quicker to leave her bike in the long grass beside Tavistock Road, scramble down the hill to the sheds, get the money, and climb back up again. Five minutes at the most.

A solitary car went by. She waited until it was out of sight, then dropped the bike in a patch of meadow-grass. No one would see it there in the dark.

There was no moon, and although her eyes had become accustomed to the night, it was hard to see where to put her feet as she picked her way down the steep hillside. The outline of the sheds loomed stark and black against the night sky as she neared the bottom, and it seemed to Amy that they were larger than they'd looked in daylight. And more ominous.

The darkness and the silence folded around her. The grass was wet. Her shoes were soaked, and she wondered what they'd look like in the morning. Better not let her mum see them. The corrugated metal was ice cold beneath her fingers as she felt her way around to the front.

She was breathing hard, and tingling with excitement. 'Second shed,' Tony had said as he stroked her hair. 'You remember, don't you, Amy?'

She remembered. She and Tony had come here one afternoon. They'd brought sandwiches and had a picnic, using an old cable reel for a table. Later, they'd made love inside the shed. That was why he'd chosen this place, she thought. Tony could be so romantic.

The big doors sagged open, but Amy hesitated to go inside. The silence was eerie; the darkness absolute. There wasn't a breath of wind; everything was still. She took out the little torch she'd brought with her and shone the tiny beam into the blackness of the interior. She could feel her heart pounding against her ribs and she wished Tony were with her now.

Amy took a deep breath and stepped through the gap.

The silence was deafening. She shone the torch around, picking out the odd bits and pieces of machinery that had been abandoned there. Beside her, at shoulder height, was the loading dock, bare and empty now as it had been for more than twenty years.

'The envelope will be taped to the back of that big old metal thing straight in front of you,' Tony had said. Neither of them knew what it was, but in fact it was the base of a winch, too big and heavy to move when the shed was cleared.

The pencil of light found the base. Gingerly, Amy worked her way in behind it. Yes! There it was. A white envelope taped to the back just as Tony had said it would be. Amy sighed with relief. She tugged at the envelope, but it had been taped on well. Her hands were sweating. She pulled harder and the envelope came away.

She tried to stuff it in her pocket, but the tape kept sticking to her jacket, and it wouldn't go in. Muttering to herself, she gave up trying. The sooner she was out of there and back up on the road the happier she would be. Tony would be pleased. She gave herself a mental hug as she followed the light of the torch to the door.

A sound! Soft, like a quiet footstep.

She froze, every nerve end suddenly alert. She wanted to turn, to see what it was, but she was too scared to move. She held her breath and strained to hear, but the pounding in her ears drowned out anything that might be there. She forced herself to turn, torch held out in front of her with both hands.

A light blazed in her eyes, blinding her. She flung up an arm to shield her face, but not before she caught a glimpse of something dark descending. Desperately, she twisted away and fell. Pain seared her skull. A black shape loomed over her. She rolled, scrambling hard to regain her feet. Someone swore behind the light. She couldn't see. Her head felt as if it would explode.

Her arm went numb. She heard it crack and felt herself falling once again. In desperation she lashed out with her foot; felt it connect, and heard a startled grunt. Blood was dripping down her face; she could feel it; taste it.

Amy scrambled around on the floor, twisting, turning this way and that to get away from her attacker. She was almost on her knees; the light was blinding her again. The weapon glinted as it rose.

She launched herself forward with every ounce of strength she had, head down to avoid the descending weapon. She felt it graze her arm as her head slammed hard into someone's chest. Amy heard the 'whoosh' of breath as her attacker staggered back and fell. The light went out.

She almost fell herself. Her legs were made of rubber and her head was full of cotton wool. She mustn't faint! She mustn't! She had to get out before the light came on again. The door! For Christ's sake, where was the door?

CHAPTER 17

Rita Thomson studied her image critically in the mirror. Her hair simply wouldn't behave this morning, but it would have to do. She glanced at the time. Quarter to six. She had to be out of the house by ten to six if she hoped to catch the bus. There wouldn't be another one along until twenty past, and that was too late to get her to work on time at the Greenfield Hotel where she worked as a dining-room supervisor.

Rita checked her lipstick one last time before turning from the mirror. 'Amy?' she called as she shrugged into her coat. 'Come on, luv. I want to hear you up before I go.' She listened.

It didn't sound as if the girl was stirring. Rita hesitated, then quickly ran upstairs. 'Amy! Time to get up,' she said sharply as she opened the bedroom door. 'You know what Mr Rudge is like if you're...'

She stopped dead. Amy wasn't there. Neither had her bed been slept in. Where the devil...? She couldn't have gone to work already. But where was she then? God! Look at the time. Rita felt her temper rising. It was always *something* with that girl!

She ran downstairs. The house was small, and it took only a minute to determine that Amy wasn't there. And her bike was gone. Come to think of it, Rita couldn't recall seeing it last night, either.

Seven minutes to six! She'd have to run if she hoped to catch the bus. Blast the girl, anyway. She'd stayed out all night; that's what she'd done. Well, just wait till she got home. She might be fifteen years old, but she could still have her behind tanned.

Rita slammed out of the house and ran down the street. If she missed her bus because of Amy...

She knew the bus driver saw her, but he would have started if she hadn't thrust her arm inside the closing door. It opened and she mounted the step and made her way to the back of the bus and a vacant seat.

She stared out of the window with troubled but unseeing eyes. She hoped Amy was all right; hoped she'd had sense enough to take the pill if she was having it off with someone. Stupid little fool!

Rita felt the sting of tears behind her eyes as her emotions swung from anger to concern. It was so *hard* to bring up a kid these days, especially a girl like Amy. She was too good-looking for her own good, and she liked the boys. And what with all this talk about AIDS...

Rita blinked rapidly and brushed a tear away. Just *wait* till she got home!

Paget knew the moment he opened his eyes that it was going to be a bad day. He'd tried to rationalize; tried to tell himself that this was just like any other day, but it wasn't, and it never would be.

Three years ago today, he had lost the most precious thing he'd ever had. Jill. Torn from him in an explosion that not only took her life, but mangled and burned her body beyond recognition.

Logically, he told himself, the date had nothing to do with it. The memory of that awful time had been just as clear, just as painful yesterday and the weeks and months before as it was today. But logic didn't enter into it. It was as if the images of that day became more sharply focused on the anniversary date, and no matter what he did, he could not escape them.

Perversely, he *wanted* to remember, terrible as those memories were. For it seemed to him that by doing so he was somehow sharing them with Jill; sharing the pain she must have suffered – even if, as he'd been told a thousand times, her death was instantaneous.

He was not a believer; nor was he a religious man, but perhaps somewhere, somehow she'd know.

This was *not* what the psychiatrist had told him to do. 'I know it's painful; I know it will leave a scar that will never go away,' he'd said. 'Yes, you must weep; yes, you must mourn, but you must also try to concentrate on the *good* things you shared together. To do otherwise is to indulge in self-pity, and that can only be destructive.'

He was probably right, Paget conceded as he forced himself to get out of bed, but that didn't make the images go away. Nor did it alter the fact that he felt as miserable as hell!

He had not slept well. His neck and shoulders were stiff. He adjusted the water in the shower until it was as hot as he could bear, then stood there and let it pound his skin. He closed his eyes, remembering the first time that he and Jill had showered together. He could see her now; eyes closed, head back as she turned her face to his and ...

'Damn!' His eyes flew open and he shook his head to clear it. He was furious with himself for allowing his mind to drift. He turned the water off and stepped out of the shower. It was just one of those silly tricks the brain played from time to time, he told himself. It didn't *mean* anything.

But for a moment – just for a fleeting second – the image of Jill's impish face had changed, and he'd seen instead the face of Andrea McMillan.

Walter Palfrey first saw the bike lying in the grass while he was on his way to work. Looked like a nice bike. Kids. Leave stuff lying about without a thought.

Palfrey saw the bike again an hour later as he was on his way to make his first delivery. He delivered motor parts from a central depot to the garages in the area. It wasn't a bad job, but it didn't pay much. By the time he'd paid the rent and bought a bit of food, there wasn't much left over for cigarettes and beer. Still, it was better than being chained to a desk.

He scanned the hillside leading down to the railway sheds, but he couldn't see any children. Besides, now that he looked more closely, the bike was too big to belong to a child. Shouldn't leave a nice bike like that lying about. Someone could come along and pinch it. It would be worth a bit.

Walter Palfrey was still thinking about the bike when he dropped off clutch parts for an Escort at Jessop's garage on the Worcester road. His next delivery would take him back across the bridge, but it wouldn't be all that far out of his way if he went back along Tavistock Road. Just to see if the bike was still there.

It was still there. Palfrey slowed and stopped the pick-up. He sat looking at the bike. Drop handlebars; ten or twelve speed; racing wheels. He got out and looked around. The nearest house was a hundred yards away, and the road was quite deserted.

Palfrey plunged into the long grass, grabbed the bike and heaved it into the back of the pick-up. He glanced around. No one had seen him. Swiftly, he covered the bike with a tarp, then got back in the pick-up. A car was coming toward him as he started off, but the driver was talking to his passenger and didn't give the pick-up so much as a glance.

Palfrey let out a long breath and lit a cigarette. He'd drive over to Welshpool tomorrow. He knew some people there. Go down the pub. Bound to be someone there who could use a bike if the price was right.

Tony Rudge fumed as he pulled the sheets from the bed and tossed them on the floor. Where the hell was Amy? Why hadn't she come to work this morning? Apart from anything else, it was her fault that he was having to help with the rooms. 'The girl's not here, so somebody's got to clean those rooms,' his father had told him bluntly, 'and I'll not have you hanging about with your hands in your pockets while there's work to be done. Now get on with it.'

She hadn't gone to pick up the money; that's what it was. And now she was too scared to come to work this morning to face him. Stupid little cow. He should have known she'd funk it. Now what was he going to do? Even if he could get away, he daren't go near the sheds himself in case the police were watching him. And he couldn't phone Amy to find out what had gone wrong because she didn't have a phone.

Tony flipped a clean sheet on the bed and tried to straighten it, but the damned thing kept sliding to one side. He went round the bed and pulled the sheet over. Too far. He went back again and pulled it back. Now there was nothing to tuck in at the bottom.

Sod it! He threw a blanket over the sheet and tucked it in. If the customers didn't like it they could make the bloody thing themselves.

Lenny Smallwood's hands tightened into fists as the shakes began again. Sweat glistened on his face. His nose was running and tears

118

started from his eyes. He needed a fix, but the bastards wouldn't give him one. He'd asked for methadone, but they'd told him it wouldn't work. Instead, they were giving him some sort of sedative that was doing bugger all as far as he was concerned.

His head throbbed with pain, and his face felt as if it had been hammered where they'd wired his jaws together.

A tremor ran through the length of his body and he felt sick. His kidneys were badly bruised, they said. One rib was broken and two were fractured. And his wrist was taped. He was lucky, they said; the arm wasn't broken after all. Lucky? Christ!

'Feeling a bit better today, is he, nurse?'

Lenny moaned. Trotter. Stupid little git! Why ask the friggin' nurse? What did she know? No, he wasn't feeling better. He felt like death! Tears trickled down his cheeks.

'He is experiencing quite a bit of pain, Doctor,' the girl said hesitantly. She was very young and she was afraid of Trotter. The word on the ward was that he had little or no respect for nurses. The charge-nurse had put it more succinctly: 'He's a jumped up little sod who thinks he's God,' she'd told them matter-of-factly, 'but he's still the doctor, so just remember that.'

'Yes,' said Trotter absently. 'Blood pressure is up, but that's to be expected under the circumstances.' He studied the chart, then handed it back to the nurse. 'I see no reason to change the medication,' he told her. 'Just make sure he drinks as much water as possible.' He turned to go.

'Please...I need something,' Lenny called after him. 'Just to tide me over. Those tablets – they're not strong enough. I need something stronger.'

Trotter returned to the bedside and stood looking down at the boy. 'I'm afraid that's not possible, Mr Smallwood,' he said. 'I know it must be unpleasant, but you'll just have to make the best of it for the next few days. I think you'll find it improves after that. And please do try to control the shaking. If you don't I shall have to order restraints, and I don't wish to resort to that.'

'Bastard!' Lenny grated. 'You could give me something if you wanted to.' He gasped as another spasm shook his body.

Trotter looked across at the nurse and shook his head. 'Keep an eye on him,' he said quietly, 'and let me know if these spasms continue. He could do himself considerable damage if this keeps up.'

Andrea McMillan was talking to the constable outside the door as Trotter left the room. 'Ah, Dr Trotter,' she greeted him. 'Just the man I'm looking for. How is the patient this morning?'

Trotter shook his head. 'Doing himself no good,' he said bluntly. 'He may have to be restrained if he keeps throwing himself about.'

Andrea McMillan pursed her lips. 'I hope it doesn't come to that,' she said. 'I thought he was coping rather well, considering what he must be going through.'

Trotter remained silent. He was the new boy here, and he wasn't about to argue with the registrar, but that didn't mean he had to like it.

'I was just telling the constable,' Andrea went on, 'that I think we can allow Chief Inspector Paget to talk to Mr Smallwood, now, but I said I would consult you first, of course. What do you think, Doctor? The boy may be in pain but he's certainly coherent.'

Trotter bridled. That should be his decision to make, not McMillan's. 'Do you really think he's ready for that?' he countered. 'It could upset him further.'

'It is his mother's murder the police are investigating,' she reminded him, 'and the police do have a right to question him. I shall insist on being present, of course.'

Trotter gave in grudgingly. 'I suppose it won't do any *permanent* damage,' he conceded.

'Good.' Andrea favoured the doctor with a smile. 'I'll arrange it then. I know you're very busy, so I'll let you get on.'

Andrea waited until Trotter was well down the corridor before turning to the constable. 'You heard that, I'm sure,' she said, 'but please make sure you tell Chief Inspector Paget that I wish to see him in my office before he visits Mr Smallwood.'

Inside the room, the young nurse had just refilled his glass with water when Lenny grabbed her arm. 'You've got to help me,' he whispered fiercely. 'Before that policewoman comes back in. The pain is killing me. Can't you get me something? Anything.'

His face was bathed in sweat, and she could see the naked agony in his eyes. 'I – I can't,' she said. 'The doctor said . . .'

'Sod the doctor!' Lenny's fingers dug deeper into her arm. 'I don't want much; just something to get me through the next few days. He said it would be better after that, but I need something now! Please?'

The girl pulled away. She felt sorry for him, but what he was asking was impossible. 'I can't,' she said. 'Besides, everything is counted and checked. It's more than my job is worth. I'm sorry.' She leaned over to wipe the sweat from his brow. 'I'll get some water and bathe your face for you,' she went on. 'Make you feel better.'

Angrily, he pushed her hand away. 'Don't bother,' he said sullenly. 'I wouldn't want you to put yourself out on my account.'

The girl looked hurt. 'It's not that I don't want to help you,' she said, 'it's just that the doctor's right. It would do more harm than good. Honestly.'

Lenny glared at her, then lay back and closed his eyes. 'All right,' he said resignedly. 'I don't want to get you in trouble, but you could still do me a small favour.'

'Like what?' the girl said cautiously.

'My girlfriend doesn't even know I'm in here,' he said. 'Ring her for me and let her know, will you? She'll be worried sick.'

'What about the police? Won't they...?'

'The police?' Lenny snorted derisively. 'They wouldn't give her the time of day even if they knew about her,' he said. 'Besides, I'd sooner they didn't. I don't want her dragged into this.'

'I don't know,' the girl said dubiously. 'I could ask the charge-nurse if it would be all right.'

Lenny groaned. 'Look, all I'm asking you to do is let her know, for God's sake!' He rolled his eyes upward and shook his head from side to side. 'It isn't much to ask – but if it's too much trouble just to pick up a phone, then...'

'It's not too much trouble,' the girl retorted, stung by his words. 'It's just that with the police here and everything, I don't want to get into trouble.'

'Never mind,' said Lenny tonelessly. 'It doesn't matter.' He sighed heavily and turned his head away.

The girl knew he was playing on her sympathy, but he he'd had a rough time of it and it didn't seem fair to keep his girlfriend in suspense.

'Do you have her number?'

Lenny turned back and looked at her with gratitude in his eyes. 'I've got two,' he said. 'If she's not at the first one, try the other. You won't tell anyone?' he added anxiously.

121

The girl hesitated, then shook her head.

'Good girl,' he said softly. 'And tell her I need the stuff in the bag. The little red one.'

'What stuff?'

'Just stuff. You know. Like my razor and comb and washing stuff. Just tell her what I said. She'll know.'

'I – I don't know ...'

Sweat ran into his eyes, and it was all he could do to stop himself from screaming at the stupid bitch. He forced himself to speak softly.

'Look, what harm can it do? Wouldn't you be upset if your boyfriend was in here like me, and nobody told you?'

The young nurse looked at Lenny for a long moment. Sincerity shone from his eyes, and she hadn't the heart to turn him down. And as he'd said, what harm could it do?

'Have you seen Paget this morning, Len? He looks as if he hasn't slept for a week.' Tregalles straddled a chair and sat down in front of Ormside's desk. 'I asked him if he was all right, and he nearly took my head off.'

Ormside tilted his chair and began to rock gently back and forth. 'He hasn't been what you might call "himself" all week,' he said, 'but you're right, he did look worse this morning. Hardly said a word when he looked in. Just checked the boards, looked at the log, grunted and left again.' He frowned. 'Is he ill?'

'I don't think so,' said Tregalles slowly. 'It's more like he has something on his mind. I was talking to him yesterday and it was just as if he'd drifted off and was thinking about something else entirely.'

'Perhaps he's got himself a woman,' Ormside suggested. 'That could account for his not getting any sleep.'

Tregalles grunted sceptically. 'If he has, he's not getting much pleasure out of it,' he declared. 'No, I don't think that's it. God, the hours he works, when would he have the time? Not that he hasn't had the chance. Grace Lovett's been trying to get him to notice her for a month or more, but he hasn't shown the slightest sign he's interested.'

'Then there must be something wrong with him,' Ormside declared. 'You'd have to be bloody dead to not notice her!'

Both men fell silent, each lost for the moment in their own particular fantasy that the name of Grace Lovett conjured in their minds. Ormside shook his head and sighed, then pulled a heavy file toward him and the spell was broken.

'Not much new this morning,' he said. 'We have a statement from the bus driver who dropped Mrs Smallwood at Farrow Lane Monday evening. He says she got on outside the bank at twenty-five to six, and he let her off about three minutes past six at Farrow Lane. He said she looked ill, and he thought she'd been crying. She would have gone right past her stop if he hadn't called out. He also said that if she fell and hurt herself it wasn't getting off his bus. He said he watched her in his mirror to make sure she was all right before he pulled away, and the last time he saw her, she was walking down Farrow Lane.'

Tregalles grimaced. 'It's beginning to look as if Paget's right,' he said. 'He's convinced that she was raped right there at work by Gresham.'

Ormside grunted. 'He'd better watch his step,' he warned. 'Gresham's well in with what passes for the upper crust round here, and I wouldn't put it past him to go running to the chief constable if Paget gets it wrong.'

Tregalles changed the subject. 'Paget's going over to the hospital this afternoon to talk to Lenny Smallwood,' he said, 'and I've been delegated to meet Mrs McLeish and take her to see her sister's body. Do you know what time her bus gets in?'

'Two thirty, assuming she caught the one she said she would.'

The telephone on Ormside's desk rang and he picked it up. He pulled a note pad toward him and began making notes. Tregalles was about to leave, but Ormside motioned him to stay.

'That was Ted Abbott,' he told Tregalles as he hung up the phone. 'He's been checking out Terrence Ling. Seems Ling wasn't exactly truthful about where he was the night Beth Smallwood died. A neighbour saw him go out about seven thirty, and says he didn't come back until well after nine.'

The early morning mist rising from the river had left behind a residue of moisture in the grass. High cloud obscured a hazy sun, and there was no warmth in it. In fact, thought Bill Tuckridge, it was bloody cold for May.

Still, at least it wasn't raining and he was able to get out. He didn't like the rain. His old bones ached enough when it was dry, but they really gave him what for after a day of rain. They were aching now as he trudged along the lane.

He'd go as far as the sheds and then turn back. Brindle, the Airedale cross, who hadn't been out for a couple of days, was enjoying himself immensely, quartering the ground ahead of him, and pausing every now and then to sniff enquiringly or to mark his territory.

Brindle should have been on a leash, but Tuckridge always let him off down here; there was nothing he could harm, and he always came when he was called.

Tuckridge stopped short of the sheds. The ground was littered with all sorts of bits and pieces half buried in the grass, and he didn't want to take a chance on turning his ankle or falling. 'Come on, then, Brindle,' he called as he turned to go back.

The dog stood and looked at him, head on one side as if to say 'Can't we stay longer?' but Tuckridge was already making his way back up the lane. The old man moved slowly, leaning heavily on his stick as he picked his way carefully over the uneven ground. Brindle remained where he was, no doubt hoping his master would change his mind, but the old man continued on.

The dog loped after him, romping through the long grass, snapping playfully at a passing bee. He stopped abruptly at the edge of a small depression, front legs stiff, eyes intent upon his new discovery. Cautiously, he approached and sniffed, then gently nudged the recumbent figure. There was no response. He barked, a short, excited sound, circling and dropping down on his front paws, trying to entice the figure to move.

'Brindle? Here, boy.' The dog's ears twitched, but he ignored the command. 'Brindle!' The tone was sharper now. The dog circled the figure once more. 'Brindle! Come! Get over here when I call you.'

Brindle whined softly, then turned and bounded across the hummocky grass to where his master waited.

'Flush a rabbit, did you, boy?' the old man said as he set off once again. Brindle wagged his tail and trotted along beside him, all thoughts of what he'd found now just a fading memory.

CHAPTER 18

Andrea McMillan threw down her pen and sat back in her chair. It was no good; she couldn't concentrate. She looked at her watch for perhaps the fifth time in the past ten minutes. Neil had said he'd try to get there by two, and it was ten past already. This was silly. She placed the tips of her fingers against her abdomen and took a deep breath; held it, then let it slowly out again. She did it several times. It was supposed to help.

It didn't.

There was a light tap on the door and Paget entered the small office hesitantly, as if not quite sure of his welcome.

'Sorry I'm late,' he apologized. 'It seems something always comes up at the last moment. I hope I haven't kept you waiting.'

'No. Not at all. I was just catching up on some paperwork. Please sit down.'

He sat down. 'It never ends, does it?' he said, indicating the files on her desk. 'The paperwork.'

'Endless,' she agreed and tried to remember all the things she'd planned to say. But all she could think of was that he looked exhausted. Probably working much too hard; not eating properly, and not getting enough sleep. She knew the symptoms all too well, having been guilty of the very same faults herself.

'I suppose it's much the same in your job?' That was *not* what she'd intended to say. Andrea busied herself gathering up papers and putting them in a folder.

'Yes.'

The silence between them lengthened.

Now that he was here, Paget wished he'd found an excuse not to come. He should have sent Tregalles in his place. And yet, perversely, he had *wanted* to come. Seeing Andrea again had made him realize just how much he'd missed the company of this woman these past few months.

Andrea had demanded nothing from him. She had just been there; a friend at a time when he needed a friend; someone to talk to; someone who had eased the pain of loneliness. Until suddenly one evening he'd realized that she had become more than just a friend, and he'd felt ashamed. Ashamed that he could so easily allow himself to be unfaithful to the memory of Jill.

There could never be another Jill. He could never love anyone the way he had loved Jill. It was just... What? Loneliness? Desire? The need to take a woman in his arms again? The whole idea was ludicrous, he told himself angrily.

But ludicrous or not, it refused to go away.

Not that Andrea had encouraged him. In fact, if anything, she'd become withdrawn. It was as if she'd sensed the change and was making it clear that she did not share his feelings.

He sighed inwardly. It had been a mistake to come here, today. On this day of all days he should be thinking of Jill, not another woman.

'I must get on,' he said briskly. 'Can we see Lenny Smallwood now?'

Andrea caught her breath. His tone was sharp and brittle, almost demanding, and the words she had rehearsed so carefully vanished from her mind. She'd thought about Neil a lot while she was away, and she had hoped today that they might talk. Hoped, too, that he might feel the same.

Obviously she'd been mistaken. Andrea closed the folder on her desk and rose swiftly to her feet. 'Of course,' she said stiffly. 'I know you must be busy.'

'How is Lenny coming along?' Paget asked as they left the office.

This was safer ground. Professional. 'He's had a very rough time of it,' Andrea told him, 'and he still has a long way to go. Did you know he's addicted to cocaine?'

'No, but I can't say I'm surprised. How is he coping?'

'About as well as can be expected, under the circumstances. Between his addiction and his injuries, he's been in a lot of pain. We're keeping him partly sedated, which means that he may find it difficult to concentrate, so you might bear that in mind.'

They walked in silence down the corridor.

Lenny's eyes were closed and he appeared to be asleep when they entered the room. His face was bruised and swollen, and dark stubble made it look even worse. Despite what he knew about the boy, Paget couldn't help but feel some pity for him. One wrist was taped; his jaw was wired, and there was a bandage on his head. A pouch dripped clear liquid into his arm through a tube, while a second tube snaked out from beneath the covers to a heavy plastic bag.

The WPC, who had been reading a magazine, jumped to her feet.

'Has he said anything about how this happened?' Paget asked quietly. 'Or about his mother?'

'No, sir. Nothing.'

'Right. Perhaps you'd like to go and have a cup of tea while we talk to him. I don't want him to feel we're ganging up on him.'

Liscombe didn't need to be told twice to take a break from what was surely one of the most boring jobs she'd ever had.

'He still insists he had an accident,' said Andrea. 'But it's quite obvious he's been beaten.'

'Right. Then let's have him awake.'

Andrea spoke softly to Lenny and shook his arm, gently coaxing him awake. Drowsily, Lenny opened his eyes and looked around. His eyes focused on Andrea and then on Paget. He blinked rapidly and became more alert. Andrea looked at Paget and nodded for him to go ahead.

'Leonard Smallwood,' he said, 'my name is Paget, Detective Chief Inspector Paget, and I'd like to ask you a few questions. Do you understand?'

Lenny was suddenly alert. He nodded cautiously.

'First, can you tell me how you came by these injuries?'

Lenny blinked rapidly and cleared his throat. 'I came off the bike,' he said. His lips moved, but his teeth remained closed due to his wired jaw.

'Where was that, exactly?'

Lenny raised a hand to touch the bandage on his head. 'Don't remember,' he said.

'I see. We didn't find your bike at the scene,' said Paget. 'Do you know what might have happened to it?'

Lenny stared at him blankly. 'Some thieving bugger must have pinched it,' he said flatly.

'According to the doctors who examined you when you were brought in, your injuries were caused by a savage beating,' Paget said. 'In fact, I'm told there is no way these injuries could have been caused by a fall from a motorbike. What do you say to that, Mr Smallwood?'

Lenny tried to shrug and winced. 'They got it wrong,' he said. His nose began to run. 'Like I said, I skidded and came off the bike.'

Paget tried another tack. 'What are you going to do when you leave here?' he asked. 'Whoever beat you up will still be out there unless you give me a name.'

Lenny rolled his eyes. 'I *told* you, nobody beat me up. I came off the bike!'

'Tell me where you went after you left your mother in the house on Monday evening.'

'Monday?' Lenny frowned in concentration and looked at Andrea. 'What day did I come in here?' he asked.

'Wednesday,' she said, 'and today is Friday.'

'I went to Tan's place. She's the girlfriend. Why?'

'How long were you there?'

'All night. You can ask her.'

'We have. She says you left earlier.'

'She made a mistake, then, didn't she?'

'I saw you myself just after midnight,' Paget said quietly. 'Outside your house. You took off when I called out to you.'

So *that's* where he'd seen this bloke before. Lenny thought he looked familiar. He'd only caught a glimpse of him in the headlight of the bike, but it was the same bloke all right.

'Yeah. Well, I thought you were someone else, didn't I? Someone I didn't want to meet just then.'

'The same person who beat you up?'

Lenny rolled his head to one side. 'I told you...' he began, but Paget brushed his words aside.

'Never mind,' he said. 'Just tell me this: when was the last time you saw your mother?'

Lenny turned back to look at him. Beads of sweat stood out upon his brow, and his nose was running freely. Andrea handed him a paper tissue.

'That night when she came home from work,' he said. 'Monday. Why? What's this all about? Fat lot she cares anyway. She hasn't even been in to see me. Neither has Tan. You keeping them away?'

Paget ignored the question. 'You had an argument with your mother that night,' he said.

Lenny sniffed and wiped his nose. He could feel the shakes coming on again, and he had cramps in his stomach. 'So?' he said belligerently.

'You had a shouting match and you hit her,' said Paget. 'Then you left the house. When did you see your mother again, Mr Small-wood?'

'I haven't. And who says I hit her? I never touched her.'

'We have a witness who says you did.'

Lenny's face gave him away. Bloody Tania! She was the only one there; it must have been her. 'So I got a bit carried away,' he mumbled. 'I didn't mean it. Mam knows I didn't mean it.'

'Did she say that when you met again in the church?'

Lenny looked puzzled. 'Church? I don't know what you mean. I told you, I haven't seen her since that night.'

'Why did you hit her? What was the argument about?'

'That's none of your business. It's private.'

'Was it money? Did it have something to do with the money your mother embezzled from the bank where she worked?'

Oh, Christ! They knew about that. Lenny closed his eyes tightly. The cramps were getting worse and he was sweating hard.

'I don't know what you're talking about,' he ground out.

'I'm afraid your mother is dead, Lenny,' said Paget softly. 'Killed by someone who attacked her in the church. Did you kill your mother, Lenny?'

The words were spoken quietly, but there couldn't have been a greater reaction if Paget had shouted them. The boy sucked in his breath; his eyes flew open to stare at Paget. He began to shake and tears ran down his face. 'Dead?' he gasped. 'She's not dead. Ask Tan. She was with me at the house. Ask Ta ... ' He choked on the word. His body arched, and Andrea grabbed him by the shoulders, straining to hold him as he tried to throw himself from side to side.

'That's enough!' she told Paget sharply. 'Ring the bell for the nurse. Four short.'

'Can I help?' Paget asked as he pressed the bell.

'Just – just leave!' she told him sharply. 'A nurse will be along in a minute. Now go! There will be no more questions today.'

Paget hesitated, but a nurse arrived on the dead run, and he was forced to move aside. Andrea began issuing instructions, and it was obvious that he would only be in the way if he remained. He thought of waiting in the corridor, but what would be the point?

What was there left to say?

CHAPTER 19

Dorothy McLeish was a small, sharp-featured woman of forty – three years older than Beth Smallwood. Her face was impassive as she looked down on the pale features of her sister. 'Yes, that's Beth,' she said quietly, and turned away. 'Is there anything else?' she asked Tregalles.

'A few formalities,' the sergeant told her, 'but they can wait if you'd rather.'

'No.' The woman's voice was firm. 'I'd like to get it all done now,' she said. 'Donald and I – he's my husband – talked it over last night, and we'll take care of the funeral arrangements. We don't have much but we can see her buried properly. I doubt that son of hers will be much help.'

'He's here in hospital at the moment,' Tregalles told her, and explained briefly what had happened. 'Perhaps you'd like to visit him?' he suggested.

'You say he's on the mend?' Mrs McLeish was English born, but she'd spent so long in Scotland that there was a discernible Scottish lilt to her words.

'That's right,' Tregalles told her. 'It may take a while, but the doctors say he'll be all right.'

'Then I'll not be bothering him,' she said flatly. 'I disliked him as a child, and he was no better for his growing up.'

'You've seen him recently, then?' Tregalles guided Mrs McLeish to the car and held the door for her, then went round and got in himself.

'He came last year. Just turned up one day with a bit of a girl in tow, and said he'd come to stay for a while. Borrowed Beth's car, he had. Said he'd come for a holiday, bold as you please. I gave him dinner, then sent him packing. I wasn't having any of *that* under my roof.'

'When was the last time you saw your sister, Mrs McLeish?'

The woman remained silent for some time. 'The last time I spoke to her was just after Lenny was born,' she said softly. 'She was seventeen, then, and I went to see her. We had a fight, and we've never spoken since.'

Tregalles frowned. 'Never?' he said. 'Yet she had your telephone number. That's how we found you.'

'She may have had it but she never used it.'

'And you never got in touch with her?'

'No. It would have done no good.'

'Are either of your parents alive?'

Dorothy McLeish stared straight ahead, but her eyes saw nothing of the road. 'I was fifteen when our mother died,' she said tonelessly. 'She'd been ill for a long time. Cancer, I think it was, although the doctor put it down as heart failure when she died. Dad wouldn't have it that she was ill. Said she was just lazy. He was a seaman, away from home half the time, thank God. We managed as best we could, but after Mum died he talked of leaving the sea. Said he'd been offered a job on the docks. We were living in Liverpool at the time.

'That's when I left home. I couldn't stand it any more. Not alone there with him. I was only sixteen, but anything was better than . . .' The words caught in her throat, and she fell silent.

They arrived at Charter Lane, and Tregalles escorted Mrs McLeish to Paget's office, which he knew would be empty. Better, he thought, than the stark surroundings of one of the interview rooms.

'Coffee?' he offered, but Dorothy McLeish shook her head.

'Is your father still alive?' he asked. 'He should be notified if he is.'

'I've no idea,' Mrs McLeish said, 'and to be quite honest, Sergeant, I hope he's not. I certainly don't want to see him again, ever.' She lifted her chin and her dark eyes met Tregalles's quizzical gaze defiantly.

'You said you haven't spoken to your sister since Lenny was a baby,' he prompted. 'Why was that?'

Mrs McLeish looked away. 'I should never have left her,' she said so softly that he could barely hear her. 'I knew what would happen.'

Tregalles waited. Dorothy McLeish turned a troubled face toward him. 'I was barely sixteen myself.' Her eyes pleaded with him to understand. 'My father had –' she swallowed hard – 'used me as a substitute for my mother since I was ten. I knew that if I stayed . . .'

She sighed regretfully as tears slowly trickled down her face. 'But I shouldn't have left Beth on her own like that.'

Tregalles left the room and returned with a cup of coffee. He set it in front of her, and she flashed him a grateful glance. He took his

131

seat again and waited as she grasped the cup with both hands and sipped the steaming liquid.

'I should have done something – anything to get Beth out of that situation,' she said wistfully, 'but I didn't, and I can't change that. She was sixteen when she met Harold Smallwood. He was eighteen; a local boy. Not much of a catch; a bit simple, but not a bad lad. Somehow or other they managed to get married. Beth lied about her age, I suppose, but she had wedding lines to prove she had really married Harold. But when it became apparent that she was pregnant, Harold couldn't handle it and he left. As far as I know, he never came back.'

'You said you fought with your sister just after Lenny was born. What was that about?'

Dorothy McLeish looked down at her hands. 'It was my fault, really,' she said quietly. 'I should have kept my mouth shut, but I was so angry!' She broke off and shook her head. 'I suppose it can't hurt her now. It was over Lenny. You see, Beth happened to mention the first time she met Harold, and I realized that Lenny couldn't be Harold's son, and I said so.'

Mrs McLeish made a helpless gesture. 'As I said, I should have kept my mouth shut, but once it was out, the damage was done. Beth flew into a rage and called me everything under the sun, and it was then I realized that she had known it all the time. Lenny wasn't Harold's son. That's why she'd rushed him into marriage.

'Lenny may carry Harold Smallwood's name, but Lenny is my father's son,' she ended. 'I know it and Beth knew it, but she refused to acknowledge it. And she never has as far as I know.'

Paget turned left into Bridge Street after leaving the hospital, but instead of returning to Charter Lane, he continued on until he came to what was still called the bypass despite the fact that the town had closed around it in recent years. There, he turned right and followed it for about half a mile before turning off on Lansdowne Drive.

The houses were set well back from the road. There was money here, attested to by paddocks bounded by white fences, and driveways lined with trees. Paget drove slowly, looking for numbers on gateposts.

He saw the sign before he saw the number; the silhouette of a Shetland Sheepdog against a white background, and the name of the kennels underneath. The house was not large compared with those around it, but it was almost twice as big as his own in Ashton Prior. Solid, two-storeyed brick, with six leaded windows across the top and four across the bottom, and the three broad steps leading up to the front door were bordered by two columns.

He rang the bell and waited. Faintly, from somewhere at the back of the house, he thought he heard the sound of a horn. He rang the bell again and heard the same sound.

'Can I help you?'

A woman had come round the side of the house and was standing with one hand on her hip. She was small and slender, and she looked as if she'd spent a lifetime out of doors. She was dressed in baggy trousers, a broadcloth shirt, and a pair of boots that had seen much better days.

'I'm looking for Mrs Gresham,' Paget said, coming down the steps. 'My name is Paget. Chief Inspector Paget of the Westvale Police.'

The woman came forward and thrust out her hand. 'I'm Lilian Gresham,' she said. 'I take it you're not looking for a dog?' The hawkish features crinkled into a smile.

'No, I'm afraid not,' he said. 'I'm looking for some information. Could you spare me a few minutes?'

'If you don't mind us talking while I get on with my work,' she said briskly. 'I'm in the middle of grooming a dog that hasn't been combed for God knows how long.'

Lilian Gresham led the way to the back of the house and down a path to a large enclosure containing covered kennels and open runs in which there must have been at least a dozen dogs. As soon as they saw her, they began running back and forth and barking excitedly.

'Quiet!' she roared in a voice that seemed to come from her boots, startling even Paget. But the dogs fell silent, except for the odd furtive 'woof!' as they settled down.

They continued on past the runs to a small building where yet another Sheltie greeted them as they entered. 'Meet Sir Gwayne of Evanloch,' said Lilian Gresham. 'Otherwise known as Gumby by his owner. Did you ever hear such a ridiculous name for a dog?' She picked up the dog and set him on a table, then went to work on him with a brush and comb.

'I presume this has something to do with that unfortunate woman's death,' she said over her shoulder. 'But I don't see how I can help. I don't think I ever met her. I haven't been in the bank in years.'

'Still, there may be a way in which you can help,' Paget told her. 'Were you here last Monday evening?'

Lilian Gresham straightened up and stretched. She pursed her lips and thought for a moment. 'Yes, I was here. That is, either out here or in the house.'

'Do you remember receiving any telephone calls that evening?'

She lifted her head and stared off into space. 'Yes. There were several, as a matter of fact. Why do you ask?'

'Were any of them for your husband?'

'Yes. Two, I believe. One was from that frightful woman, Gretchen Middlehurst. Something to do with the cricket club. Arthur is on the committee, you see. She blethered on and on about it. I did leave a message for Arthur, so I assume he has taken care of it.'

'And the other call?'

Lilian Gresham frowned. 'That one was a bit odd,' she said slowly. 'He insisted on speaking to Arthur even after I told him Arthur wasn't here. He didn't actually call me a liar, but he certainly implied it. Said Arthur was avoiding him, and it wasn't good enough. Quite belligerent. I didn't like his tone and I told him so, then I hung up. I half expected him to ring back, but he didn't. Foreign, I think. Spoke very good English but I'm sure he was foreign. Oriental, I should think.'

'I see. Do you have any idea what time that was?'

Lilian Gresham thought about that. 'I was still out here when he rang.' She indicated the telephone on the wall. 'Both lines on it are extensions from the house,' she explained. 'One is for everyday use, and the other is for the kennels. Whenever I'm out here and Arthur's out, I switch them through. I suppose it would be easier if we had an answering machine, but I hate those damned mechanical voices.' She picked up the brush and comb and began working on the dog once more.

'I think it must have been about nine o'clock,' she said, referring to his question. 'Yes, it was, because I was tidying up and getting ready to go back into the house. Sorry, but that's the best I can do. Is it important?'

'Probably not,' said Paget, 'but we do have to check everything out. There were no other calls for Mr Gresham?'

'No, I'm sure there weren't.'

'I take it your husband was out most of the evening, then?'

'That's right. He went to visit his father in Golden Meadows. He often goes up there in the evening.'

'Do you recall what time it was when he left the house, Mrs Gresham?'

'Some time around seven, I should think. I can't say I was paying that much attention to the time.' The woman paused, then turned to face him, frowning. 'Why are you asking all these questions, Chief Inspector?' she asked. 'Surely you can't think that Arthur...' She made a dismissive gesture.

'We believe that Elizabeth Smallwood was killed by someone she knew,' he said. 'As a matter of routine, we must check out where everyone was when she died. Once we can confirm their stories, we can eliminate them from our enquiries and concentrate our efforts elsewhere.'

'I see.' Lilian Gresham looked thoughtful as she returned to her task. 'Is there anything else you wish to know?'

'Do you recall what time it was when Mr Gresham returned that night?'

The woman didn't reply immediately, seeming to concentrate on stripping handfuls of hair from the heavy coat. 'I can't be sure,' she said at last. 'After I finished here, I went in, had a bath, and went straight to bed. That would be about ten or a little after. I vaguely remember hearing Arthur come in, but I don't know what time it was. And he was gone before eight the next morning, which was quite unusual for him. Had some sort of meeting to attend, I believe he said.'

Lilian Gresham turned her full attention back to the dog. 'I don't think there is anything else I can tell you,' she said. 'Sorry if I haven't been much help. Would you mind seeing yourself out?'

Traffic was heavy along Tavistock Road at this time of day, and Peggy Mycroft kept well over to the side as she cycled home from school. She didn't like this stretch of road at all. Cars travelled far too fast, and they came too close.

This part was particularly bad because of the narrow verge and the steep slope that dropped away to the railway sheds below. One slip and she'd be over, and there would be no stopping until she hit the bottom. She kept her eyes fixed firmly on the strip of road in front of her, concentrating on keeping her balance as another string of cars whizzed past. Only another fifty yards or so to go before she could turn off the busy road, she thought thankfully.

A movement caught her eye, and suddenly a bedraggled figure rose up beside her and staggered into the road. Peggy screamed and fell off her bike. The driver of a car about to pass blanched and cursed her roundly as he swung out to avoid the girl, then slammed on his brakes as he realized what he'd seen.

CHAPTER 20

Amy Thomson lay with her eyes closed, listening to the activity around her. They had kept her awake when all she wanted to do was sleep; probing, shining lights into her eyes, holding up different numbers of fingers in front of her face and asking repeatedly how many she saw. What was her name? Where did she live? Could she count backward from ten to one?

They had done something to her shoulder. It felt dead, even when she tried to move it. She thought it might be bandaged, but she hadn't the energy to find out.

Now, finally, they had given her something for the pain in her head, and it was beginning to work. But she still felt cold despite the blankets tucked in around her. She didn't think that she would ever be warm again.

The policeman, who had stayed with her until the ambulance came, was still there. She could hear him talking to someone in a low voice. He was waiting to talk to her again, but she wanted to think before she told him anything. He was saying something about another girl; the girl on the bike. Just a grazed knee and elbow and shaken up a bit.

She'd pretended not to hear when he'd asked her what she'd been doing down there in the sheds; she had to get it sorted in her mind before she told him anything.

136

Why would *anyone* want to kill her? She'd done nothing except pick up the money as Tony had asked her to. Oh, God! The money! What had happened to the money? She didn't even know how much it was, but Tony had offered her twenty quid just for picking it up, so there must have been quite a bit.

Amy groaned. Tony would be furious!

So what? she thought rebelliously. He should be happy she wasn't killed. After all, she'd been doing him a favour, and he could have gone there himself. No one would have seen him.

Amy hadn't given that much thought until now because she'd been so anxious to please Tony – that's what people did for one another when they were in love. But now, in the light of what had happened, doubt crept into her mind, and the story he had told her didn't sound as plausible as it had when they lay together on the bed.

Had he known that someone might be there?

Even as the thought formed in her mind, Amy knew instinctively that Tony *had* known there might be someone waiting in the darkness. And still he'd sent her there.

To be killed? The thought chilled her to the bone.

No! Tony wouldn't do that, she told herself fiercely. Not Tony. He loved her.

Then, why didn't he come to look for you when you didn't turn up for work? He knew where you'd gone. If he really loved you, wouldn't he have been concerned? Wouldn't he have come looking for you?

But he hadn't come, had he? *Because he thought that you were dead!*

Amy trembled beneath the covers as suspicion grew. Could it have been Tony behind the light inside the shed? The more she thought about it, the more it seemed possible.

But why would Tony want her dead? What had she done? Why...?

'Oohh, Jesus!' she said aloud, and began to shake. Someone put a cool hand on her forehead and murmured something soothing, but Amy wasn't listening to the words. She was remembering Tony's behaviour that night in the belfry. She had only his word for it that he had found that woman dead. How did she know that he hadn't killed her? Amy remembered how he'd acted in the car as they drove away. How he'd made her promise to forget she'd ever seen a body in the church. She remembered how his fingers had dug into her flesh; how he'd looked at her.

137

There was a dark side to Tony; a side of which she'd been secretly afraid. Deliciously afraid until now; sensing it as one might sense a dangerous undertow beneath the surface of a placid pool.

The throbbing in her head was gone. She tried to think, but everything seemed fuzzy. The sound of voices faded. She was getting warm. Disjointed thoughts drifted through her mind: crouching in her shallow hiding place and trembling with fear as the beam of the torch swept past; listening to her attacker stumbling across uneven ground as he searched for her; the sporadic hum of traffic on the road above; shivering long after the sounds were gone, too scared to move in case the killer was still out there waiting for her.

Then nothing. She must have passed out. For how long, she had no idea, but it was daylight when she opened her eyes. She remembered trying to move; remembered the searing pain before everything went black once more.

But she must have moved because the next thing she remembered was crawling through mud and wondering what her mother was going to say when she saw the state of her clothes; clawing her way up the embankment inch by hard-won inch.

The memories became jumbled. Her mother was calling to her, stroking her hair, but she couldn't answer.

'Good. She's asleep,' the nurse said quietly to the constable. 'You might as well go and have something to eat while you can. She'll be out for hours.'

Although Amy Thomson didn't remember it, she had wakened in the ambulance, and when the attendant asked her if she could tell him what had happened, she'd said somebody had tried to kill her in the sheds. Then she passed out again.

The ambulance attendant gave the information to the constable who had followed them in, and the constable had in turn radioed the information into Charter Lane.

Which was why the railway sheds were now cordoned off, and men were slowly searching the area. It was a thankless task. The area was littered with rusting pieces of machinery and broken cable reels, an accumulation of discarded take-away cartons, bottles and rusty tins; a shoe; cardboard boxes; several tyres; and burnt patches in the grass where children had built fires.

They found bloodstains on a tuft of grass in a small depression in the ground some distance from the sheds. The grass around it was pressed flat. Other bloodstains were found outside the nearest shed, and on the concrete floor of the shed itself, but there was little else to show there'd been a struggle there.

Paget glanced at the time. Still time for one more call, he decided. He should be calling it a day, but he didn't want to go home. Didn't want to be alone with his thoughts. Not tonight.

Terry Ling lived in Tyler Road on the edge of what was known as the 'Old Town'. A row of Georgian houses had been converted into flats in the 1970s, and Ling lived on the first floor of number 33.

A removal van stood outside. The front door was propped open and furniture was being moved into a ground-floor flat. Paget entered the building and climbed the stairs to the first floor. The hallway was dark, and the carpet on the floor was wearing thin, but apart from that the place seemed to be well maintained. Ling's flat was at the very end of the hall, overlooking the street. Paget knocked.

Terry Ling opened the door. He started at Paget blankly for a second, then his brows drew together in a puzzled frown. 'Chief Inspector?' he said questioningly.

'Sorry to trouble you at home, Mr Ling,' said Paget perfunctorily, 'but I wonder if I might have a word? May I come in?'

Still looking puzzled, Terry Ling stood aside for Paget to enter. The flat was small and sparsely furnished, but everything was spotless. Small carpets of oriental design dotted the polished floor, while framed photographs of what Paget took to be scenes of Hong Kong by day and night took up much of one wall.

'Your work, Mr Ling?' Paget indicated the photographs as they both sat down.

Ling made a deprecating gesture. 'I used to dabble,' he said, 'but I haven't done any since coming to this country.'

'You have an eye for composition,' Paget said. He, too, had 'dabbled' in photography in his younger days, but came to realize that he lacked that crucial 'something' that changed a picture into a work of art.

Ling shrugged modestly.

'Your wife ... ?' Paget glanced around. 'Is she at home?'

Ling shook his head. 'As I told you the other day, my wife works.' His chin came up and his eyes seemed to challenge Paget. 'She cleans offices. She is a doctor of philosophy, and she cleans offices so that we can enjoy the luxury of this.' His tone was bitter as he flicked a hand to indicate the flat.

'So you spend most of your evenings alone here in the flat, as I believe you said was the case last Monday?'

Ling nodded but remained silent.

'One of your neighbours claims he saw you leave here that evening, and he says you were gone for some time.'

Ling's gaze never wavered. 'He was mistaken,' he said tonelessly.

'He has made a sworn statement, Mr Ling.' Ling looked away. Paget waited. 'Where did you go?' he prompted.

'I told you, I...'

'It won't wash, you know,' Paget broke in softly. 'I should tell you that the man also saw you return, and I don't know why he would want to lie about a thing like that.'

Terry Ling looked down at the floor. He shrugged. 'I went for a drive,' he said. 'There was no one here; I was restless. I had a lot to think about.'

'Such as Beth Smallwood's promotion?'

Ling's head came up sharply and his eyes flashed. 'Among other things, yes.'

'Such as?'

Ling regarded Paget stonily, then sighed resignedly. 'If you must know, I wanted to think about my position. It became very clear last Monday that I have no future with this bank – at least while Gresham is in charge.' Ling got up and walked to the window and stood looking out. 'I am supposed to be in training for a management position,' he said dully, 'but they will use almost any excuse to keep me out of their exclusive club. I thought Birmingham was bad, but these small country towns are ten times worse.'

He turned to face Paget. 'Just give it time, old chap,' he mimicked. 'Not *quite* the way we do things here, you know. I'm sure you'll learn. Just give it time.' Ling's imitation of Arthur Gresham, including the accompanying mime of pushing out his lips and polishing his glasses, was almost perfect.

'Time,' he said contemptuously. 'I know more about banking than Gresham will ever know. I could do his job tomorrow, and I could bring in more business.'

Paget doubted that. Not in Broadminster. Whether Ling liked it or not, the people here accepted change very slowly. It wasn't just a matter of his being Chinese – at least, not entirely – it was a matter of trust and acceptance, and Terry Ling simply did not fit the mould. Apart from anything else, he was too aggressive. Paget didn't doubt that Ling was clever, but that was part of his problem. He wanted everyone to know it, and that wouldn't sit well at all.

The question was: did Ling see Beth Smallwood's promotion as the final indignity? There could be little doubt that it was a slap in the face, and Ling would not take kindly to that.

Ling sat down again and faced Paget. 'You must understand, I had a great deal to think about, Chief Inspector,' he said earnestly. 'We are expecting our first child in October. I have to do *something*. That's why I went out. I needed to think things through.'

'Where did you go?'

'Nowhere in particular. I just drove around. I like to drive; I think better when I'm driving. Sorry, but quite honestly I can't tell you where I went.'

'Were you anywhere near Farrow Lane?'

'I don't know where Farrow Lane is.'

Paget let it go. 'Why didn't you tell me this when we spoke the other day?'

Ling grimaced. 'Isn't it obvious? I hadn't done anything wrong, but I knew that if I told you that I had been out just driving around, you would have jumped to the wrong conclusion as you have now. Yes, I'm unhappy about the way I have been treated by the bank; yes, I believe I can do a far better job than Beth Smallwood would have done, but I certainly wouldn't regard killing her as a solution to my problems. Give me a little credit, Chief Inspector.'

'What about the telephone call?'

Ling's eyes narrowed. 'What telephone call?'

Paget sighed heavily. 'Let's not play games, Mr Ling,' he said. 'The call you made to Gresham's house. You spoke to Mrs Gresham. She recognized your voice.'

'How could she? We've never...?' Ling stopped and his mouth twisted into a wry smile. 'She didn't, did she?' he said softly. 'She's never heard my voice as far as I know.'

'Her description was accurate enough for me to guess it was you,' said Paget. 'Especially when she said you sounded hostile. What did you intend to say to Mr Gresham, had he been there?'

Terry Ling stared at the floor and shook his head. 'I really don't know,' he said wearily. 'I was so upset by then that I might have said anything.' He lifted his head. 'Perhaps it is just as well that he was out.'

Rita Thomson stared out of the window of the police car. The doctor had said there wasn't any point in staying. Amy would sleep until morning, and she would probably feel more like talking then. Go home and get some rest, he'd advised.

Rest. That was a good one. How were you supposed to rest with your daughter in hospital after she'd been out all night, and some-one had tried to kill her?

It had been a close thing, the doctor said. The blow had been a glancing one, but it was hard enough to crack her skull and break Amy's collar-bone. Even half an inch to the left and ... Rita pressed her lips together. She was close to tears. What was Amy thinking of, going down there in the middle of the night? She must have gone to meet some boy. Stupid, stupid girl! Hadn't she been warned often enough?

The car pulled up beside the house, and people in the street stopped to stare. The driver, a uniformed WPC, helped Rita out, and she hurried to the door without looking to right or left. Let them stare. There would be all sorts of rumours flying round within the hour. She found her key and opened the door.

'We'll see you inside, Mrs Thomson,' said the man in plain clothes. Vickers, he'd said his name was. Detective Sergeant.

Rita walked unsteadily down the narrow passage and made straight for the kitchen. She paused. 'Her bike,' she said, surveying the space it normally occupied. She turned to Vickers. 'What hap-pened to Amy's bike?'

'Are you sure she used it last night, Mrs Thomson? There was no bike found at the scene. Could it be outside?'

Rita tried to think. 'It was gone this morning,' she said. 'I just assumed ...'

'Have a quick look round outside,' Vickers said to the constable. 'What is it we're looking for, Mrs Thomson? Colour? Make?'

Rita described the bike. 'It cost a lot of money,' she ended. 'We can't afford to lose it. Apart from anything else, Amy needs it for work.' It suddenly hit her that Amy wouldn't be going to work for a while, and tears spilled down her face.

Vickers guided her to a chair and sat her down. 'You'll feel better for a cup of tea,' he said. 'Just tell me where it is and I'll put the kettle on.'

Tom Vickers ambled around the kitchen as if he'd lived there all his life. He seemed to know instinctively where everything would be even before she told him. And she didn't mind. Normally, she wouldn't have anyone, other than Amy, of course, messing about in her kitchen, but there was something comfortable about Vickers.

He wasn't a young man. Fiftyish, she guessed. Grey hair, ruddy face, kindly eyes, and an easy manner. He looked like somebody's uncle, and while he busied himself making the tea, he talked.

Rita found herself responding. She told him everything: how she had discovered that Amy was not in the house; how she'd felt; why she hadn't reported Amy missing. She even told him about Amy's father; the divorce; things she'd never spoken of to anyone before, not even Amy.

The WPC had returned to say there was no sign of Amy's bike, and she had radioed a description into Charter Lane. Some kid might have picked it up and taken it home, but whether anyone would report it was very much open to question.

Vickers filled Rita's cup again. 'Do you mind if I have a look round Amy's room?' he asked casually. 'It seems she won't be able to talk to us until tomorrow, and there might be something that will give us a clue as to why she was down at the sheds at that time of night. The sooner we can start looking for the person who attacked her, the better for everyone.'

Rita half rose from her chair. 'I haven't had a chance to tidy her room,' she began, but Vickers put his hands on her shoulders and pushed her gently down again.

'Not to worry, Mrs Thomson,' he told her. 'I've seen untidy rooms before. You just sit still and finish your tea. Top of the stairs, is it?'

'Back bedroom,' said Rita automatically, settling back in her seat. She felt too tired to object. Besides, it might help.

Upstairs, in Amy's room, Rita would have been surprised at how swiftly Vickers moved. The room was small, and there was hardly room to move between the wardrobe, a small chest of drawers, and a narrow single bed. There were film magazines and romance novels everywhere; in the drawers; in the bottom of the wardrobe; on top of the wardrobe; under the bed.

And it was on top of the wardrobe, well hidden behind a stack of books, that Vickers found the diary. He sat down on the bed and opened it and flipped through the pages, then turned to the most recent entry and began working his way back.

Fifteen years old! Vickers shook his head. Either Amy had a very active imagination or she led an extremely interesting life. Especially with someone called Tony. He came to the previous Monday, read the entry, then whistled softly.

Vickers made his way downstairs and showed the diary to Rita Thomson. 'Have you ever seen this before?' he asked. She looked blankly at the book and shook her head. 'I'm sure that's not our Amy's,' she said. 'Can I see?'

Vickers hesitated, then handed her the diary. 'I shall have to take it with me,' he told her. 'I'll give you a receipt for it, of course.'

Rita slowly turned the pages. What little colour there had been in her face drained away. Tears trickled down her face as she shoved the book back into Vickers' hands. 'Take it,' she whispered hoarsely. 'Take it away. I don't want to see it. I didn't know. Honestly, I didn't know.'

'Is there anyone who could come and stay with you tonight?' Vickers asked.

Rita shook her head. 'I don't want *anyone* here,' she said fiercely. 'Please go, now. I'll be all right.' She saw the doubt in Vickers' eyes. 'I will,' she insisted. 'Now, please go. You've been very kind, but please, just leave me alone.'

Paget was hungry, but the thought of having to prepare a meal when he got home didn't appeal to him at all. Neither did he feel much like going to a restaurant; not on his own.

He compromised by stopping at the fish and chip shop at the bottom end of Church Street, and had to stand in line for more than twenty minutes before being served. The shop was warm, and he almost fell asleep standing there, but by the time his order had been filled, the hot smell of fat had put him off the food.

He sat in the car and picked at the meal. The chips weren't bad but the batter on the fish was soggy and his appetite had gone. He got out of the car and dumped the remains of the meal into the bin.

He was tired. He'd have to be careful driving home. It would be so easy to fall asleep. A sudden gust of wind splattered rain against the windscreen. Another cold and wet weekend?

The day was almost over. Jill's day, and all he wanted to do was sleep. He should be feeling something, he told himself, but there was nothing. Nothing but an emptiness that refused to go away.

CHAPTER 21

Saturday – 18 May

Paget arrived at the hospital shortly after seven, happy to have something positive to do on this rainy Saturday. Tom Vickers had telephoned him at home the night before to tell him of the diary he'd found in Amy Thomson's room, and now he found the girl awake and more than willing to talk.

Amy's night had been filled with dreams, and she woke up bathed in sweat. Memories flooded in, and the more that she remembered, the more certain she became that it was Tony who had tried to kill her. He was the one who had killed the woman in the church. He'd just made up that story about there being money in the shed. He'd even gone to the trouble of putting an envelope there so she would see it and go right in, but she wouldn't mind betting there wasn't any money in it.

When Paget arrived, Amy couldn't talk fast enough. She told him everything: about Tony Rudge taking her to the church on Monday evening; his having a key to the church and the belfry; even having sex with him. She held back nothing, describing the panic Tony had been in when he'd shaken her awake in the belfry.

'You were asleep when he left the room?' Paget asked. 'You don't know what made him go down in the first place?'

Amy shook her head. 'All I know is what he told me when he woke me up and started throwing everything into the sleeping bag.' She went on to describe how she had gone down into the church to see the body for herself because she hadn't believed Tony, then told Paget what had happened in the car.

'He had me so scared. I couldn't think straight,' she went on. 'And he warned me not to say anything to anybody when he dropped me off at the end of our street. But I couldn't just let her lie there with nobody knowing what had happened to her, could I? I kept thinking, What if she's still alive? I couldn't see how she could be, but what if she was? That's why I rang the police.'

Both Ormside and Tregalles were in the incident room when Paget arrived. Len Ormside had planned on coming in to do some work as it was, but Tregalles had promised Audrey that he would take the children to their swimming lessons this Saturday morning, and she had objected strenuously when he'd told her he had to work.

'You haven't had a Saturday off in weeks,' she flared, 'and the kids were so looking forward to you going with them to the baths. Can't Mr Paget get someone else for a change?'

'It's not his fault, luv,' Tregalles had told her soothingly. 'It *is* a murder investigation, and we have to follow up these things straightaway.'

'Hmph! I might have known you'd take his side, but what am I going to tell the kids?'

Tregalles sighed. 'Sorry, luv, but I don't have much choice, do I?' he said. 'And they're old enough to understand.'

But would they understand? he wondered now.

'Are you with us, Tregalles?' Paget's left eyebrow was raised to its fullest as he fixed the sergeant with a penetrating stare.

'Sorry, sir. Thinking of something,' Tregalles said as he searched his memory for what had just been said. Ah, yes. Rudge. 'So Tony Rudge *was* there when the murder was committed,' he said. 'And he had a motive.'

'But if Rudge just wanted to kill Amy Thomson,' Ormside put in, 'why bother putting the envelope there at all?'

'Amy seems to think it was to make sure she went all the way into the back of the shed,' Paget told him. 'But there's something odd about that whole business, so let's have him in and he can tell us for himself.'

Tony Rudge shook his head sadly and spread his hands. 'She's a nice kid, but she's lying, Mr Paget. Like I said, she's got this sort of crush on me. Follows me about. Wants me to take her out. It's a bit embarrassing, really. I've tried to be nice to her; tried to tell her to find a boyfriend more her own age, but it's no use. It's spite, that's what it is. She's doing this to get back at me, that's all. She made it all up.'

Tony tilted the wooden chair back, trying to appear at ease, but inside his head thoughts were whirling madly. How much did they *really* know? he wondered. More to the point: how much could they prove?

The interview room was warm, and the only sound was the quiet hum of the tape recorder. He was dying for a cigarette, but when he'd reached for one, the sergeant had pointed to the No Smoking sign and shaken a warning finger.

'My super doesn't think Amy's lying, and neither do I,' said Paget. 'He wants you charged with murder in the case of Beth Smallwood, and attempted murder in the case of Amy Thomson.'

Tony laughed nervously. 'That's bullshit, and you know it,' he scoffed.

'Is it? We know that you and Amy were together in the church the night Beth Smallwood was killed.' Paget held up his hand as Tony opened his mouth to protest. 'And it's no good denying it because we have the evidence to prove it. Both of you left your prints behind in the belfry, and I'm told that not only do we have your prints on the condoms, but also two distinct samples of public hair, which I have no doubt will prove to be yours and Amy's once tests are completed. I should think that bit of information will be of great interest to a jury, especially since Amy is only fifteen.

'We also have Amy's prints on the candle she dropped close to the body, and we have a detailed account of what happened in her diary.'

'Just because it's in her diary doesn't mean it's true,' protested Rudge.

Paget ignored the comment. 'You went downstairs while Amy was still asleep, and you found Beth Smallwood there – the very woman who had testified that Lenny was at home when Walter Latham was hit on the head when he caught you in his house. You took all the blame for that crime, so you had every reason to hate Beth Smallwood.'

Paget eyed Tony Rudge stonily. 'Perhaps you didn't go down there with the *intention* of killing her,' he went on. 'It seems more likely to me that there was an argument and you grabbed a candlestick and hit her with it. Then, realizing what you'd done, you tried to make it look like a robbery gone wrong, then ran back upstairs, woke Amy and gave her some cock-and-bull story about finding a dead woman downstairs.

'You made Amy promise not to say anything to anyone, and you thought you'd succeeded. You didn't think anyone would discover the body for some time, did you? But suddenly the police were there, and it didn't take you long to figure out who had told them, did it? Only one person could have told them, and that was Amy. Which meant that she'd become a liability. You couldn't trust her, could you, Tony? She had to be silenced, which was why you persuaded her to go out there to the railway sheds in the middle of the night. You were waiting for her, weren't you? Waiting there to kill her.'

Tony Rudge laughed nervously. 'That's bloody ridiculous,' he said, but his voice shook and he couldn't keep his hands still. 'Me? Kill someone?' His voice rose. 'You must be joking!' He made an effort to steady his voice. 'Look, Mr Paget, I admit I didn't like Lenny's mum, not after what she did to me in court, but I didn't kill her. Besides, like I said, you've got it wrong. I wasn't there with Amy. I was with this bird I met in a pub, but not last Monday. It was a couple of weeks before.'

Paget rose from his seat and stood looking down at Tony Rudge. 'On your feet, Rudge,' he said roughly. 'You are to be charged with the murder of Elizabeth Smallwood, and the attempted murder of Amy Thomson. This interview is now terminated at –' he glanced at the time – '13.21. Bring him along, Tregalles.'

Tony gaped at him. He couldn't believe what he was hearing. He shrank back in his chair as Tregalles came round the table and grasped his arm. Paget was already making for the door.

'It wasn't me! Honest to God, it wasn't me!' Tony shouted. 'Mr Paget, wait! Please. I know who killed Lenny's mum. I know . . .'

He fell back into the chair as Tregalles released his arm, his whole body shaking as if about to fall apart.

Paget had his hand on the door. 'I don't believe you, Tony,' he said over his shoulder. 'I've had enough of your lies. Get him on his feet, Tregalles.'

'I was there!' Tony shouted hoarsely. 'I know I said I wasn't, but I was. I *saw* who killed her. You have to believe me,' he pleaded.

Paget hesitated, then turned slowly as if reluctant to waste any more time on the boy. 'And Amy?' he said.

Tony groaned. 'She – she was there,' he admitted. 'She's telling the truth. We were in the church that night.'

'And the railway sheds? You sent her there?'

'I didn't think there was any danger. Honest to God, I didn't.'

Paget returned to the table and stood looking down at the young man. 'I'm waiting,' he said.

Now that he had Paget's attention, Tony suddenly became cautious, and a crafty look came into his eyes. 'If I tell you what I know, what's in it for me?' he asked.

Paget turned on his heel. 'Forget it,' he said roughly. 'Carry on, Sergeant.'

'All right. All right!' Tony scrambled to his feet and tried to push past Tregalles, so anxious was he to stop Paget from leaving. 'I'll tell you everything. Look, just put the tape back on.' He was gabbling now. 'Please, Mr Paget...?'

Paget sighed heavily and turned back once more. He nodded to Tregalles to start the tape. 'This had better be good, Tony,' he said as he sat down. 'It had better be damned good.'

For the second time in less than a week, Paget stood on the doorstep of number 83 Hawthorn Drive, waiting for someone to answer the door. But this time he was accompanied by Tregalles and WPC Jane Whitby. A white van containing three men stood at the kerb.

Once more, it was Harry Beecham who answered the door. If anything, Paget thought he looked worse than before. Beecham blinked at them owlishly, shielding his eyes as if unused to daylight.

'Oh! It's you, Chief Inspector,' he said shakily.

'May we come in, Mr Beecham?'

Beecham looked at each of them in turn. 'You mean all three of you?'

'If you don't mind, sir.'

Harry Beecham seemed to gather his wits. 'I'm not sure that I should,' he said uncertainly. 'What's this all about?'

'It would be best if we talked inside,' said Paget. 'Is your wife at home?'

'Of course she's at home,' said Beecham with some asperity. 'And I don't want her disturbed. She...'

Paget's voice hardened. 'I do have a warrant to search this house,' he said, producing it for Beecham to see. 'Now, please stand aside.'

'But why search my house? I've told you everything I know.'

'Unfortunately, sir, some of your answers are not consistent with information recently received, and the sooner we can clear the matter up, the better.'

Beecham wavered, then gave way, standing back as Paget and the others filed into the hall. 'Where is Mrs Beecham, sir?' Paget asked.

'Look, I've let you in, but I will not have you disturbing my wife,' said Beecham. 'I told you before, she's ill, and I don't want her upset.'

'Is she under the care of a doctor?'

'Yes. Well, no, not exactly; not at the moment, but...'

Paget nodded to Jane Whitby. 'Take a look,' he said tersely.

The WPC moved off down the hall. Beecham made as if to go after her, but Tregalles blocked him. 'You can't *do* this,' Beecham protested angrily. 'You have no right. My wife is not well.'

Jane Whitby pushed open the door to the kitchen. It was a long, narrow room at the back of the house, with a window overlooking the garden.

A woman standing at the sink looked up and her eyes opened wide when she saw the policewoman standing there. She was very thin and pale, and her skin looked almost translucent in the afternoon light. Her grey hair was short, uneven, cropped close to her head. It looked, Jane thought, as if it had been cut with dull scissors. She looked old, but when the policewoman drew nearer, she could see that her first impression was wrong. The woman was probably not much more than forty.

'Who are you? What do you want?' The woman began to back away and raised her arms in front of her face as if afraid of being attacked.

'Mrs Beecham? Helen Beecham? My name is Whitby. Constable Whitby of the Westvale Constabulary, and I'd like to ask you a few questions.'

'What are you doing here? Where's Harry? Where's my husband?' Helen Beecham's voice began to rise, and she looked scared to death.

'It's all right, Mrs Beecham,' Jane Whitby said soothingly. 'Mr Beecham is talking to Chief Inspector Paget in the hall. May I sit down?'

Helen Beecham's slender hands twisted the tea-towel she was holding into a tight ball. 'Harry won't like it,' she said. 'You're not supposed to be here.' Her eyes flicked to the door as if she sought escape, but Jane Whitby was directly in her path. 'I shouldn't be talking to you. Please go away.'

There was fear in the woman's eyes, and Jane Whitby hesitated. She'd been told that the woman was ill, but something was wrong here. This woman was scared out of her wits.

'It's all right, Mrs Beecham,' she said again. 'I won't sit down if you don't want me to. If you'll just...'

Behind her, Jane heard the sound of running feet, and the door was suddenly flung open. Harry Beecham burst into the room, followed closely by Paget and Tregalles. He pushed Jane Whitby aside as he went to his wife. 'It's all right, my dear,' he said softly as he pulled her to him. 'It's all right. Don't worry. I have to go out for a little while, but you'll be all right. I shall be back shortly.' He kissed his wife lightly on the forehead and turned to go, but she clung to him.

'I don't want you to go,' she whispered. 'Do you have to, Harry?'

'I'm afraid I must,' said Beecham, 'but I shan't be long. This lady will stay with you while I'm gone, so you'll be all right. You don't have to talk to her. Just remember that. You don't have to talk to her.' He turned to face Jane Whitby. 'And I don't want you badgering her,' he said sternly.

'You need have no fear of that, sir,' Paget said coldly.

'And if you run like that again,' Tregalles put in, 'you'll find yourself in a great deal of trouble, Mr Beecham. Shall we go?'

Behind him, Paget stared. He'd never met Helen Beecham in his life, but there was something terribly familiar about this woman. He knew he'd seen her before. Or a picture of her...

A picture!

He felt the chill of recognition, and yet it couldn't be. Not this frail, grey-haired old woman. Their eyes met and he knew he wasn't wrong.

Helen Beecham was the dancer in the charcoal sketch.

CHAPTER 22

'Hello, Bernie. How's business, then? Doing all right, are you?'

Bernie Striker froze. He hadn't heard the sound of the shop door opening, neither had he heard anyone approach. But he knew the voice. Must have come in through the back. That was Archie Stern's style.

Bernie fixed the closest thing he could manage in the way of a smile on his round face, and turned to face the speaker.

'Didn't hear you come in, Archie,' he said nervously. 'Sorry. Busy. You know how it is?' His hands were sweaty; he wiped them on his shirt.

'I asked you how business was, Bernie?' said Stern pleasantly.

The big man shrugged. 'Times aren't what they used to be,' he said cautiously. 'Not that much money about, but I scratch a living.'

'Really?' Stern seemed surprised. 'Funny, but I heard you were doing quite well, Bernie. The only shop in town. All those bikers coming in. They never seem to be short of money. Seems to me you've got it made.'

Bernie shrugged again. 'There's good days and bad days,' he admitted. He wiped his brow. What the hell did Archie want? He wasn't here just for chat. 'Was there something you wanted?' he ventured tentatively. 'I mean, I didn't think...'

'Best not to,' said Archie. Then, seeing Bernie's puzzled frown, he added, 'Think, that is.' He glanced around as if looking for something. 'I don't see it,' he said, frowning. 'What happened to it, Bernie?'

Bernie blinked at him. 'I – I don't know what you mean,' he said, thoroughly mystified. 'What don't you see, Archie?'

'Lenny's bike. I understand he left it here. He owes me, Bernie, and I've come for it.'

'Ah!' It wasn't warm in the shop, but Bernie could feel the sweat beading on his brow. He closed his eyes and tried to think. What the hell was he going to say? 'I didn't realize...I mean I stripped it down. See, I didn't want it here in the shop in case the police came round after Lenny – after he left, like.'

152

Archie Stern tilted his head and raised a brow in mild surprise. 'You didn't think he'd be back for the bike?'

'Well, I . . .' Bernie stopped. He didn't know what to say, and he wanted desperately to get it right. 'I *did* ring to let you know he was here,' he said.

Archie nodded. 'True,' he said, 'but that does leave us with a problem, doesn't it, Bernie. I mean, what would I do with a bunch of parts? Eh? What was the bike worth, Bernie? Eight, nine thou?'

The fat man spread his hands and shook his head. 'Probably more like four, maybe five,' he said.

Archie frowned. 'I heard that Lenny put five thousand down on the bike when he bought it, and he still owed you four, plus interest.'

'Ahh – yes, well, yes, that's right; I remember now,' said Bernie.

'And you financed the rest yourself at twenty per cent, I'm told.'

A sickly smile came over Bernie's face. 'It's just business,' he shrugged. 'The kid couldn't get a loan from anyone else. There was a risk. You have to charge a bit extra for that.'

Archie nodded. 'Oh, I agree, Bernie,' he said earnestly, 'but the fact remains that it was *my* money Lenny used for the down payment. Now Lenny can't pay it back, and you've dismantled the bike. My bike, Bernie.'

Bernie swallowed hard. 'I didn't know it was your money, Archie, or I'd never have sold him the bike,' he said. 'If it's the money –' he felt as if he were about to choke on the words – 'I think I could manage to raise the five thou b-by next week.'

Archie Stern slowly shook his head. 'Not good enough, Bernie,' he said sadly. 'See, Lenny didn't steal money. He stole merchandise. Merchandise that belonged to me, and he sold it at cut-rate prices. It grieves me, Bernie, but I have to recover what I lost. It's business, Bernie. You understand business, don't you?'

Bernie nodded miserably. 'I did give you a bell when Lenny showed up here the other night,' he reminded Stern again. 'I mean I did try to help.'

'Which is why I'm going to be reasonable,' said Stern. He glanced around the shop as if taking stock. 'Twenty should just about cover it,' he said as his eyes met Bernie Striker's. 'And I'm doing myself down at that, Bernie.'

'Twenty *thousand*?' Bernie squeaked. 'Jesus, Archie, where am I going to get twenty thou? I'd have to mortgage the shop, stock and all to get that kind of money.'

Stern sighed heavily. 'Like you said, Bernie, there's good days and bad days.' He seemed suddenly to tire of the conversation. 'No need to bring it round, Bernie. The boys will be in to collect it,' he said as he moved toward the door. 'Have it here by Friday. No excuses. You've got a nice little business going here. I'd hate to see anything happen to it – or to you.'

Superintendent Alcott was on the phone when Paget knocked and stuck his head round the door. Alcott motioned for him to come in and sit down. Paget dropped into a seat and stared blankly out of the window.

Alcott finished his conversation and hung up. 'Hell of a way to spend a Saturday,' he growled. 'So what have we got?'

Paget remained silent for several seconds. 'Jane Whitby just rang from the hospital,' he said quietly. 'Helen Beecham has been admitted for treatment and further examination, but it appears that she is the victim of systematic physical and mental abuse. The Casualty officer won't commit himself as to the cause, but he did say that Helen Beecham's body has been subjected to, and I quote, "severe trauma over an extended period of time".

'Jane became suspicious just after we left. She said she could see that Mrs Beecham was in pain, but the woman denied it; said it was nothing. She became quite agitated when Jane tried to pursue it.

'The long and the short of it is that Jane persisted. Mrs Beecham became more and more agitated, then collapsed without warning. Jane loosened the woman's clothing and found bruises and welts all over the upper body, and she thought that one of the ribs might be fractured by the way Helen Beecham reacted when the area was touched. Jane rang for an ambulance, and while they waited for it to arrive, she questioned Mrs Beecham about the bruises.

'At first, Helen Beecham insisted that the bruises were caused by her falling, but when Jane persisted, she admitted that her husband was responsible.' Paget shook his head in a bewildered sort of way because what he was about to say was barely comprehensible to him. 'But Helen Beecham also kept insisting that Beecham had only punished her because she deserved it. She told Jane that she'd always been a bad wife; that she'd never been able to live up to Harry's standards. She said she'd let him down at the very beginning when they were first married, and when Jane asked her why she thought that, she said it was because she had been selfish in wanting to pursue a career rather than look after her husband's needs.

'There was more, but I think you get the picture. Even now, Jane says, the woman is terrified that Harry will find out that she's left the house without his permission.'

'Have you confronted Beecham with this?'

'No. Jane Whitby only informed us a few minutes ago, so I haven't had a chance.'

'What about the rest of it? The murder of Mrs Smallwood and the beating of Amy Thomson.'

'He's denying everything, but we found an anorak and a pair of trousers with what appear to be bloodstains on them in the house. Someone has tried to wash the stains out, but they didn't get everything out of the lining. We also found a pair of shoes with the clothes, so they've been sent along to the lab for comparison with soil samples taken from the area around the railway sheds, and with scrapings from the floor of the church. If we can prove that the blood on the clothing matches Amy Thomson's, then we've got him.'

Paget drew a deep breath and let it out again. 'And, if that's the case, then we have to assume that Rudge was telling the truth, and Beecham *was* in the church the night Beth Smallwood was killed; otherwise, why would he have responded to Rudge's threat of blackmail? Beecham himself swears he was never in the church; that he knows nothing about bloodstained clothing; nothing about blackmail; and nothing about the attack on Amy Thomson.

'The circumstantial evidence ties Beecham to the attack on Amy, but we still lack solid evidence that he actually killed Beth Smallwood. I've sent his prints over to be checked against those we found inside the church, but if we can't come up with a match, then we have nothing but Tony Rudge's word for it that Beecham was ever there. And a good brief could make mincemeat out of anything Rudge has to say.'

'What about the girl? Amy Thomson. Can she back up Rudge's statement about Beecham being in the church?'

'No. Rudge says she didn't see Beecham because she was still asleep in the belfry when he went downstairs to find out what was going on. He says he heard the main door bang shut, so he crept down the stairs to find out who was there. He opened the door at the bottom of the belfry steps, saw the light on in the nave, then saw Beecham come running out. Rudge says he waited until he heard a car start up outside before he ventured into the nave. That's when he says he first saw the body of Beth Smallwood.'

Alcott squinted at Paget through a haze of smoke. 'You said earlier that Rudge claims he recognized Beecham as the man his father had dealt with when he was negotiating a loan from the bank. Do you think that's the truth? Or is there some other connection he's not telling us about?'

Paget shrugged. 'I don't know. Rudge says he was with his father when he got the loan from the bank, and he met Beecham briefly then. That can be checked easily enough. But he couldn't remember Beecham's name, so he dug out the papers from his father's desk to find the name, then looked up Beecham's address in the telephone book. It could be true. There's only one H. Beecham listed.'

Alcott scowled and drew heavily on his cigarette. 'And on that flimsy bit of information, he shoves a blackmail note through Beecham's front door,' he said ruminatively. 'I find that hard to believe.'

'So did I,' said Paget, 'but once he realized we were serious about charging *him* with the murder of Beth Smallwood, he couldn't get the words out fast enough, even to the point of admitting to attempted blackmail. You've heard the tape. Tony Rudge is not the brightest lad in the world, and I think he was so blinded by the prospect of money and his own brilliance that he just charged ahead.'

'He was bright enough to have his girlfriend go along to pick up the money,' Alcott pointed out. 'How is she, by the way?'

'Doing remarkably well, considering she came within a hair of being killed.'

Alcott nodded. 'Good,' he said. 'What do you plan to do with Beecham?'

Paget glanced at the clock. 'We won't get anything out of Forensic until at least Monday afternoon,' he said, 'and if we can't come up with more than we have by this evening, we'll have to let him go. I hate to do it, but on the other hand I don't think he's likely to run.'

Alcott grimaced. He didn't like the idea of having to let Beecham go either, but they wouldn't be able to hold him without more evidence against him. 'Right,' he said. 'Keep me informed.'

'There is one other thing,' said Paget as he rose to leave. 'Tregalles has been checking on Beecham's background. Helen Beecham is his second wife. His first wife died as a result of a fall down the stairs. There was an inquest, but no blame was attached to Beecham. In fact, he came out of it with the sympathy of the court. Her death was attributed to a weakened condition brought about by chronic anorexia. According to Beecham, she was unsteady on her feet and prone to falling, and there were bruises on her body confirming that. Unfortunately, the last time she fell she happened to be at the top of the stairs.'

Alcott stared. '*Two* of them?' he breathed.

'Two of them,' said Paget quietly, 'but we may never prove it.'

Before leaving for the night, Paget went over the results of the day's enquiries in the incident room. Tania Costello seemed to have vanished from the face of the earth; not that Paget found that surprising. Probably gone to one of the larger cities where she could lose herself until all this had blown over; Birmingham or London, most likely. Not that he believed that she had been involved in the murder of her boyfriend's mother, but she might have shed some light on what had happened in the house that night before Beth Smallwood went along to the church.

As for Lenny himself, Paget felt confident that he had not known his mother was dead, and as a consequence, he had ordered the constable in the boy's room to be withdrawn. The shock in Lenny's eyes when Paget had told him of his mother's death had been genuine, though whether because of some affection for her, or because he realized that he would have to fend for himself from now on was open to conjecture.

Being Saturday, nothing had come in from Forensic, neither had there been anything further from the hospital regarding Helen Beecham's condition. Paget read the latest notes on the status board with a growing sense of frustration. The most galling thing of all was having to release Harry Beecham. Paget had argued passionately that Beecham should at least be charged with the abuse of his wife, but the CPS refused to touch it. The fact, they said, that Helen Beecham had collapsed while in the sole charge of WPC Whitby *could* be construed as due to pressure applied by Whitby to force Mrs Beecham to testify against her husband.

There were no witnesses to back up WPC Whitby's statement, and given the fact that Helen Beecham was insisting that she deserved to be punished, there was every chance that she would deny or retract in court any previous statements she was alleged to have made.

Besides, they said, it was after all, merely a domestic affair.

Paget's reply to *that* observation was unprintable.

It was late but there was still light in the sky when Paget garaged his car for the night. A broad band of red covered the western sky, and the breeze felt soft and warm against his face as he walked to the front door. About time, he thought; here it was almost the end of May and it seemed as if winter had never ended.

He was tired. He felt as if he hadn't slept for a week, but his mind refused to let him rest even as he prepared for bed. There *had* to be some evidence, other than Tony Rudge's word for it, that would tie Beecham convincingly to the death of Beth Smallwood. Always assuming, he reminded himself, that Beecham was in fact guilty.

Rudge might be a dodgy witness, but Paget didn't doubt his story about *seeing* Beecham at the church, but what had *really* happened there? After spending the day drinking and brooding over his abrupt dismissal, would Beecham just charge into the church, seize a candlestick, and strike Beth Smallwood down without a word? Without argument? Without recriminations?

But Rudge had insisted he had heard nothing. No voices raised; no cry from Beth. Nothing.

Paget had questioned him closely about that, but Rudge had stuck to his story. He said he'd gone down the belfry steps after hearing the front door bang shut. 'I was half awake and it sounded like a bloody cannon,' he said.

That made sense. Mrs Turvey had said Beecham had been pounding on Beth's door, and he'd been belligerent when she spoke to him. Paget didn't believe for a moment that Beecham would not have gone to the church. And he'd be even more angry by that time, so he wouldn't care how much noise he made. He was going to have it out with the woman he thought had betrayed him.

But there was something wrong with what followed. Rudge claimed that he was at the bottom of the belfry steps in a matter of seconds. He opened the door a crack and stood there listening. He could see the light on in the nave, but couldn't see what was happening down by the chancel.

And he'd heard nothing!

Rudge had gone on to say that he was about to step out to take a closer look when Beecham came running out and left the church.

'How did he look?' Tregalles had asked.

'Like he'd just committed murder. Chalk white, he was.'

A few seconds later, Rudge said, he heard a car start up and take off in a hurry. Charlie's people had scoured the area thoroughly immediately following the murder, but they'd found nothing to prove that Beecham's car was ever there. The rains had seen to that.

Rudge had gone on to say that it was only then that he ventured out and found Beth Smallwood's body. He said he'd panicked because he knew that people might think that he had killed Beth because of what she had done to him in court.

It all sounded very plausible, Paget thought as he made his way to bed. But what if it had happened the other way round? What if Rudge had known that Beth was down there that evening; perhaps seen her come in? Then, while Amy was asleep, he'd crept down and killed her? But just as he was about to leave, Beecham had come storming into the church, angry and all set to have it out with Beth. Rudge could have concealed himself, watched while Beecham discovered the body then ran from the church. Beecham would of course deny all knowledge of ever having been there for fear of being accused of killing Beth Smallwood, and Rudge, having recognized Beecham, would consider the idea of blackmailing him a bonus.

Paget stared into the darkness. Was Tony Rudge clever enough to have lied convincingly to them about what had happened that night? Possibly. Anyone facing the prospect of being charged with murder might well become exceedingly inventive.

But one big question still remained: why would Rudge insist there had been no noise? Surely, if only to make his story more convincing, he would have spoken of hearing a struggle; a cry from Beth – anything but complete silence.

So what about Amy? All the hard evidence pointed to Beecham. If Beecham had killed Beth Smallwood, he might not hesitate to kill his blackmailer to protect himself. But if he was being black-mailed for something he did not do, would he go there prepared to kill?

He might, especially if he feared an investigation into his private life. He might go to any lengths to avoid that. Anyone who could do what Beecham had done to his wife was capable of anything in Paget's estimation.

He slid into bed and was about to switch off the light when his eyes were drawn to the framed photograph of Jill. He picked it up and studied it as he had so many times before. Thoughts of Beecham vanished as he allowed his mind to drift, remembering.

Her dark eyes met his solemnly, and suddenly he heard her voice inside his head as clearly as if she were in the room.

'I'm all right. Really, I'm all right. Please let me go, Neil. You're suffocating me.'

He remembered the scene vividly. It was a Sunday and they had gone down to Eastbourne for the day. The weather had been perfect, and they were enjoying a final walk along the cliffs before returning home when Jill suddenly turned her ankle and stumbled toward the edge. The ground had started to give way. The sea pounded on the rocks below. He'd reached out and grabbed her arm as she started to go down. The grass was torn apart as the earth beneath it crumbled and began its long slow plunge toward the waiting sea and rocks below.

He'd pulled her clear and clutched her to him, his own heart beating wildly as he fought for breath himself. He remembered vividly the terror of that moment; remembered how he'd held her in such a fierce embrace that she'd cried out to be released.

He set the picture down and turned out the light, but Jill's breathless words still echoed in the darkness. *'You're suffocating me, Neil. Please let me go.'*

CHAPTER 23

Sunday – 19 May

The sound of distant drums dragged Paget back to consciousness. He lay with his eyes closed, trying to get his mind to work, trying to identify the sound.

Rain. He groaned aloud. So much for 'red sky at night', he thought gloomily. The bloody shepherd had got it wrong again.

He made breakfast and sat down to read the paper, but his thoughts from the night before kept intruding. Jill's words still echoed in his head, and he was troubled by their insistence. Why should he think of that particular incident now? He wandered disconsolately from room to room, growing more irritable by the minute.

By ten o'clock he could stand it no longer. He left the house and drove into town.

His original intention was to go to the office, but once in town he changed his mind and drove to the hospital instead.

Paget stopped at the desk to speak to the senior nurse on duty, a short, stout, grey-haired woman of about fifty. Her face was round; her skin was the colour of polished mahogany, and her eyes were the liveliest Paget had ever seen. Originally from Jamaica, Rose Tremonte had been at the Royal Broadminster hospital for much of her working life.

'Good morning, Rose,' Paget greeted her. 'Still working the weekends, I see. Don't you ever get tired of it?'

Rose glanced around as if afraid of being overheard, and lowered her voice to a conspiratorial whisper. 'No bosses on the weekends,' she confided. Her face broke into a broad smile, and a deep chuckle rumbled in her ample throat.

They chatted for a few minutes, and Paget asked about Amy.

'She's coming along just fine,' said Rose. 'She's a nice kid. She's going to be all right.'

'Can I talk to her?'

'No reason why not,' Rose told him agreeably.

Amy looked very young and vulnerable as she lay there against the pillows. Even at fifteen, she was a very pretty girl; in two or three more years she would an extremely attractive young woman. Paget only hoped that her recent brush with death would make her more cautious about whom she trusted in the future.

He led her through her story once more, but learned nothing new. Her memory seemed clear, and she was extremely frank about her relationship with Tony Rudge, although she came close to tears when she described how she had been attacked in the railway shed.

'You seem quite convinced that it was Tony who attacked you,' he said. 'What makes you so certain?'

Amy's face clouded. 'It had to be him, didn't it?' she said. 'I mean it had to be Tony who killed that woman in the church. Lenny's

161

mum. See, I didn't know it was her at the time, so I believed Tony when he said he'd heard something and gone down to have a look round and found her dead. But he'd told me a bit about Lenny Smallwood, and I knew he hated him and his mum, so when I heard who she was, I did wonder.'

The girl plucked at the sheet and kept her eyes lowered. 'But I didn't want to believe that, because...Well, you know.' She fell silent for a long moment, then looked up at Paget and shrugged. 'It's just that it all fits together,' she said, 'and I must have been daft to have believed all that rubbish about this bloke owing him money and being afraid to show his face and all that. I mean, where would Tony get that sort of money in prison anyway? And he's not really the lending sort.'

'You're sure you neither saw nor heard anyone else in the church that night?'

'No. There was no one; I'm sure of that.'

'But you said yourself that you were asleep until Tony woke you and said you had to get out of there, so someone could have been in the church without your knowledge.'

'I suppose,' she said dubiously. 'Are you saying you *believe* him?'

Paget didn't answer directly. 'Tell me, could you hear if someone was, say, having an argument in the church while you were in that room in the belfry?'

'No. You can't hear anything either way. That's why it was so good for us. Nobody could hear us, and with the door locked and that sign about the tower being unsafe, we didn't have to be quiet.'

'What about the main door? It's pretty heavy. Could you hear that if it banged shut?'

'Oh, yes. You can hear that,' the girl agreed. 'It sort of echoes; sort of goes "boom," if you know what I mean. But you can't hear voices.'

'Right. Now, Amy, I know it must be painful for you, but I'd like you to try to remember everything you saw or heard when you first entered that railway shed. You said you thought you were just going in to pick up an envelope. Did you have any idea that someone might be there?'

'I shouldn't have gone in if I'd thought there was someone in there,' Amy said emphatically. 'I was dead scared as it was.'

'So take me through the steps again. You went inside and used the torch. What did you see?'

'Just an empty shed. Well, bits and pieces of old machinery; that sort of thing.'

'And ...?'

'This big old metal thing where Tony said the envelope would be, and it was. It was stuck on tight, so I had to really pull hard to get it off. And it wouldn't go into my pocket because the tape kept sticking to my clothes.'

'So you had the envelope in your hand? Is that right?'

'Yes. That's when I heard a noise.' Amy gave an involuntary shiver.

'What sort of noise?'

'I don't know. Just a noise.'

'All right. Then what happened?'

'I tried to see what it was, but that's when he shone this big torch in my eyes, and I couldn't see a thing. Then he hit me with this metal thing alongside the head, and ...'

'You said "metal thing". You didn't say that before. How do you know it was metal? Did you see it?'

Amy frowned, trying to concentrate. 'I just saw this sort of glint as it came down, and I tried to stop it ... Yes! That's right. I remember, now. I tried to grab hold of it. It was cold and hard. It was metal, like a bar.'

'Flat? Round?'

'Flat – I think. I'm not sure. Sorry.'

'It's all right, Amy. You're doing very well. What else do you remember?'

'I went down. I thought my head was split. He had another go and hit me on the shoulder, and he was swearing like ...' Amy stopped in mid-sentence, and her eyes opened wide. 'I'd forgotten that,' she breathed. 'He was lashing out and swearing because he'd missed me.'

'Did you recognize the voice? Think, now. Was it Tony's voice?'

Amy closed her eyes and remained silent as she relived that moment of the attack. Her eyes flew open. 'It wasn't Tony,' she said with something like relief. 'I'm sure it wasn't Tony.' Tears trickled down her face as she began to cry.

'He did set you up, though,' Paget reminded her. He didn't want her to have any illusions about Tony Rudge. 'Please go on.'

Amy sniffed loudly and wiped away the tears with her hands. 'That's when I reckoned my only chance was to knock him off

163

balance so's I could run,' she said. 'So I butted him as hard as I could and ran like hell.'

Her memory of events after that was confused and hazy until she woke up in hospital, and Paget didn't press her. She was tiring, so he thanked her warmly and asked if there was anything she needed.

'No, thanks,' she said. 'Besides, my mum will be here soon, and she's bringing some things.'

'How is your mother taking all this? It must have been very hard on her, not knowing where you were.'

Amy shot him a glance that was a mixture of guilt and impishness. 'She didn't half give me what for last night,' she said, 'but then she cried and she's coming in this morning, so I reckon it'll be all right.'

He couldn't help but like the girl, he thought as he left the room. She'd been extremely foolish, and she was damned lucky to be alive, but she was a plucky little thing. He just hoped she'd learned her lesson.

Before leaving the floor, Paget sought out Rose once again and asked about Helen Beecham.

'She's down in C Ward, now,' she told him. C Ward was the hospital's psychiatric section. 'They moved her down there last night for observation after they caught her trying to sneak out. Said she had to get home to her husband because he'd be wanting his tea.'

Paget thought of the free spirit portrayed in the charcoal sketch, and compared it to the image of the woman he'd seen standing at the kitchen sink. What Beecham had done to her filled him with revulsion, and he hoped Forensic would find sufficient evidence of his crimes to put the man away for a very long time.

He was about to leave when another thought occurred to him. 'Tell me, Rose, when did Dr McMillan come back to work here?'

Rose thought for a moment. 'About a month ago,' she said. 'Mr Stone's been trying for months to get a registrar to work with him in orthopaedics, but he couldn't find anyone who was interested.' Rose lowered her voice. 'Between you and me, Mr Paget, I'm not surprised; he's a miserable old devil and so demanding that there's not many who'll work with him, but he is a brilliant consultant. So, he went to see Dr McMillan and persuaded her to come back to work with him.'

Rose grinned. 'She has his measure,' she chuckled. 'She doesn't stand any nonsense from him, and he's been a lot easier to work with since she came back. And she's got herself a good teacher. I hope she stays.'

So did he, thought Paget. So did he.

CHAPTER 24

The incident room was silent. The investigation into the death of Beth Smallwood had, to all intents and purposes, ground to a halt. Any information that did come in would be handled by the regular Sunday staff, and anything urgent would be relayed immediately to the appropriate officer.

Paget sat in Ormside's chair and stared disconsolately at the wall-charts linking and cross-referencing names, dates, times, alibis and movements. Beecham was certainly the prime suspect, but Tony Rudge came in a close second, and Terry Ling could not be dismissed. Ling was clever and he'd had a rough time of it since leaving Hong Kong. Now, with the imminent arrival of his first child, he may have felt that Beth Smallwood's promotion was the last straw. He claimed he did not know where Farrow Lane was, but that could be a lie. On the other hand, how would he know that Beth was in the church that night, and not at home?

So much depended upon what the lab could tell them, and some of that information might not be available for several days.

But as far as Paget was concerned, there were still some disturbing questions to be answered, starting with the autopsy report. Beth Smallwood had been sexually assaulted several hours prior to her death, and no matter how he reconstructed events, Paget couldn't help but conclude that the assault had taken place at the bank.

Beth's behaviour, as Ginny Holbrook had described it, did not sound like that of someone who had just been promoted, although Rachel Fairmont seemed to think that Beth had simply been overwhelmed by the sudden turn of events. The bus driver who had picked Beth up outside the bank had thought she was ill.

Gresham had made a point of telling Paget how emotional and high-strung Beth was, but that could have been a deliberate attempt to forestall questions that might arise concerning her behaviour after she left his office. Beecham had made no bones about how he believed Beth had got his old job, but anything that man said was suspect now. Terry Ling had said that Beth had been promoted because she was a woman, but had backed off when asked to explain, while Ginny Holbrook had said – after he'd backed her into a corner – that Gresham couldn't keep his hands to himself, and she and the other women at the bank used to have a 'bit of a giggle' over Gresham's pursuit of Beth Smallwood.

Put all that together, and it seemed to Paget that Beth had indeed paid Gresham's price for her promotion. But not all that willingly, according to Starkie's findings.

And how had Gresham known that Beth wouldn't be in on Tuesday morning? Neither Beth nor Rachel had phoned Gresham's house, according to Lilian Gresham, so how did he know that Beth had phoned Rachel?

Also, there was Gresham's statement regarding his whereabouts on Monday evening. He'd made it sound as if he'd spent most of the evening visiting his father, but Claude had admitted falling asleep, so there was no telling what time Gresham had left there. Broadminster was not a big town; you could drive from Golden Meadows to St Justin's church in less than ten minutes. The question was: why would Gresham do that? And how would he know where to find Beth? She couldn't have told him earlier because she didn't know that she would be at the church until Parslow telephoned her at home.

Unless Rachel had told him of the phone call. But if that were the case, how had she managed to get in touch with him? Arthur Gresham did not have a phone in his car, nor did he carry a pocket pager; Paget had already checked into that. And why had Gresham arrived late that Tuesday morning? His wife had said he left early for a meeting, which might explain his late arrival at the bank if the meeting had been held elsewhere. But if that were the case, why had Rachel Fairmont – Gresham's own secretary – known nothing about it?

Paget thought about Alcott's warning, and hesitated – but not for long. Gresham was hiding something. It might or might not have a bearing on Beth Smallwood's death, but Paget wouldn't be satisfied until he had the answer.

'I must apologize for coming round on a Sunday,' Paget said as Rachel Fairmont ushered him into the room. 'I hope I'm not interfering with anything?'

'No. No, it's all right. It's just that your call rather took me by surprise, that's all. It being the weekend, I mean.' Rachel turned to face him, then simply stood there as if not quite sure what to do next. She looked, Paget thought, as if she had dressed hastily, and her hair was slightly damp. 'Would you like a cup of tea?' she asked hopefully.

'Only if you were about to have one yourself,' said Paget.

'I think I will make some,' she said. 'Please sit down.' She picked up a damp towel from the back of a chair, and left the room before Paget could reply.

The flat was one of a block of twelve behind a shopping precinct on the south side of King George Way. The room was small but tastefully furnished. Rachel Fairmont had a good eye for colour and style, and she had made the most of the space, although it seemed to Paget that the emphasis was on style rather than comfort.

He sat down in an overstuffed chair as Rachel re-entered the room carrying a tray. She set the tray on a low table, poured the tea, then pulled up an ottoman and sat down facing him, hands clasped around her knees.

She looked so different from the secretary he'd first seen at the bank. Gone was the tailored look of blouse and skirt and the carefully made-up face; gone, too, was the severe hair-style that made her face look fuller than it really was. The Rachel Fairmont who faced him across the table looked more feminine. Instead of a blouse, she wore a bulky, oatmeal-coloured sweater that fell in loose folds around her hips, and a denim skirt that all but covered her long bare legs and open-toed sandals. Her hair fell in gentle folds around her face and rested on her shoulders, softening the lines and making her look younger than he'd first thought. And there was something different about her eyes. Of course! She'd been wearing glasses at the office, and now she wore none. Contacts, perhaps?

This Rachel Fairmont was a very attractive woman.

Rachel coloured slightly beneath his gaze and shrugged an apology. 'Sorry I look such a mess,' she said. 'My hair isn't quite dry from the shower.'

'Not at all,' said Paget. 'I'm afraid I did call at a bad time after all. I could come back again later if you'd rather.'

'No, really, it's all right,' she assured him. Rachel picked up her cup and sipped her tea. But her eyes were watchful as she looked at him over the rim of the cup.

'Have you lived here long?' he asked by way of opening the conversation.

'Six years.' A slight frown creased her brow. 'Why do you ask?'

He smiled. 'No particular reason,' he said. 'Just curiosity. I'm afraid it's an occupational disease. Asking questions.'

A token smile touched Rachel's face, but it was gone almost as soon as it appeared. 'I'm not quite sure why you're here,' she said hesitantly. 'I really don't know how I can help you.'

'I'd like you to think back to the conversation you had with Beth Smallwood when she rang last Monday evening,' he said. 'I know I asked you about it before, but I'd appreciate it if you would go over it again for me. What time did you say it was when she rang?'

Her brows drew together. 'I'm pretty sure it was very close to eight o'clock. I didn't know who it was at first – Beth sounded so strange. But then she explained that she'd bitten her tongue when she fell, and it was hard for her to talk.'

'And what exactly did she say?'

'Just that she wouldn't be in to work the next day, and she asked me to tell Mr Gresham in the morning.'

'Did she say why she was ringing you rather than Mr Gresham?'

Rachel frowned. 'No – at least I don't remember if she did. She may have tried to reach him and couldn't. I didn't think to ask.'

'Do you recall anything else she said, now that you've had more time to think about it?'

'No. As I said, it was hard for her to talk, so she wasn't on long.'

Paget gave a small sigh. 'I must admit I'm having trouble getting a clear picture of Beth Smallwood,' he confided. 'I know you said you never did really get to know her, but you must have formed some impressions. What sort of person was she? Did you ever visit her at home? Did she ever come here?'

Rachel looked off into the distance for a long moment, then slowly shook her head. 'I wish I could help you, Chief Inspector,' she said. 'I know it sounds strange, but I can't say I knew Beth at all. She kept very much to herself, and –' Rachel broke off and looked down at her hands – 'I'm afraid I'm rather like that myself, so we just seemed to go our separate ways when we left work.'

'But you must have talked at work now and again. Over coffee; at lunch time. Did she ever mention any friends outside of work? Anyone she'd met, perhaps?'

'No, I don't think so.'

'Steady worker, was she? I mean, she wasn't one who took a lot of time off during business hours or anything like that?'

'No.' Rachel seemed puzzled by the question. 'I can't remember the last time Beth took any time off even when she wasn't feeling well.'

'And she was there at the bank all day Monday?'

'Yes.'

'She didn't, for example, have an extra long lunch hour or slip out for an hour sometime during the day?'

Rachel seemed mystified by the question. 'No. The only time I ever remember Beth taking time off was when she was having her teeth done a year or so ago. And she hardly ever went out at lunch time; she always brought her lunch with her and ate it at her desk.' Rachel hesitated as if uncertain about how what she was about to say would be taken. 'You see, Beth was – I was about to say "conscientious", but I think it had more to do with the fear of losing her job. That threat has been hanging over all our heads for months, now, but Beth seemed particularly concerned because of her son.'

'So she did talk about her son, then?'

'Well, not really, but one picks up the odd bits and pieces.' Rachel wrinkled her nose. 'My *impression* of her son was that he was little better than a layabout, always sponging off his mother, but I would never have said that to Beth. She doted on the boy.'

'Have you met him? Was he ever at the bank?'

'No. I've heard the rumours of course, but that's all.'

'Rumours?'

Rachel looked uncomfortable. 'I feel as if I'm telling tales out of school,' she said, 'but someone said that the real reason she'd been away that time was not because of her teeth, but because she'd had to go to court. Lenny had been in some scrape or other, but I don't know the details.'

'Do you recall who told you that?'

'No. And come to think of it, I'm not sure now whether I heard it at work or read something in the local paper. Sorry.'

Paget sipped his tea in silence for a moment. 'Can you describe what Beth Smallwood was wearing that last day at the bank?'

Rachel gave him an odd look as if trying to decide whether the question was a serious one or not. 'She was wearing a dark blue dress – very dark; almost black – with a V-neck insert covered with tiny –' she hesitated – 'daisies, I think. It had buttons to the waist, and I think there was a belt.' Her brows drew together. 'Yes, there was. It was the same colour as the dress. She wore that dress quite often...' She stopped and caught her lower lip between her teeth. 'I'm sorry, I didn't mean to sound...I just meant that – well, Beth wasn't very well off for clothes.'

'No need to apologize. I understand,' he assured her.

'Do you mind telling me why you wanted to know what Beth was wearing?'

'Not at all. I simply wanted to know whether she'd had time to change before going to the church.' He paused. 'You told me you saw her when she came out of Mr Gresham's office that day,' he went on. 'Tell me again how she seemed to you.'

Rachel picked up her cup, found that it was almost empty, and set it down again. 'More tea?' she asked, holding the teapot ready to pour.

'No more for me, thank you,' he said.

Rachel refilled her own cup, put in a spoonful of sugar and stirred it vigorously. She appeared to be considering how best to answer Paget's question. 'I think she was concerned about whether she was up to the job,' she said finally. 'A bit overwhelmed, perhaps.'

Rachel seemed to have modified her opinion of Beth Smallwood's behaviour since he had last spoken to her, but Paget let it pass.

'Did Beth ever speak to you or complain to you of sexual harassment at work, Miss Fairmont?'

For a moment, there was no reaction. Then two bright spots appeared on Rachel's cheeks. She drew back as if burned and stared at Paget as if he'd made some sort of lewd suggestion. '*Really!* Chief Inspector,' she said breathlessly. 'I – I can't think where you got that idea.' She drew in a long breath. 'I don't know what to say.'

'An answer to the question would be helpful,' said Paget mildly.

The woman didn't seem to know where to look, and the colour in her face was spreading. 'I – I don't think that sort of thing deserves an answer,' she said shakily.

Paget sighed. 'It's a simple question, Miss Fairmont, and I would like an answer.'

'Then the answer is no!'

'Thank you.' Obviously he'd touched a nerve. 'And thank you for the tea. I think that's all for now.' He set his cup aside and pushed himself out of the chair. Rachel rose and followed quickly as he moved toward the door.

'There is just one more thing you may be able to help me with,' he said as if the thought had just occurred to him. 'The other day you told me that you hadn't had a chance to tell Mr Gresham about Beth Smallwood's call to you on Monday evening, and yet he knew about that call on Tuesday morning when I first spoke to him. How do you suppose he knew about that?'

Rachel held his gaze, and yet he had the impression that shutters had come down behind her eyes and she wasn't seeing him at all. The silence between them lengthened. 'I've no idea,' she said at last. 'But I'm sure there's some quite simple explanation.'

'Oh, I'm sure there is, Miss Fairmont,' said Paget amiably as he opened the door. 'Thank you again. You've been extremely helpful.'

CHAPTER 25

Monday – 20 May

It was always a bit of a madhouse first thing Monday morning in the incident room as everyone prepared for another week of intensive activity.

'Let's have a bit of hush, then, shall we?' Len Ormside's normally quiet voice was raised just enough to cut through the wall of noise, which gradually subsided. 'Even those of you who weren't here on Saturday no doubt know by now that a suspect by the name of Harry Beecham was questioned and released for lack of evidence. However, as far as we are concerned, he is still our prime suspect in the attempted murder of Amy Thomson. We believe there is evidence to support that, but we will have to wait for the report from Forensic before we'll know for certain. He is also the prime suspect in the murder of Beth Smallwood, but we have only Tony Rudge's word for it that Beecham was in the church that night. There is no physical evidence to back that up as yet.

'Rudge claims that he delivered a blackmail letter to Beecham's house in the early hours of Thursday morning. You have a description of his car; it's old and it's noisy, so someone may have noticed it. I want every possibility checked. Pearson, you take charge of that. The same applies to the early hours of Friday morning when we believe that Beecham drove from his house to the railway sheds, parked his car nearby while he waited for the blackmailer to arrive, then drove home again after attacking Amy Thomson. It's a long shot, but someone may have seen him.

'Now then, most of you already know your assignments, so I don't want to see you hanging about in here. As for the others, I'll get to you in a few minutes, but right now I want Ingram, and Falkner over here at the desk. I've got jobs for you.'

Ormside looked up as DC Graham Ingram and DC Esme Falkner came up to his desk. 'Rachel Fairmont,' he said. 'Mr Paget thinks we should know more about her, so I want you to make discreet enquiries among the neighbours, shopkeepers, and anyone else you think might help. And I *mean* discreet. She's not a suspect, but Mr Paget feels she might be withholding information. Now, here is what he's after...'

'Chief Inspector Paget?' Grace Lovett spoke the words on a rising inflection, and to anyone attuned to the nuances of the human voice it was obvious she spoke the words with pleasure. But at the other end of the telephone, Paget's mind was on other things.

'Grace, Charlie suggested that I speak to you directly,' he said. 'When you were in Beth Smallwood's house last Tuesday, do you recall seeing a dark blue dress with a broad V-neck with some sort of small flowers on it; buttons to the waist, and a belt?'

'Yes.' Grace's answer was swift and unequivocal. 'It was stuffed in a bin bag along with some underclothes in the bathroom. I remember wondering why they weren't with the other things waiting to be washed. Why? Is it important? I could come over if you think...'

'No, no, thank you, Grace; that won't be necessary; you've told me what I wanted to know.' Paget paused. 'In the bathroom, you say? Not in the bedroom?'

'No. Definitely in the bathroom. As a matter of fact it seemed out of keeping with the rest of the place in that it was the only room in the house that wasn't clean. Someone, presumably Beth Smallwood herself, had taken a bath and hadn't cleaned it afterwards. I say presumably Beth because there was a residue of bath salts in the bottom of the tub, and I did wonder if she'd had to leave in a hurry, expecting to clean it later.'

'Do we still have access to the house?'

'I believe we do.'

'Good. I'd like you to go back there, pick up that dress and the underclothes and have them sent to the lab for examination. Can you do that?'

'It's no trouble at all,' said Grace agreeably, 'and if there is any other way I can help, I'd be happy to...'

'Grace, thank you,' Paget said with feeling, 'but you've already done more than enough. But if I should find I need anything else along that line, do you mind if I ring you directly?'

'Please do,' she said. '*Please* do,' she repeated wistfully as she replaced the phone gently in its cradle.

Paget replaced the phone, and for a moment thought of Grace. She was a lovely girl; pleasant, hard-working, extremely observant, and always willing to help. She was far and away the best analyst Charlie had, and he had a good team. But Grace had that something extra; a sort of sixth sense; an intuition that allowed her to glean more from her findings than most. Good-looking woman, too.

He glanced at the time and Grace vanished from his mind. There was work to be done, and the sooner he got over to the hospital the better. He thought of ringing Andrea first, but decided it would be better to see her when he got there.

But Dr McMillan was in a meeting, he was told when he arrived on the fourth floor. And Dr Trotter was away, but the staff nurse on duty, whom Paget knew slightly, raised no objection to his talking to Lenny.

The police guard was gone. Technically, Lenny was still a suspect in the murder of his mother, but his reaction to the news of her death had been one of genuine shock in Paget's opinion. The boy was a lout and a trouble-maker, but the chief inspector couldn't see him as his mother's killer. As for the people who had beaten him up and left him on the road, they could have killed him then if that was

173

their intention. They weren't likely to come back to finish the job at this late stage. They'd made their point.

If anything, Lenny looked worse than he had the previous Friday. He watched with sullen eyes as Paget approached the bed.

'How is it today, Lenny?' Paget greeted him.

'None the better for seeing you,' the boy grated through wired teeth.

'I need a couple of straight answers,' Paget told him. 'And the sooner I get them the sooner you'll be rid of me. I want to know what your mother was wearing when you last saw her?'

The boy shivered and wrapped his arms around himself. 'Dressing-gown,' he muttered. 'Why?'

'Why was she in a dressing-gown at that time of day?'

'Why do you think?' he asked contemptuously. 'She'd just come out of the bath, hadn't she.'

'When was this exactly?'

'I dunno. She was in there when we got there; me and Tan. Why? What's this all about?'

Paget ignored the questions. 'Did she usually take a bath when she got home?'

Lenny eased himself up on the pillows. His eyes closed for a moment as a spasm racked his thin body. 'I need a jolt,' he gasped. 'For Christ's sake, man, can't you make them give me something?'

'They are giving you something, Lenny,' said Paget. 'If they weren't, you'd be in far more pain than you are. If you stick with it, you've got a chance to kick this. It may be your only chance.'

Lenny shook his head angrily. 'Don't give me that shit, man,' he grated. 'It ain't ever going to be any better.' He slid down in the bed and turned his face into the pillow.

'Answer the question, Lenny. Did your mother usually take a bath when she got home from work?'

Lenny lay there for a long moment, then slowly turned his head to face Paget. 'No,' he said. He sounded puzzled, as if only now had he thought about it and found it odd. 'No,' he said again. 'She always had one before she went to bed. Always.'

Tregalles was also at the hospital that morning, but in another wing entirely. He'd arranged a meeting with a psychiatrist by the name of Sandra Chandler, and now they sat facing one another across a small table in her office. A coffee-maker gurgled softly in the background, and each held a mug of coffee in their hands.

'But why didn't Helen Beecham just leave him?' Tregalles said. 'He was away at work all day. She had all sorts of opportunities to leave.'

Sandra Chandler was a big, comfortable-looking woman with a pleasant face and natural smile, but she wasn't smiling now.

'Where would she go?' she countered. 'She had no relatives; no friends. Bad as it was at home, it was safer than the unknown. It's not at all uncommon in cases such as these, and it is one of the hardest hurdles to overcome when we are trying to encourage women to make the break.

'You see, by the time anyone becomes aware of what's happening, a woman is convinced that everything that has happened to her is her own fault. That it's *her* fault that dinner is never satisfactory; that *she* is to blame because the house is never clean enough to satisfy her husband; and she is absolutely convinced that it is *her* fault that their sex life is a failure, no matter how hard she tries to please.'

Sandra swirled the coffee around inside the mug, then took a drink. 'A woman in that situation has been so completely brainwashed that she no longer has a standard of her own. Everything is measured by the standard set by her husband; a standard that is constantly adjusted so that it is just beyond her reach. She tries desperately to please a husband who refuses to be pleased.'

'But she's free now,' Tregalles objected.

'Is she? How do you get rid of years of mental conditioning? How do you convince her that her husband can no longer hurt her? How do you give her back her confidence and self-respect?'

'But the beatings . . .? Surely she can't possibly want to go back to that?'

Sandra Chandler smiled sadly and shook her head. 'In many cases, women in that position come to believe that they *deserve* to be punished for failing so miserably. Once they reach the stage where they are fearful of making a mistake, they make more mistakes; they can't seem to do anything right no matter how hard they try. So they're bad; they deserve what they get. It's the same way with children; if they are told often enough that they are worthless, they come to believe it.'

Tregalles felt a cold shiver run through him. He thought of Harry Beecham sitting there so calmly in the interview room, assuring them that he'd done nothing wrong. That he loved his wife. *Five years!* That was how long this had been going on. Virtually ever since the day they were married. And no one had noticed. No one had cared enough to find out why Helen Beecham had never appeared in public again. He voiced his thoughts to Sandra Chandler.

'Helen was probably a very solitary child,' she said. 'You say she was an artist? Creative people often immerse themselves in their work. They have little time to form relationships with other people. It's quite possible that she had no friends – no real friends, that is – and if her husband is the type of man you suggest, then he would discourage anyone who might have tried to keep in touch with her until she was completely cut off from help. As for her talent as a painter, he would see that as a threat. It gave her an identity as an individual – drew the spotlight to her rather than to him – and he could never allow that. He would ridicule her efforts; undermine whatever confidence she'd developed over the years, until at last she would come to believe that she had no talent and it would be pointless to continue.'

Tregalles remained silent for some time as he digested the information. 'How long will it be before Mrs Beecham can be made to realize the truth?' he asked at last.

The psychiatrist shrugged and shook her head. 'It's impossible to say. Everyone is different. But there is a ray of hope in Mrs Beecham's case. When I talked with her yesterday, I'm sure I detected a spark of resentment at the way she'd been treated. If that's true, it's a start. It means that deep down she still retains a shred of self-esteem, and we can build on that. But how long it will take is anybody's guess. Sorry, Sergeant, but that's the best I can do at the moment.'

CHAPTER 26

Sergeant Ormside put the phone down and looked up at the uniformed constable hovering over him. 'What is it this time,

Dandridge?' he asked wearily. 'I thought you were supposed to be out knocking on doors.'

Dandridge fidgeted. 'It's just that I was wondering whether you'd heard anything, Sarge? You know, about that run-in with the motorist last Tuesday?'

Ormside sighed. 'I told you the other day to check with Sergeant Nolan. The complaint should go to him, not me.'

Dandridge fiddled with his cap. 'Yes, but with me being seconded to the Smallwood investigation, I thought it might have come to you.'

'Well, it hasn't! So stop hanging about here and get out there. If you've heard nothing by now, chances are that he was just blowing hot air. Think yourself lucky.'

Dandridge looked anything but reassured. 'It's just that with him being who he is, I thought he'd be bound to follow it up,' he said. 'Tore a right strip off me, he did. Still . . .' He began to move away.

'Hold on. I thought you said you didn't know who he was,' said Ormside. 'You told me that he wouldn't give his name.'

'He wouldn't. Just drove off in his Rover when I asked.'

'Which you forgot to take the number of,' Ormside reminded him.

'Yes, well, I did explain that,' said Dandridge. 'But see, I didn't know who he was then; it was only when I saw his picture in the paper the other day that . . .'

'Picture? What picture, Dandridge?'

'In Saturday's *Star*, Sarge. On the sports page. It had to do with that land the cricket club's been after for years. Well, now they've got it, and there was this picture of him shaking hands with one of the councillors. Gresham – that's his name. Arthur Gresham, chairman or some such thing of the Cricket Association.'

Paget had just left the hospital when Len Ormside's call came through on the car phone. He had, he told Paget cryptically, information that he thought would be of interest to the chief inspector. Could he return to headquarters?

Knowing Ormside would not have asked him to return unless it was important, Paget was there in less than ten minutes.

Ormside wasted no time on preliminaries when Paget arrived. 'This is PC Dandridge,' he said. 'He was on traffic duty at the head of Farrow Lane last Tuesday morning. A man in a maroon Rover attempted to turn down the lane, but Dandridge stopped him and asked if he lived there. When the man said he didn't but had business there, Dandridge informed him that the road was closed temporarily to everyone but local residents. According to Dandridge, the man became abusive and said he would report him and have his job, but refused to give his name. Then he drove off.'

Ormside glowered at Dandridge as he continued. 'Unfortunately for us, PC Dandridge failed to read the number plate of the car, being too preoccupied with his own future or lack of it, and it was only when he saw the man's picture in the newspaper last Saturday that he found out that his name was Arthur Gresham.'

'Gresham?' Paget shot the constable a hard look. 'Are you quite sure, Dandridge?'

'Yes, sir.'

'Did he lay a complaint?'

'No. I phoned around and checked,' said Ormside, 'and there is nothing on record.'

'What time was this, Dandridge?'

The constable fumbled with his notebook. 'Eight forty-one, sir.'

'Did he say why he wanted to go down Farrow Lane?'

'Just that he had business there, sir.'

Paget was fast losing patience. 'Did he mention any names? Good God, man, there are only four small cottages down there. What *did* he say exactly?'

'Just that he had to get down there, and he'd have my job if I didn't bloody well get out of his way,' blurted Dandridge. He hurried on. 'He said he had friends on the Watch Committee, and that I'd regret holding him up, and it was only after I explained why he couldn't go down there that he finally drove off, sir.'

'Explained, Dandridge?' Ormside raked the man with a look. His voice was ominously low as he asked the next question. 'Just what do you mean by "explained"?'

Dandridge shifted uncomfortably in his seat. 'Well ... That there was a murder investigation in progress, like,' he stammered. The constable knew he was in trouble but the penny hadn't dropped as yet.

Ormside shook his head despairingly. 'You told him there was a murder investigation in progress,' he said, 'and suddenly he changes his mind about having to get down Farrow Lane, and drives off.' Ormside's voice sank even lower. 'You didn't by any chance tell him the name of the person killed, did you, Dandridge?'

'Well, I . . .' Colour flooded into the constable's face and he ran a finger round the inside of a tightening collar. 'I – I might have done, Sarge,' he said weakly. He turned to Paget. 'I was just trying to make him understand, sir,' he said desperately.

Paget sighed. There was nothing to be gained by berating the man now. Better to salvage whatever they could. 'What was Gresham's reaction when you told him the name of the victim?' he asked.

Dandridge glanced down at his notebook, decided it wasn't going to help him, and put it away. 'He looked . . . sort of, well, sort of stunned, sir,' he said slowly.

'He wasn't the only bloody one,' Ormside muttered. He cocked an eye at Paget, but the chief inspector shook his head. 'All right, Dandridge,' he said brusquely. 'Make a full report. Include everything you've told us here, and let Sergeant Nolan have a copy. I'll be having a word with him myself,' he added ominously. 'Now, get out there and do something useful for a change; you've wasted enough time for one day. You can make it up by working an extra hour tonight. But –' Ormside raised a warning finger – 'I'd better not see your name on the overtime sheet tomorrow, m'lad, or I'll have you. Got it?'

'Yes, Sarge.' The constable avoided Paget's eyes as he turned and made for the door on the double.

'God! but you're a tyrant, Len,' said Paget as Dandridge left the room. 'That lad was quaking in his boots.'

'And so he should be!' Ormside growled. 'Put a bit of ginger up his arse, perhaps he'll remember to keep his mouth shut in future.'

Sylvia Brown was a slim, energetic woman of about twenty-five. She lived with her husband and two daughters in a semi-detached house in Valencia Crescent. The crescent was in one of the new housing estates that had mushroomed on the edge of Broadminster in the early 'eighties – and all but died a few years later.

Mrs Brown was in the middle of baking scones when Paget arrived. 'I hope you don't mind if I carry on,' she said as she led him through to the kitchen, 'but I must get these done so I can get on with Trevor's dinner. He's a teacher at the school across the way,' she explained. 'He comes home for his dinner every day.'

She brushed a straying strand of hair away from her face with the back of a floury hand. 'I'm sorry, but I'm not quite sure what it was you wanted,' she said. 'Something to do with Claude Gresham, wasn't it?'

'That's right,' Paget said. 'Although it has more to do with his son, actually.'

'Arthur?' A frown of disapproval crossed her face.

'That's right. I'm told that he visits his father quite regularly, and that he was there last Monday evening. Do you recall seeing him there that night?'

Sylvia began to work the dough gently with her fingers. 'Last Monday,' she said ruminatively. 'No, he wasn't there last Monday; at least I didn't see him. Mind you, that's not surprising. He usually makes sure he's gone before I get there.'

'Oh? Why is that, Mrs Brown?'

Sylvia Brown wrinkled her nose. 'Let's just say we don't get along.'

'May I ask why?'

Sylvia picked up a cutter and began to lift rounds from the pastry and place them on a metal tray. 'He can't keep his hands to himself,' she said without looking up. 'Takes after his father. Claude is just as bad but he's barely mobile, so he's not a problem. But Arthur . . . Take a look at his left hand the next time you see him. You'll see four little marks just above the knuckles. He made the mistake of trying it on when I was setting out Claude's tray. He was lucky I only had a fork in my hand at the time. I told him if he ever tried it on again it would be his balls.'

A grim smile tugged at the corners of her mouth as she glanced at Paget. 'Haven't seen much of him since then.'

Paget couldn't help but return the smile. 'So you didn't see him at all that night?'

'No, and I was in and out of the room several times from about seven thirty on. Claude was there, sleeping in his chair, but I didn't see Arthur.'

'Claude seems to think his son came about seven,' Paget prompted.

Sylvia nodded. 'Yes, if he was there at all that night, that would be about right. He never stays long. Sometimes no more than a few minutes. I think that's why Arthur reads to his father. Claude nods off after ten or fifteen minutes, and he quite often doesn't wake up until it's time to go to bed.'

'When is that?'

'I start getting them into their beds by eight fifteen,' Sylvia said. 'By the time they are all settled down it's usually between nine fifteen and nine thirty.' She grinned. 'They're worse than kids, some of them, wanting this and wanting that just so they don't have to put out the light.'

Sylvia Brown picked up the cutter again and began to lift more rounds. 'Funny, really,' she mused. 'He comes two or three times a week, and yet he's always looking at his watch as if he can't wait to be gone. Sometimes I wonder why he comes at all.'

Which was exactly what Paget wondered as he drove back into town.

Ivor Trent confirmed that he had met Arthur Gresham in the Three Crowns the previous Monday evening. Trent was a short, stubby man with a florid face and bulging midriff. 'He wanted to talk to me about a proposal the cricket club will be putting forward to enlarge their club house,' he said. 'All perfectly above-board,' he added defensively.

'I'm sure it was,' said Paget, and wondered why Trent was so defensive. 'Do you recall what time it was when Mr Gresham arrived?'

'A few minutes after nine. I got there spot on nine, and he came in a few minutes later. Arthur had suggested ten, originally, but I had another appointment later on, so he agreed to nine o'clock.'

'So he arrived about five or ten minutes past nine? You're quite sure about the time?'

'Quite sure.'

'I see. And how did he seem when he arrived?'

'Funny you should ask that,' said Trent. 'He seemed a bit upset. In fact I got the impression that his mind wasn't really on our discussion at all. Which was why I suggested we meet again the following morning in my office. As I said, I had another appointment and had to leave by twenty to ten.'

'So you met again next morning?'

'Actually, no. Arthur rang me at home later that night and cancelled. We met later in the week.'

Although Paget questioned Trent closely, he couldn't shake him on the time Gresham had arrived. So where had Gresham been between the time he left his father shortly after seven, and ten past nine?

And what was he doing at Farrow Lane the following morning, when he'd told his wife he had a meeting to attend? A meeting that his secretary knew nothing about.

Returning to his office, Paget found a note from Ormside waiting for him. He picked up the phone and rang the sergeant's desk.

'We've traced Beecham's movements for a good part of the time after he left the bank,' Ormside said. 'He appears to have made a round of the country pubs south of here, drinking whisky everywhere he went. The last one was the Waddling Duck at Cricklade. He was drinking doubles there.'

Cricklade was a small village about a mile from Broadminster's southern boundary, and no more than a few minutes away from Farrow Lane.

'Did he talk to anyone? Utter threats? Anything like that?'

'Apparently not. Just sat off in a corner and drank steadily wherever he went. The landlord of the Waddling Duck says he didn't see Beecham go, but he thinks it was somewhere around eight.'

It didn't help. The case against Beecham still hinged on Rudge's testimony, and even the greenest of briefs could blow that away without half trying.

'I hate to say it, but I think Harry Beecham was right about one thing,' said Paget. 'Beth Smallwood paid a very high price for her promotion. I think Gresham either raped her, or left her with so little choice that she was forced to submit.'

Paget sipped his coffee without really tasting it. He and Tregalles had retired to the relative quiet of Paget's office to review what they had.

'Knowing what we do now, that Beth was embezzling money, she might well have agreed to anything to avoid exposure,' Paget continued. 'But let's suppose for a moment that Gresham had reason to believe that Beth had had a change of heart and intended to lay a complaint against him. Wouldn't his reaction be to try to stop her?'

'But why would Beth Smallwood submit to him in the office in the afternoon, then change her mind later on?' Tregalles asked reasonably. 'Even assuming that she did – and I think that's a hell of a big assumption – how would Gresham know that? And how would he know that she'd be in the church? She didn't know herself until the vicar rang her.'

'But we do know that she rang Nancy King to say she wanted to come in and set the record straight about her testimony in Lenny's court case,' said Paget. 'What if she mentioned that to Rachel, and Rachel got it wrong? She had difficulty understanding Beth, if you remember. If I'm right, Beth had suffered badly at the hands of Gresham in the office and she'd been knocked about by Lenny when she got home. She had been physically and mentally battered throughout the day, and even without a swollen tongue, I doubt if she'd be all that coherent. What if Rachel thought Beth meant she was going to the police to tell them about what had happened in Gresham's office that afternoon, and Rachel passed it on to Gresham?'

Tregalles thought about that. 'That not only assumes that Rachel knew what had happened in the office,' he said slowly, 'but implies some sort of complicity if she informed Gresham of what she thought Beth was about to do.'

'Not necessarily. What if Beth told Rachel that she wouldn't be in to work because she was . . . oh, let's say: "going to the police station in the morning to tell them everything," for example. It may not have made any sense to Rachel, but it might have scared the hell out of Gresham if she told him.'

'But she said she didn't ring Gresham that night, and Mrs Gresham confirmed that,' Tregalles objected. 'And she didn't have a chance to talk to him next morning because you were there before Gresham arrived.'

'Perhaps she didn't have to,' said Paget quietly. 'Perhaps Gresham was with Rachel when Beth rang.'

CHAPTER 27

It had been a long and difficult day, and Andrea McMillan was looking forward to going home. Hands thrust deep inside the pockets of her white coat, she made her way along the corridor toward the desk.

She was almost past the door to Lenny Smallwood's room before she realized that it was closed. Strange. She grasped the handle and pushed the door open.

Lenny was half out of bed, leaning down toward a girl, hands to his face, covering his nose. The girl was holding something in cupped hands. Like an offering, thought Andrea. Both Lenny and the girl looked startled.

Andrea moved forward swiftly as she realized what was happening. The girl shrank back, but Lenny reached out and snatched something from her lap and began cramming it into his mouth. Andrea grasped his wrist, but he pulled away, face buried in his hands, snuffling, rooting like a pig as he gulped the substance down. White powder flew everywhere.

'Bitch!' Lenny screamed as he lunged upward and grasped her by the throat. Andrea twisted away, slipped and fell across the girl. She tried to get up, but Lenny was out of bed, astride her back, fingers digging into her throat. She couldn't breathe, couldn't cry out...

The girl wrenched herself free and scrambled to her feet. Lenny's fingers dug in deeper, pulling Andrea's head back until she thought her neck would snap. From the corner of her eye, she saw the girl reach for the water jug beside the bed. She felt the splash of water on her face, then nothing.

'Haversall, here, sir. There's been an incident at the hospital involving Lenny Smallwood, sir. The duty sergeant instructed me to call you. It seems a doctor found a girl in Smallwood's room. She was giving him cocaine, and when the doctor tried to stop her there was a scuffle and the doctor was knocked unconscious. They're searching for the girl now, but so far they've...'

'The doctor?' Paget broke in. 'What was the name of the doctor?' He gripped the phone, fearful of the answer.

'The name, sir? Just a moment. Yes, here it is. Dr McMillan. Apparently she...'

Haversall looked startled as the line went dead. 'Well thank you very much, *sir!*' she muttered indignantly as she too hung up.

Normally, it took twenty minutes to drive from his home in Ashton Prior to the centre of Broadminster, but Paget made it to the hospital in thirteen minutes flat. He dashed up the steps and ran headlong into a cluster of police and hospital security staff.

'Fourth floor, sir,' said one of the men in answer to Paget's enquiry. 'Would you like me to...?'

But Paget was gone.

He ran into more hospital security people as he stepped out of the lift on the fourth floor, but his eyes went immediately to Andrea, who was sitting in a wheelchair beside the work station desk, a blanket draped around her shoulders. Her eyes were closed and her face was almost as white as the bulky dressing covering the left side of her head.

A nurse hovered over her. She said something Paget could not hear, but Andrea waved her away without opening her eyes.

The sight of Andrea in pain chilled him to the core. What the devil were they thinking about? She ought to be in bed! He moved swiftly to her side.

'Andrea, I... Are you all right?'

Of course she's not all right, you idiot! Why was it, he thought desperately, that he could never seem to find the right words when he was near this woman?

Her eyes opened in surprise. She tilted her head to look up at him, and winced. 'Neil...' she said, and stopped. He could see bruises on her throat.

'Don't try to talk,' he told her swiftly. 'You ought to be in bed.' He glanced accusingly at the nurse.

'Don't tell me, tell Dr McMillan,' the woman bridled. 'God knows we've tried.'

'I'm all right,' Andrea insisted hoarsely, but the weariness in her voice belied her words. 'Besides, I have to get home.'

'You'll do no such thing,' a voice boomed beside Paget's ear. 'Take her down to 428, Nurse, and don't listen to anything she says to the contrary. Understand?'

'Yes, Mr Stone.'

'But Sarah...'

'Sarah will be well taken care of by your Mrs Ansell,' Stone said flatly. 'I'll telephone her myself. Now get on with it, Nurse.' He turned and glared at Paget through steel-rimmed glasses as if expecting an argument from him.

Paget watched as Andrea was wheeled away. He wished he could go with her, but at least he felt better now that someone was insisting that she receive the attention she deserved.

He introduced himself to Stone. The consultant was a big man, heavily built, and taller than Paget by a couple of inches. He wore his hair long, and his plump face was almost lost in a mass of straggling whiskers.

'Ah! Paget. Yes. Andrea spoke of you,' he said. 'The Smallwood boy. Mother murdered. Read about it last week. Well, he's done it now. Don't know what the stupid little bugger thought he was trying to achieve, stuffing himself with cocaine like that. He'll be lucky if he lives. Swallowed the lot, packets and all, and they could do some *real* damage.'

'But what about Andrea? How badly is she hurt?'

Stone eyed him curiously. 'She'll be fine after a good night's rest,' he said. 'We'll keep an eye on her for any after-effects from the head injury, but there is no indication at present that there will be. Throat will be sore as hell, of course, but no permanent damage.'

'Tell me what happened,' said Paget.

Stone shrugged. 'Your people can probably tell you more than I can,' he said, 'but I gather she walked into Smallwood's room and caught some girl feeding him cocaine. When he saw Andrea, he started shoving everything into his mouth. She tried to stop him, and that's when he attacked her. Andrea remembers Smallwood trying to choke her, and she saw the girl pick up the jug, but she can't remember anything after that.'

'And Smallwood?'

'Hard to say. They're working on him now. Apart from anything else, he seems to have done himself some internal damage when he jumped out of bed, so it's impossible at this stage to say what they'll find.'

'What about the girl?' No one had mentioned a name, but Paget was prepared to bet the girl was Tania Costello.

'No idea. She seems to have vanished. I heard one of your chaps say he thought she'd escaped on a moped.'

The light was fading in room 428, and Andrea McMillan felt that she was fading with it. The throbbing in her head seemed to be subsiding, although her throat still felt as if it were on fire, and it was agony to swallow.

But as shadows deepened in the room, she recalled the anguish in Neil Paget's face as he'd looked at her tonight. It was as if he were sharing in her pain, and she knew that he had come because of her; not because of Lenny; not because a crime had been committed, but because of her and her alone.

Tuesday – 21 May

Despite the best efforts of the doctors, Lenny Smallwood died at 4.32 a.m. No one knew how much cocaine he'd stuffed into his mouth – just that it was a lot, and there was little they could do. And that, together with his other injuries – made worse by his diving out of bed – had finished him.

Sergeant Ormside gave Paget the news when he arrived that morning. 'I don't think there's any doubt that the girl was Tania Costello,' he said. 'The description fits.'

Paget grunted. 'Better make sure that Mrs McLeish is informed,' he said. 'Poor woman came down for one funeral and now she has two.'

'Right, sir.' Ormside picked up a report and handed it to Paget. 'It looks as if your instincts were right,' he said. 'It seems that Miss Fairmont has a gentleman-friend who visits her regularly two or three nights a week.' He grinned crookedly. 'Descriptions vary, depending on who you talk to, but most of them agree the man is middle-aged, and he drives a Rover – a dark red Rover – which he parks in the next street beside a butcher's shop. We haven't found anyone who can confirm the car was parked there last Monday evening, but chances are we will if we keep at it.'

Paget skimmed through the notes and nodded with satisfaction. 'Rachel Fairmont is a good-looking woman,' he observed. 'I couldn't see Gresham keeping his hands off her for long. But she plays her part well at work. Not one of the girls I questioned even suggested that there was anything going on between them.

'Which accounts for how he knew about Beth Smallwood's call to Rachel. He was there with her in her flat when Beth rang. He visited his father for a few minutes earlier in the evening, then went on to the flat. Now we know why he has been visiting his father so regularly. He uses that as an excuse to visit Rachel.

'If Beth did mention going to the police,' he continued, 'and Rachel told Gresham what she'd said, he was almost bound to draw the wrong conclusion. He would have insisted on Rachel telling him everything that Beth had said, so he would know that

Beth would be alone in the church. He had more than enough time to drive over there to try to dissuade her or try to buy her off. What happened then is anyone's guess. Perhaps Beth did try to explain but he didn't give her a chance.

'And when Gresham arrived at the pub that night, he was so preoccupied that Trent suggested they meet again the following day.'

Paget handed the notes back to Ormside. 'But it's all conjecture at the moment, isn't it? What we need is proof. I think it's time we had another talk with Gresham and Miss Fairmont.'

'We'll walk,' said Paget as he and Tregalles left the building. 'Fresh air will do us good. Besides, parking is impossible over there.'

He needed to walk; needed to get rid of some of the tension. He'd spent at least half the night lying awake thinking and worrying about Andrea. He wished he could have done more, but comforted himself with the thought that she was in capable hands.

He'd left the house half an hour early and gone straight to the hospital before coming in to work, but Andrea was not in her room. She'd been taken down for 'tests', whatever that might mean. When he tried to press for details, the staff nurse took pity on him.

'Believe me, Chief Inspector, there's no need to worry,' she assured him. 'It's simply routine work. Dr McMillan will be back to work in a couple of days, I'm sure. But I'll let her know you were here when she returns to this floor.'

It seemed to Paget that Rachel Fairmont looked apprehensive as he and Tregalles approached her. She smiled mechanically, and after checking with Gresham via the intercom, ushered them into his office before retreating to her own desk.

Arthur Gresham was at his most affable. He came forward to greet them, and waited until they were seated before returning to his own chair.

'This is a coincidence,' he told them. 'I was just about to ring you, Chief Inspector.' He removed his glasses and began to polish them. 'Miss Fairmont told me yesterday that you had been to see her. She said you were puzzled by the fact that I knew about Beth Smallwood's call to her on that tragic evening. I meant to call you yesterday to clear the matter up, but I'm afraid I became busy and it slipped my mind.'

Paget doubted that, but decided to remain silent and listen to what Gresham had to say. The man might hang himself yet.

Gresham pursed his lips and moistened them. 'To tell you the truth,' he said in a confidential tone, 'Miss Fairmont is more than a little embarrassed about it. It's not like her at all. I think it must have been the shock of hearing about poor Beth that drove it completely out of her mind. You see, she simply forgot about my call to her that night. She was extremely upset when I reminded her of it, and as I said, embarrassed.'

'What call was that, sir?'

Gresham slipped his glasses back in place. 'The one I made to her after talking to Ivor Trent in the Three Crowns that night. You see, we'd agreed to have a meeting in his office first thing the following morning, and I rang Miss Fairmont to let her know that I'd be late. It was then that she told me about Beth telephoning to say she wouldn't be in the following day, but as I say, it completely slipped her mind. I'm sorry if it's caused you any inconvenience, Chief Inspector, although, quite frankly, I can't see what it has to do with Beth Smallwood's death.'

Tregalles spoke up. 'But I understand that you cancelled that meeting with Mr Trent,' he said. 'Why was that, sir?'

'Ah! Yes.' Gresham pursed judicial lips once more and clasped plump hands across his stomach, and when he spoke again it was to Paget rather than Tregalles.

'You see, I'm afraid I wasn't quite straight with you the other day, Chief Inspector,' he said apologetically. 'In retrospect, it was foolish of me, I know. But when Miss Fairmont told me about Beth, I was concerned about her. It sounded as if she had taken a nasty tumble, and I wanted to make sure that she was all right. It was getting late and I didn't want to disturb her if she was already in bed, so I decided to go out there first thing the following morning. I rang Trent and explained the situation, and we set up another time.'

'And did you go out the following morning?' Tregalles asked.

Gresham was forced to face him. 'Yes, I did, Sergeant,' he said brusquely, 'but I couldn't get through because the road was cordoned off by your people.'

'I see. And what time was it when you rang Miss Fairmont?'

Gresham frowned his irritation. 'I don't know *exactly*,' he said. 'Ten o'clock or thereabouts, I suppose.'

'And you rang Miss Fairmont from where, sir?'

Gresham snorted. 'Oh, really, Sergeant! Does it matter?'

'We won't know until you tell us, will we, sir?'

Gresham looked to Paget, but found no comfort there. He sighed resignedly. 'There's a public telephone outside the Three Crowns,' he said. 'I rang from there.'

'Thank you, sir.' Tregalles made a note in his notebook. 'You say you found Farrow Lane cordoned off when you tried to go down there on the Tuesday morning. Did anyone tell you why it was blocked off?'

Gresham looked disconcerted, and a slow flush began to rise above his collar. 'Actually, it was mentioned by one of your men at the barrier,' he said, 'but I had no idea that the person who had been attacked was Beth Smallwood.' Gresham turned to Paget and spread his hands. 'I'm sorry I misled you when you came to see me later that morning, Chief Inspector, but I really didn't see any point in mentioning I'd been out there, since it had absolutely nothing to do with your investigation. Now, of course, I see I should have said something, and I do apologize.'

Paget's grunt was non-committal. 'Could we have Miss Fairmont in?' he asked.

Gresham pursed his lips again. 'I do hope you won't be too hard on her, poor girl,' he said. 'She feels terrible about her lapse of memory.'

'I don't think there is any fear of that, sir,' said Paget.

Rachel Fairmont entered the office in the manner of a schoolgirl summoned to the headmaster's office, fearful of the consequences. In a voice barely above a whisper, she verified in every detail what Gresham had just told them about the telephone call to her. 'I simply don't know how it could have gone so completely from my mind, Chief Inspector,' she ended distractedly. 'I should have remembered when you asked me on Sunday, but by then I'm afraid I was so confused . . .' The words seemed to catch in her throat, and she looked as if she might cry.

Paget looked at Gresham. 'Do you have anything to add to that?' he asked.

The manager sat back in his chair, folded his hands over his stomach once more and returned Paget's gaze. 'I think we have covered everything, Chief Inspector,' he said. 'I do apologize again. I hope we haven't caused you too much inconvenience. Now, what was it you wished to see me about?'

Paget rose to his feet and Tregalles followed. 'I believe you have told us what we wanted to know,' he said carefully. 'Of course, I shall need revised statements from you both. Shall we say four o'clock this afternoon at Charter Lane?'

'Ah!' Gresham came out from behind his desk as Tregalles also rose. 'I'm afraid that's a bit awkward,' he said. 'You see, the auditors are presenting their report this afternoon, and a VIP from head office will be here. I have been instructed to attend, and Miss Fairmont will be required to take the minutes. Perhaps tomorrow morning...?'

Paget eyed the manager stonily. He hated to concede anything to this man, but there was nothing to be gained by making an issue over a few hours. 'Very well,' he said. 'Nine o'clock tomorrow morning.'

As they came out into brilliant sunshine, Tregalles blew out his cheeks and shook his head in wonder. 'That's the biggest load of codswallop I've heard in years!' he declared. 'Surely to God Gresham can't think he's going to get away with a story like that? And that secretary of his. She was lying her head off for him.'

'I suspect that Arthur Gresham believes he can get away with anything if he puts his mind to it,' said Paget. He remained silent for a moment. 'But I'm not at all sure about Miss Fairmont. Perhaps we'll find out tomorrow.'

The same staff nurse who had been on duty earlier in the day was still there. 'I told Dr McMillan you were here earlier, Chief Inspector,' she said as Paget approached the desk, 'but I'm afraid you've missed her again. She's been discharged.'

'Discharged? Why? She isn't fit. Who gave...?'

'She discharged herself, Mr Paget,' the nurse said flatly. 'We would have preferred to have her stay another day, but she wanted to get home, and there was no reason for us to keep her here, provided she is careful for the next few days. Her injuries are by no means life-threatening.'

'They looked pretty serious to me,' said Paget bluntly.

The staff nurse's lips settled into a thin line. 'We *do* know what we're doing here,' she said stiffly, 'and so does Dr McMillan. She was given a thorough examination before she left, and I'm quite sure she is capable of looking after herself at home.'

Paget felt chastened, and deservedly so. It was hardly the fault of the nurse that Andrea had insisted on leaving. 'I'm sorry,' he apologized. 'I wasn't criticizing you. It's just that, after seeing Dr McMillan's injuries last night, I was concerned. I just want to make sure that she'll be all right.'

The nurse's face relaxed. 'I'm sure she will be, Mr Paget,' she said soothingly. 'And I think it is very good of you to show so much concern.' A tiny smile tugged at the corner of her mouth as if she found something amusing.

On his way back to the office, Paget took a detour through Market Square. Finding an empty parking slot seemed like a good omen, but still he hesitated. Perhaps it wasn't such a good idea after all. But on the other hand, what was there to lose?

Still not quite convinced he was doing the right thing, he got out of the car and made his way to a small shop on the corner. He hesitated at the door, then grasped the handle firmly and went inside.

CHAPTER 28

Graffiti covered much of the walls and glass of the phone booth outside the Three Crowns. The bottom panels had been kicked out, and the floor was littered with broken glass, cigarette butts, chips, and crumpled newspaper.

Tregalles wiped the telephone earpiece on his sleeve before putting it to his ear. Dead, as he'd suspected.

Inside the pub, the landlord told him that he couldn't remember when the telephone outside had not been like that. 'I used to report it regularly,' he said, 'but even when they did come and see to it, it only stayed mended a couple of days. People are always coming in here asking to use the phone, but if you start that they'll all try it on, so I say no to everyone.'

'What about when you're not here? Might one of the staff let someone use the phone?'

'Not a chance. There's only me and Flo – that's the wife – and Ernie behind the bar of a night, and they know the rules.'

'Any other phones round here?'

'There's one at the bottom of the hill outside the post office, but that's out of order half the time as well.'

The local BT service supervisor admitted, reluctantly, that he had all but given up on the phone outside the Three Crowns. Yes, according to his records it had been out of order now for almost three weeks. 'It's a waste of time and money,' he insisted. 'It only lasts a couple of days at most if we do repair it, and we have more pressing priorities. Sorry, but that's the way it is.'

To his surprise, Tregalles seemed pleased. 'I think my DCI will like that,' he told the man. 'In fact I'm sure he will.'

Sandra Chandler looked thoughtful as she glanced at the clock. She gathered up her notes and put them in the drawer of her desk and locked it. She had promised to meet a colleague for lunch, but there was still time to pop in to see Helen Beecham on the way. Even a few minutes together could help to strengthen the bond between them; help build that fragile bridge of trust.

They'd already started serving meals down on C Ward, and she had to edge her way past several trolleys as she made her way down the corridor. The double doors were open. They shouldn't have been, of course. They were supposed to be closed and attended at all times to comply with safety regulations, but it was almost impossible to manoeuvre the unwieldy trolleys back and forth at mealtimes without propping the doors open.

Deep in thought, Sandra Chandler was almost past the couple coming toward her before she realized that one of them was Helen Beecham. Her head was turned away, and a bony hand clutched claw-like at her dressing-gown, holding it tightly at the throat. Shuffling along in open slippers, she leaned heavily on the arm of the man beside her.

'Helen?' said Sandra gently. 'Where are you going?'

Helen Beecham's only response was to bury her head deeper into the shoulder of her companion. He was a small man; grey hair, small moustache, sallow skin.

'And you are...?' she asked pleasantly.

'I'm her brother,' the man said. 'I came as soon as I heard. I couldn't believe it...I mean I had no idea. We're just going for a little walk while we talk. I do have her doctor's permission.'

'Do you really? That's odd; I don't recall giving it.'

Alarm flared in his eyes, swiftly replaced by a shrug of apology. 'I'm sorry,' he said. 'I was under the impression that the person I spoke to was Helen's doctor. I must have been mistaken.'

Sandra planted herself in front of him. 'You're damned right you were mistaken,' she said softly. 'Now let go of Helen's arm. You're not going anywhere – Mr Beecham.'

Sandra Chandler had no fear of the man, but she was not prepared for what happened next. Face contorted, Harry Beecham pulled free of Helen's grasp and slammed his fist into Sandra's stomach. She gasped and doubled up with pain. A fist smashed into her face, and she felt herself sliding to the floor.

Beecham grabbed his wife's arm and dragged her with him as he made for the door, but the trolleys blocked his way. Behind him, Sandra Chandler struggled to regain her breath. She tried to call out but no sound would come.

A trolley crashed into the wall, spilling trays and dinners across the floor. Helen stumbled and fell amidst the food and broken crockery, but Beecham pulled her to her feet and charged ahead. A nurse came running down the hall, but Beecham shoved her out of the way and ploughed on.

'Please! Harry, please!' Helen pleaded feebly as she staggered in his wake, but Beecham paid no heed. 'You're coming home,' he grated as he dragged her to a small side door marked 'Exit – For Emergency Use Only'. Raw sunshine made her blink and turn her head away as Beecham dragged her to the car parked beside the door. He opened the rear door and shoved her inside. She sprawled across the seat, then fell to the floor as Beecham jumped in the driver's seat and slammed the car into reverse. The tyres screamed. She could smell the burning rubber.

'We've got the bastard!' Ormside growled.

He greeted Paget with the words as the chief inspector walked through the door of the incident room. The sergeant was itemizing the information from Forensic on a blackboard.

'Beecham,' he elaborated. 'The bloodstains on Beecham's clothing are Group B, the same as Amy Thomson's blood. Beecham is Group O. Now, Forensic warn us in their report that that in itself proves nothing, but they also point out that Group B is not all that common in this country, so it's a step in the right direction. DNA tests will prove conclusively whether they are the same, but that will take quite a bit more time.

'But there's more. Samples of grit taken from the tyres of Beecham's car are identical to those taken at the scene down by the railway sheds. And a metal bar found buried in one of the plant boxes in the greenhouse in Beecham's garden has bloodstains on it. Group B again.

'That,' the sergeant went on, 'ties him to the attack on Amy Thomson, but there's more. Several partial fingerprints and palm prints found in the church have been identified as Beecham's. They were found on the main door of the church and on one of the pews close to the chancel steps. Which,' he concluded, 'ties him to the killing of Beth Smallwood.'

Paget stood before the blackboard and nodded slowly. 'Good work, Len,' he said quietly. 'We'll have him in for questioning.' He glanced at the time. 'Where's Tregalles?'

'I think he's upstairs working on reports,' Ormside said.

'Right. Give him a shout. Tell him to meet me at the car. We'll pick up Beecham now.'

Harry Beecham dragged his protesting wife into the house and locked the door. He cursed when she fell as he tried to drag her up the stairs. 'It's no good pretending that you're ill,' he screamed. 'Bone bloody idle, that's your trouble. Get up! Move, you useless cow!'

Helen Beecham struggled to her feet. She'd lost her slippers when she'd fallen at the hospital. Dully, she saw one foot was bleeding where she'd gashed it on the broken crockery. Harry was screaming at her again. She moaned as he pulled her up the stairs. Her arm felt as if it were being torn from its socket.

He literally hurled her into the bedroom, then slammed the door behind her. She heard the key turn in the lock as she sank exhausted to the floor and closed her eyes. She wanted only to be left alone; left alone to die.

Downstairs once more, Harry Beecham sat on the bottom step, panting hard. He'd shown them, he thought triumphantly. They couldn't take *his* wife away from him. She was *his* property; *his* to do with as he wished. No one had the right to interfere with what went on in a man's own home. No one!

It was all Gresham's fault, he told himself bitterly. If it hadn't been for that sex-crazed bastard, everything would have been all right. Beth should have been the one to leave the bank, by rights, not him. She wasn't capable of doing the job. Not his job. It was a man's job; always had been; always would be. She'd have made a right balls of it. Besides, she was supposed to have been his friend. Some bloody friend she turned out to be! As soon as Gresham had offered her the job, she'd jumped at it – or let Gresham jump on her.

Beecham snickered at the thought. Fat lot of good it had done her. Look where she was now. He was glad she was dead. He felt again the excitement, the rush of adrenalin as he'd looked down on her staring eyes and watched the blood oozing from her head. Served her right!

Women! they were all the same. Couldn't trust them. Let you down every time. His first wife, Esther, had been the same. Wanted to go back to work, to help them get ahead, she'd said. But he knew what she was up to. He wasn't born yesterday. She'd get ahead all right. Get ahead of him! She'd have her own money and start telling *him* how things should be. Well, look what happened to *her!* He'd tamed her! He'd shown her who was boss.

She'd tried to pretend that she was sick as well; too sick to keep the house as she should; too sick to get his meals; too sick...He snorted in disgust.

He saw her in his mind's eye, standing there clinging to the newel post at the top of the stairs, making those awful mewling sounds. The very sight of her had sickened him. All it had taken was a slight push.

He'd thought Helen would be better. Quiet, submissive, plain. She'd know her place. He'd expected her to give up all that nonsense about painting when they were married – or at least keep it to a nice little hobby that wouldn't interfere with her wifely duties. But, oh, no. She wanted to 'express' herself; be creative; sell her paintings. She wanted to be better then he was; show him up.

Beecham smirked. Well, he'd soon put a stop to *that* little scheme! He'd shown *her* where her duty lay.

196

He became aware of the sound of cars pulling up outside. Doors slammed, and someone shouted. He darted into the front room and lifted the edge of the lace curtain.

Police! Grim-faced; determined. How...?

He dropped the curtain as if it were hot and backed away from the window. He saw shadows flitting past as men ran round the side of the house, and suddenly he was bathed in sweat.

'Police! Open the door!' Fists were pounding on the door.

He went cold. Bile rose like acid in his throat, choking him, suffocating him. He ran into the hall. Now fists were hammering on the back door as well. He put his hands over his ears, but he couldn't shut out the sound. He heard a crash. They'd smashed the glass in the back door; they'd be in the house in seconds.

He went up the stairs, whimpering and scrambling on all fours as he slipped and scraped his shins. The whole house seemed to shake as a burly shoulder crashed into the door below. Sweat and tears ran down his face. His vision blurred. His foot caught on the top step and he sprawled across the landing.

He regained his feet and staggered to an open door. Behind him he heard the splintering crash as the front door caved in. Booted feet thundered in the hall below. Someone shouted, 'Check upstairs!'

He slammed the door and turned the key.

CHAPTER 29

Paget knocked and entered, closing the door behind him.

Superintendent Alcott was standing at the window, hands clasped behind his back as he looked out across the playing fields. The ever-present cigarette burned between his fingers.

Paget waited.

'Messy,' Alcott said without turning round. 'Could it have been prevented?'

'No.' Paget was emphatic. 'We were actually on our way to pick him up when the call came through from the hospital that Beecham had abducted his wife. Three cars responded, and we all arrived at the house more or less at the same time. It took us less than two minutes to break in, but we were too late. By the time we'd kicked in the bathroom door, Beecham was dead. Throat cut from ear to ear.'

'And Mrs Beecham?'

'We found her locked in a bedroom. She's back in hospital now.'

Alcott left the window and took his seat behind the desk. 'I don't know,' he sighed. 'I've been in this business for almost thirty years, and I still find it hard to believe some of the things that people do to each other. I suppose he was mad?'

Paget sat down himself. 'I don't think he was,' he said, 'at least, not in the sense that he didn't know right from wrong. I think Beecham knew exactly what he was doing, and he went to great pains to hide his actions from the outside world. He was very clever, and he was looked upon with a great deal of sympathy by his co-workers for looking after his "sick wife" with such fortitude.'

Alcott grimaced his distaste. 'Give me a detailed report as soon as you can,' he said. 'The press officer needs a summary, and I suppose I'd better brief Mr Brock myself. He feels that a senior officer should be present when the announcement is made that a major crime has been resolved.'

'Resolved, sir?' Paget looked dubious. 'Don't you think it might be a bit premature?'

Alcott eyed Paget narrowly through the smoke. 'What are you trying to tell me?' he demanded roughly. 'That Harry Beecham is *not* guilty?'

Paget shook his head. 'No. I don't think there is the slightest doubt that he is guilty of the assault on Amy Thomson, and of holding his wife a virtual prisoner, but I would like more time to study the evidence against Beecham in the matter of Beth Smallwood's death. Much of the evidence we have is purely circumstantial, and I hesitate to attribute everything to Harry Beecham until Forensic have completed their tests. In my view, it would be better to delay that announcement for a day or two rather than take the chance of having to retract it later.'

Alcott shook his head impatiently. 'Good God, man, what more do we need?' he demanded. 'We have Beecham's palm and finger-prints in the church; we have Rudge's testimony that he saw Beecham running from the scene; we have motive – Beecham him-self told you that he wanted to confront Beth Smallwood because he was convinced that she had sold herself to Gresham in order to get his job – not that we need to offer that as evidence since it was only speculation on Beecham's part; and this Mrs whatever-her-name from next door says Beecham was pounding on Smallwood's door, and she told him where Beth was.'

Alcott leaned back and glowered at Paget.

The chief inspector nodded slowly. 'I agree,' he said simply. 'We do have all those things, but none of them prove conclusively that Beecham actually killed Beth Smallwood. It can be argued equally well that Beth Smallwood was dead when Beecham got there, and that his subsequent actions were those of a man who realized how incriminating it would look if he were found there, and he simply panicked and ran.'

'And the blackmail?' Alcott demanded. 'Why did he respond to Rudge's attempt to blackmail him if he didn't kill Beth Smallwood? And he didn't hesitate to try to kill young Amy.'

'Same argument,' said Paget. 'Beecham couldn't afford to let it be known that he had been in the church that night.'

Alcott suddenly rose to his feet. 'You've still got this bee in your bonnet about Gresham, haven't you?' he accused.

'If not being satisfied with some of the things Gresham has told us, then, yes, I do have a "bee in my bonnet" as you put it, sir,' said Paget evenly. 'The man is lying to us, and his explanation of how he knew Beth Smallwood would not be coming in on Tuesday morning is ludicrous. Not only that, but he has his secretary, with whom he's having an affair, lying to us as well.'

Paget, too, rose to his feet. 'Look, sir,' he said earnestly, 'all I'm asking for is a little more time to follow this up. I don't know whether Gresham had anything to do with Beth Smallwood's death or not, but I do know that if we simply lay the blame at Beecham's door and let it go at that, we could well be letting a murderer go free.'

Alcott turned his back on Paget and stared out across the playing fields. Chief Superintendent Brock wasn't going to like this. As far as he was concerned, the case was in the bag, and no doubt he was already preening himself for his appearance before the cameras. On the other hand, it might be the lesser of two evils to risk the man's displeasure now rather than drop him in deep shit later.

Alcott sucked deeply on his cigarette. Past experience had taught him to listen when Paget advised caution, but could he convince Brock of that? Perhaps, if he held back the information about Beecham's prints having been identified in the church...

He turned to face Paget and eyed the chief inspector gravely. 'Very well,' he growled, 'but I want this resolved one way or another within the next couple of days, understand?'

Paget breathed easier. He didn't like the time frame, but he wasn't about to argue the point with Alcott. 'Understood, sir,' he said – and departed quickly before Alcott could change his mind.

The telephone was ringing as Paget entered his office. 'There's a Miss Fairmont asking to see you, sir,' the duty officer told him when he answered. 'Shall I have someone bring her up?'

Rachel Fairmont? That was odd. Wasn't she supposed to be taking the minutes of the meeting at the bank this afternoon? 'Is anyone with her?' he asked.

'No, sir.'

'Right, then. Give me five minutes, then send her up.'

Paget rang the incident room and asked for Tregalles. 'Rachel Fairmont will be in my office in the next few minutes,' he told the sergeant. 'I'd like you to sit in; we may need notes.'

Rachel Fairmont and Tregalles arrived at the same time. While Paget directed her to a comfortable seat in front of the desk, Tregalles settled himself unobtrusively just inside the door. Paget took his own seat behind the desk and looked enquiringly at Rachel.

'I was under the impression that you would be in a meeting this afternoon,' he said, glancing at the clock.

Rachel moistened her lips. Her fingers gripped the handbag in her lap as if she feared someone might snatch it from her.

'I – I should be,' she said nervously, 'but I told Mr Gresham I wasn't feeling very well. I said I wanted to go home. I didn't like to lie to him, but I thought he might try to stop me coming if I told him the truth.'

'I see. And why would he do that?'

'It's just that...' Rachel hesitated, then lowered her chin as if steeling herself. 'I'm afraid I lied to you this morning,' she burst out. 'I'm sorry. I know I shouldn't have. I could see you didn't believe me. I told Mr Gresham that you hadn't believed either of us, but he said it would be all right if we...'

She stopped abruptly and caught her lower lip between her teeth.

'Just take your time,' Paget advised. 'You say you lied. I take it you mean you lied about the phone call you are supposed to have received from Mr Gresham on the night Beth Smallwood was killed?'

Rachel nodded vigorously. 'Yes.'

'There was no such call?'

'No.'

'But Mr Gresham knew about Mrs Smallwood's call to you?'

Rachel hesitated. 'Yes,' she said in a barely audible voice.

'Because he was with you when she rang?'

The woman's eyes widened, but she nodded slowly. 'Yes.'

'In fact, Miss Fairmont, you and Arthur Gresham are lovers. Is that not true?'

Rachel must have guessed it was coming, but even so, she flinched at the word. She looked down at her hands. 'Yes,' she said softly. She seemed relieved now that her secret was out in the open. 'I know it was wrong to lie to you, but I did it for Arthur's sake. He was afraid. His job at the bank; his wife – he hasn't told her about us yet. It's difficult. We don't want to hurt Lilian any more than we have to – it's not her fault that we fell in love – so he's waiting for the right time. You see, we intend to be married.'

Rachel's fingers kneaded her handbag as she looked imploringly at Paget. 'None of this has to come out, does it?' she asked anxiously. 'Now that I've told you the truth. I mean, it has nothing to do with what happened.'

Paget eyed Rachel speculatively. 'Tell me everything Beth Smallwood told you on the telephone the night she was killed?' he said.

Rachel frowned. 'I've told you...' she began, but Paget stopped her.

'You told me only what you wanted me to hear,' he said. 'Each time I asked you about that conversation, you were evasive, Miss Fairmont. If you expect me to co-operate with you, I must have the truth. What else did Beth say when she rang?'

Rachel gnawed at her lip once more, then looked at Paget with pleading eyes. 'I didn't mean to mislead you, Chief Inspector,' she said earnestly. 'It's just that what she said didn't make any sense, and Arthur said there was no point in mentioning it to you because it would only lead to confusion. He said he'd have to talk to Beth to find out what it was all about.'

'When was he going to do that?'

'I don't know. He didn't say.'

'Then I come back to the question, Miss Fairmont: what did Beth tell you on the phone that night?'

Rachel lowered her eyes. 'It wasn't the doctor she was going to see in the morning. It was the police,' she said huskily.

Paget flicked a glance at Tregalles. Now they were coming to it. Mrs Turvey had said that Beth Smallwood had spoken to her about going to the police, and Nancy King had told them that she'd set up an appointment with Beth for nine o'clock Tuesday morning.

'The police?' he said as if surprised. 'Did she say why?'

'It was all so muddled. It was hard to understand her because of her swollen tongue. What I *think* she said was that she had made an appointment to see the police the next day, and she was going to tell them everything. She said she would have gone to see them that night but she had to go to the church. Something about a wedding. I didn't understand that part. And she said she didn't care what happened to her.

'In retrospect, I suppose she must have been talking about her embezzling the money from the bank, but at the time it didn't make any sense to me or to Arthur. Neither of us could think why Beth would want to talk to the police. Arthur was very upset about it.'

Rachel leaned forward earnestly. 'You see, Arthur is very sensitive about anything that might reflect badly on the bank, so he was anxious to talk to Beth as soon as possible to find out what sort of trouble she was in. Talk of the police disturbed him.'

'I see. Did you get the impression he meant to speak to her that evening?'

'Oh, no. I'm sure he didn't mean that. Well, he couldn't very well, could he? At least, not immediately. Not without letting Beth know that he was with me, and we didn't want anyone to know that.' She shot him a quizzical look. 'How did *you* know?' she asked curiously. 'About us, I mean?'

'I couldn't help wondering why Gresham acted so formally with you,' Paget told her. 'And after seeing you at home, I wondered why you dress the way you do at the office. I thought at first that it was to avoid Gresham's advances, considering his reputation in the office, but your reaction when I mentioned that made me wonder all the more. A few discreet enquiries confirmed my suspicions, and I realized you must have been together when Beth rang that night.'

Rachel's eyes flashed. 'That's not true!' she flared. 'About Arthur, I mean. He ... It's just his way. He's a very tactile person. Sometimes he might put his arm round someone's shoulder or touch them on the arm, but it doesn't *mean* anything.'

Paget ignored the outburst. 'Why do you think Beth Smallwood was in such a state when she left the office that Monday afternoon?' he asked.

'She was excited about the prospects of her new job, I expect. Why? What does that have to do with anything?'

Paget took out a notebook and flipped through the pages. ' "It was a bit embarrassing, really," ' he quoted. ' "She kept apologizing for the way she looked and for being so silly . . . she dropped her handbag and spilled everything on the floor." That was what you told me, Miss Fairmont, and another employee described Beth's face as "all puffy and white . . . she'd been crying and I thought she was ill." And the bus driver said, "I thought she was ill and she'd been crying." ' '

He closed the notebook. 'How long had she been out of Mr Gresham's office when you saw her in that state, Miss Fairmont?'

'Half an hour; perhaps a little more,' she said stiffly.

Paget eyed the secretary speculatively for several seconds. 'Half an hour,' he repeated. 'And still in a state of great agitation over what amounted to a relatively small promotion.

'I'm sorry, but I'm afraid I don't buy that,' he went on. 'What you have described sounds more like the reaction of someone who has suffered an extremely traumatic experience. And we know that Beth Smallwood *did* suffer such an experience that afternoon. We know it from the medical evidence; we know it from the bruises on Beth Smallwood's body. We know it from the condition of her clothing. What you have described seems far more consistent with *that* explanation than it does with the reaction of someone who has just been promoted.'

Rachel had gone very pale, and her teeth pressed hard against her lower lip.

Paget eyed the woman dispassionately. 'You were there outside Gresham's office, Miss Fairmont,' he said. 'You must have some idea what happened to Beth Smallwood in there.'

Rachel Fairmont closed her eyes tightly and shook her head. 'No! I won't listen to this,' she whispered. 'Arthur would never . . . Beth was just . . . She was surprised, that's all. She told me she almost fainted when she heard the news.'

'Why do *you* think Beth Smallwood was promoted, Miss Fairmont?'

Rachel tilted her head defiantly. 'Because,' she said, 'as Arthur explained to me, he had no choice. He was forced to cut staff, and it was "suggested" by head office that he cut senior staff rather than junior staff in order to save more money. It would have made more sense to let Beth go rather than Harry, but as I say, he had no choice. He didn't do it because he *wanted* to do it; he did it because he *had* to do it.'

'And you knew nothing of this beforehand?'

'No. Arthur called me into his office after Beth left, and asked me to take a memo announcing Harry Beecham's leaving and Beth's appointment. That was when I first learned that Beth was to take Harry's place.'

Paget shook his head impatiently. 'You have worked for Arthur Gresham as his private secretary for years, Miss Fairmont. Not only that, but by your own admission the two of you are lovers. And yet you say you had no idea that Gresham intended to get rid of Harry Beecham and promote Beth Smallwood in his place? – a person who, by all accounts, was neither equipped nor ready for the job. Why do you think that was, Miss Fairmont? Why do you think he never mentioned it to you? Weren't you just a little bit suspicious about what had gone on between Arthur Gresham – the man you say you intend to marry – and Beth Smallwood when you saw the state she was in when she left his office?'

Colour flared in Rachel's cheeks.

'Weren't you jealous, Miss Fairmont? Weren't you upset?'

'No! Of course not. Arthur isn't...It wasn't like that,' she protested, but her voice trembled and she looked as if she were on the verge of tears.

'What time did Mr Gresham leave your flat that Monday evening?'

The question caught Rachel by surprise. She looked confused. 'I – I don't know, exactly,' she said. 'Why? What are you getting at?'

'Please try to think. It is important.'

Rachel tried to look at him, but her eyes slid away before his penetrating gaze. 'It wasn't long after Beth rang,' she said in a subdued voice. 'We talked about what she'd said for a few minutes and then he left because he had a meeting with Ivor Trent.'

'And Beth rang about eight?'

'Yes. About then. It was about fifteen minutes after Arthur arrived, and he usually gets there about quarter to eight.'

'And he left shortly after Beth called.'

'Yes.'

'So that would be what? Quarter-past eight? Twenty past?'

Rachel sighed. 'Something like that,' she agreed wearily. 'But I fail to see what...'

'Certainly no later than half-past? Right?'

Rachel hung her head. 'I-don't-know!' she said despairingly through clenched teeth. 'I *told* you: I-wasn't-watching-the-damned-clock!'

'No, of course you wouldn't be,' said Paget quietly. 'I'm sorry if my questions have upset you, Miss Fairmont, but we do have to make sure we have things clear in our minds. You did the right thing by coming in, and I do appreciate it.' He glanced at the time. 'Was there anything else?'

Rachel shook her head. She looked utterly miserable, and it was clear she was far from convinced that she had done the right thing by coming in.

Paget stood up and came round the desk. 'Sergeant Tregalles will take you downstairs where your statement will be recorded and typed up,' he told her. 'Do you need a lift home?'

'No, I have my car,' she said dully as she rose to her feet. Her eyes sought Paget's. 'You're wrong about Arthur,' she said. 'I *know* him. I know him better than anyone. He isn't like that. You must believe me; he isn't like that at all.'

Tregalles had just returned with a copy of Rachel Fairmont's statement when Grace Lovett appeared in the open doorway. She looked tall and slim and elegant in her two-piece linen suit with shoes to match. Her blonde hair rested gently on her shoulders, glinting softly beneath the office lights, and her eyes were the colour of a summer sea.

'Am I interrupting?' she asked hesitantly. 'I could come back again at a more convenient time.'

'No, no. Not at all, Grace,' said Paget, motioning her to come in. 'Tregalles and I were just about to call it a day. What brings you here?'

Tregalles stood aside for Grace to enter. She entered like a breath of spring, fresh and clean and tantalizingly fragrant, and the sergeant sighed inwardly. He couldn't for the life of him imagine why

Grace Lovett was still single. Nor could he understand Paget's apparent indifference to her charms.

Paget waved her to a seat. 'Now, what can we do for you?'

Grace undid the tie on the folder she'd been carrying, and pulled out several sheets of paper stapled together. 'I had to come over this way,' she said by way of explanation, 'so I brought this with me. It's the report on Mrs Smallwood's clothing – the items you asked me to recover from her house and send over for analysis.'

'That was very good of you, Grace,' said Paget as he took the report from her. 'Does it help us at all?'

'I think it does, sir. As you will see, the condition of the under-garments tends to confirm that there was sexual activity, but it is impossible to state accurately when that activity took place. How-ever, given the condition of the rest of Beth Smallwood's clothing, and the manner in which she kept them, I think it would be safe to assume that she changed her underclothes daily, and they would then be washed, so it could be inferred that the activity took place earlier that day. Also, there are traces of seminal fluids, but they will have to undergo further tests before any conclusions can be drawn.'

Grace delivered the information dispassionately as if giving evidence in court, and Paget found himself admiring her for it.

'But the most interesting part – at least I think so,' Grace continued, 'is the information regarding the fibres found in Beth Smallwood's hair and on her undergarments. As you will see, sir, they are carpet fibres, easily identifiable if only – and here's the catch – you have some idea where to look for the carpet.'

Paget, who had been skim-reading as she talked, looked at her for a moment, then smiled. 'I think I know exactly where to look,' he said quietly. 'Can I keep this?' He tapped the report.

'Of, course, sir. That is your copy.'

Paget rose to his feet, and Grace had no option but to follow his example. 'Thank you, Grace,' he said warmly. 'I appreciate your bringing this over here personally. This could help a lot.'

Grace Lovett smiled in return and allowed herself to be shep-herded to the door. She had hoped to stay longer, but she had been late getting there, and now everyone else had gone home. Still, he had said he appreciated what she'd done.

Tregalles was on his feet, holding the door. His face was solemn but his eyes twinkled. His glance flicked toward Paget then back to her. He winked.

Grace felt her face grow warm, and she could feel the sergeant's eyes upon her all the way down the corridor. *Next* time, she promised herself, she would make damned sure that Tregalles was somewhere else before she came to see his boss.

CHAPTER 30

Paget took copies of the forensic reports home with him that evening, but by the time he'd waded through the jargon and officialese, and mentally followed the movements of everyone who had been in the church the night Beth Smallwood died, he found himself nodding off.

The answer, he felt sure, lay in the reports before him, but he couldn't see it. There was something he had read that had triggered a response, and yet for the life of him he could not bring it into focus.

He yawned and glanced at the time. It was only nine o'clock, but perhaps a shower and an early night would clear his head. Perhaps a fresh look at things would bring the answer in the morning.

The phone rang. He groaned. It was bound to be something to do with work. He scooped it up. 'Paget.' His tone was clipped.

'Neil?'

'Andrea?'

'It *is* you,' she said. 'For a moment there I thought...' Andrea laughed nervously. 'Sorry, Neil. What I meant to say was, thank you very much for the flowers and the card. The flowers are beautiful, and the verse was lovely. You really shouldn't have. But I'm glad you did. They really cheered me up. I should have rung earlier, but...' Andrea's voice took on an anxious tone. 'I'm not interrupting anything, am I?'

'No, no, of course not,' he assured her. 'I'm glad you liked the flowers.' His mind raced. Andrea sounded so pleased.

'They're lovely,' Andrea said again. She paused, hesitated. 'I'm told you were enquiring about me at the hospital today. It was very good of you to come. Sorry I wasn't there, but I was anxious to get home as soon as possible. I didn't want Sarah to worry.'

'It was ...' He was about to lie; to say he just happened to be there. He changed his mind. 'I was worried about you, Andrea,' he said. 'You could have been killed by that crazy pair. Are you quite sure you're all right?'

'I'm fine. Really.' Andrea gripped the phone a little tighter and took a deep breath. 'Neil ...'

'Yes?'

'I – I was wondering ... I mean, I really do appreciate your concern, and I'd like to thank you, well, personally.' Her face felt warm and her mouth was suddenly dry. 'Perhaps ...' Her courage failed her. All the things she'd so carefully rehearsed vanished in a cloud of self-doubt. 'Perhaps, next time you're in the hospital I'll have a chance to do that,' she finished lamely.

Somehow he had expected more. There had been something in her voice, a warmth that had made him think ... He dismissed the thought impatiently.

'There's really no need,' he said gruffly.

'Well ... In any case, thanks again, Neil. Goodbye.'

Andrea set the phone gently in its cradle and closed her eyes. 'Why?' she demanded despairingly of the empty room. 'Why is it so damned hard to simply ask the man to dinner? What is it that makes me so unsure of myself when I'm talking to him?'

A sound came from the partly open bedroom door, and Andrea rose to her feet, still mentally shaking her head at her own cowardice. She stood for a moment inside the doorway, watching Sarah as she slept. The child had kicked the covers off in her sleep, and lay with one arm hanging over the side. As Andrea went to her, she recalled the terror of the night she'd thought Sarah was in Victor's hands, and she shivered violently. She'd trusted a man once, and it could have cost Sarah her life; she dare not make the same mistake again. Not that Neil could be compared to Victor. But then, Victor had seemed all right at first ...

Suddenly everything boiled up inside her. Why couldn't she and Neil have just remained friends? It had been all right, then. She had felt safe with him. Comfortable. Until that night before Christmas when he'd looked at her and she knew; knew that he wanted to be more than 'just a friend'. Not that he'd said anything, but she could see it in his eyes; sense it in his voice – and she'd wanted to respond.

208

And that had frightened her, because she knew she could not – dare not allow this man to get too close to her. And then it was too late.

Andrea sighed softly as she moved to the bedside. Why did everything have to be so damned complicated?

Wednesday – 22 May

As Paget was about to enter the building, a fair-haired young man burst through the doors and almost knocked the chief inspector over. Maltby. A junior member of the CPS, and certainly the most impetuous.

'Oh, God! Sorry, sir,' he apologized as he recognized the chief inspector. 'I didn't mean...I really am sorry, sir, but it's the wife. I mean I'm going to see the wife...It's a boy! Seven pounds four ounces. I was supposed to be there, but it came early. I mean *he* came early. Janet will kill me.' The prospect didn't seem to worry him.

'Your first, I take it?' said Paget, hiding his amusement.

'Yes, sir. Oh, God! I almost forgot. Have one of these, sir.' Maltby reached into an inside pocket and took out a handful of cigars. He thrust one into Paget's hand. 'And I really am sorry, sir.' He patted Paget's arms as if to make sure he was all right, then leapt the remaining steps and was off like a hare.

Paget still had the cigar in his hand when he reached his office. He had no intention of smoking it, but no doubt Alcott would take it off his hands. He smiled as he rolled the Cellophane-wrapped cigar between his fingers and thought about young Maltby. A son. Must be quite a feeling.

He was about to put the cigar away when he paused. Cellophane, and a partial print – and something he'd meant to check on with Forensic at the beginning of the week. It might mean nothing, but then again...

He picked up the phone.

Arthur Gresham arrived alone. Miss Fairmont, he explained, was not well, and had not come in this morning.

'Nothing serious, I hope?' said Paget as he led the way into the interview room.

Gresham looked around the room with obvious distaste as he took his seat at the table. 'No,' he said, dismissing the idea with a shrug. 'Touch of flu or some such thing, I expect. Came on yesterday afternoon and she left early. Made it damned awkward at the audit meeting, I can tell you. Had to bring in one of the other girls to take the minutes, and she didn't have shorthand. Went on till after six.'

Gresham frowned as Tregalles switched on the tape recorder and entered the time and date and those present.

Gresham looked at his watch. 'Is all this really necessary, Chief Inspector?' he asked irritably. 'I thought that all I had to do this morning was correct my statement. I do have other business to attend to, you know.'

'I appreciate that, sir,' said Paget blandly, 'but there are one or two other matters that have arisen since last we spoke. You don't *object* to helping us with our enquiries, do you, sir?'

Gresham eyed the tape recorder speculatively. 'Of course not,' he said in a milder tone. 'That is why I'm here.'

'Good.' Paget leaned back in his chair and nodded at Tregalles.

The sergeant opened the file in front of him. 'Let's begin with what you told us yesterday,' he said. 'You told us that you rang Miss Fairmont about ten o'clock on the night Beth Smallwood was killed, and she told you of the call she had received from Mrs Smallwood. Is that correct, sir?'

Gresham scowled. The fact that it was the sergeant rather then the chief inspector who was asking the questions irritated the bank manager.

'That's what I said, Sergeant, and Miss Fairmont confirmed it if you recall.'

'And you say you made that call from the public telephone outside the Three Crowns. Is that correct?'

Gresham appealed to Paget. 'You know all this already,' he said.

'If you'll just bear with us, Mr Gresham. We do have to make sure we have everything straight before it is committed to paper.'

Gresham looked less than mollified as he turned to Tregalles. 'What was the question?' he asked sharply. Tregalles repeated the question. 'Yes, yes,' he said irritably, 'that is what I said.'

'You are quite sure of that, sir?'

'I wouldn't have said it if I didn't mean it, Sergeant,' Gresham flared.

Tregalles was unperturbed. 'You see, sir, the reason I wanted you to be sure is because that particular telephone has not been working for more than three weeks. How do you account for that?'

'Well, it was working when I used it,' Gresham said belligerently. I should know. And as I said, Miss Fairmont will back me up.'

'Yes, well, we'll come to that in a moment, sir. But I'm afraid British Telecom's records don't back you up.'

Gresham turned to Paget once again. 'Obviously the records are wrong,' he blustered. 'Besides, what difference does it make which telephone I used? Miss Fairmont has told you ...'

'Miss Fairmont,' Tregalles broke in smoothly, 'has retracted the statement she made in your office yesterday. She now says there was no such call made that night.' Tregalles tapped the folder. 'She says you were with her in her flat when Mrs Smallwood rang.'

Gresham's eyes widened. 'That's preposterous!' he said. 'When did she tell you this?'

'Late yesterday afternoon.'

Gresham shook his head as if in disbelief. He took off his glasses and began to polish them.

'Miss Fairmont came in,' Tregalles went on, 'because she realized that we did not believe the fabrication about the phone call – to say nothing of her purported lapse of memory regarding that call – and she hoped to clear things up by telling us the truth. She also confirmed something we had discovered for ourselves – that you and she were lovers.'

Gresham opened his mouth and closed it again. 'I don't believe you,' he said unsteadily.

'That we knew about it or that Miss Fairmont confirmed it?' Paget put in. 'I can assure you, sir, that both statements are correct. We have witnesses who have seen you visit Miss Fairmont's flat a number of times; witnesses who have seen you park your distinctive car beside the butcher's shop in Lyall Street, and others who will testify that you were *not* at Golden Meadows when you said you were.'

Gresham's face had paled. He moistened his lips. 'There is no need to go on,' he said stiffly. 'You have made your point, Chief Inspector. What is it you want of me?'

'Miss Fairmont told us that Beth Smallwood intended to talk to the police on Tuesday morning,' Tregalles said. 'She says that news upset you. Why was that, sir?'

Gresham half closed his eyes. God! What else had that woman said? 'I didn't know what Beth was talking about,' he said. 'I wondered if it had something to do with the bank. And if it had, I wondered why Beth hadn't spoken to me first.'

'I think you knew very well – or thought you knew – what Beth Smallwood was talking about,' said Paget. 'And I think you were scared to death.'

Gresham's face reddened. 'I don't know ...' he began, but Paget cut him off.

'Then let me remind you, sir. You thought that Beth was going to tell the police about what happened in your office that afternoon. You thought she was going to tell them how she'd been raped on your office floor. But you couldn't let that happen, could you? You couldn't allow Beth Smallwood to go to the police with her story. Even if the charge could not be proved, an investigation into your activities would soon reveal your affair with Miss Fairmont, and if that became public knowledge, you'd be on very shaky ground with the bank. Neither, I suspect, would your wife be all that pleased, and you couldn't afford that, could you? Especially if she wanted a divorce. That possibility alone would spell financial disaster for you, wouldn't it, Mr Gresham?'

Gresham's glasses came off again. 'That's ...' he began shakily, but Paget cut him off again.

'Beth Smallwood was raped that Monday afternoon,' he said harshly. 'When she came out of your office she was in tears. She dashed straight into the Ladies and stayed there out of sight until Miss Fairmont went in to find out what was wrong. That was at least half an hour after Beth Smallwood left your office, Mr Gresham, and she was still so agitated that she couldn't even hold her handbag without spilling everything on the floor. Does that sound like the behaviour of a woman who is happy about an unexpected promotion?'

All colour had deserted Gresham's face. Sweat glistened on his brow. 'You can't prove any ...' he began, but Paget cut him off yet again.

'Can't *prove* it?' he echoed contemptuously. 'We know from the medical evidence that Beth Smallwood was raped. We know it happened in the afternoon. We know that you had been pursuing her for weeks; your own staff will testify to that! You, sir, cannot keep your hands off women, and there are those who would be only too happy to testify to that!' Paget reached across the table and grabbed Gresham's hand. He turned it palm down and jabbed an accusing finger at the four small marks where a fork had once pierced the skin. Gresham snatched his hand away.

'There were fibres found on Beth Smallwood's clothing,' he went on as he released the hand. 'Her underclothing, Mr Gresham. Carpet fibres which will be compared with the carpet in your office.'

Gresham's face was ashen. His lips trembled but no words would come.

'I think that when you left Rachel Fairmont's flat that Monday night,' Paget continued, 'you went directly to the church where you knew the woman you had raped would be alone. You went inside and found her by the chancel steps, preparing to put new candles in their holders. You grabbed one of the candlesticks and struck her, then struck again to make sure that she was dead.

'But you had to make sure that no one looked in your direction for a motive. You had to make it look as if someone else had done it; a random killing by some unknown. You wiped the candlesticks, set them on the altar and lit them, then took money and credit cards from Beth's handbag to make it look as if she had been attacked while praying.'

Gresham was shaking his head violently. 'You're wrong!' he gasped. 'I didn't kill Beth. I wasn't anywhere near the church. I had to go to a meeting with the city planner. I . . .'

'Your meeting with Ivor Trent was for nine o'clock,' Tregalles interjected coldly. 'You left your lover's flat before eight thirty, and it takes no more than three minutes to drive to the Three Crowns from there. Yet you didn't arrive until just after nine, and you were so preoccupied that Trent put the meeting off until the following day. Where were you during that half-hour, Mr Gresham? Where were you at the very time that Beth Smallwood was being beaten to death?'

Gresham's glasses skittered out of his hands and slid across the table, but he made no attempt to retrieve them. 'I swear I didn't kill her,' he whispered. 'I was driving. Rachel kept going on and on at me about that afternoon until I was sick of it. I just wanted to get away. I didn't know what to do. I still didn't know what to do when I realized it was nine o'clock and I had to go and meet Trent.'

The bank manager drew in a shaky breath, and with it tried to rally. 'It – it wasn't rape,' he stammered. 'Beth was grateful. She was attracted to me, and ...' He broke off as he saw the expression on the sergeant's face.

'Would you like to see the photographs of her body?' Tregalles growled. 'See the bruises? The gouges in her flesh? Don't try to tell me it wasn't rape! And once they've seen the pictures, I don't think a jury would think so either.'

Gresham slumped in his chair and closed his eyes. His face glistened.

Paget eyed him with contempt. He felt no pity for the man. But for all the circumstantial evidence, there was not a single piece of hard evidence that put Gresham at the church when Beth was killed.

'Why did you try to return to the church the following morning?' he asked abruptly.

Gresham seized on the question. 'I wasn't trying to go to the church,' he said. 'Why would I? I didn't know Beth was dead. I was going to catch her before she had a chance to go to the police. I was going to try to talk her out of it. Offer her money if I had to. Anything ...'

'Including murder?' Tregalles said.

'No! For God's sake, why won't you believe me? All right! Perhaps I was a bit ... a bit rough on Beth, but I didn't kill her. Why would I go back to see her in the morning if I'd killed her the night before?'

'But we don't know that for certain, do we, sir?' Tregalles countered. 'You *say* you were going to Beth's house, but you could have been returning to the church. Seeing the police there must have come as a shock. You hadn't expected the body to be discovered quite so soon, had you, sir? So you started to turn to make it *look* as if you intended to go down Farrow Lane – even made a point of it by arguing with the policeman on duty. But I'm curious, Mr Gresham: what was it that you thought you'd left behind?'

Blood rose in Gresham's neck and his face became contorted as he half rose in his seat. 'I wasn't *going* to the damned church,' he screamed across the table. Spittle flew from his mouth. 'I keep telling you, I didn't know that Beth was dead!'

CHAPTER 31

Paget tossed Gresham's statement on the desk. 'We still need proof,' he said wearily. 'There is nothing here to show that Gresham was ever in that church. Nothing at all.' He leaned back in his chair and stared at the ceiling as if searching for inspiration. 'Why *did* he go back on Tuesday morning?'

Tregalles shrugged and shook his head. 'I spoke to Dandridge again, and he insists that Gresham was trying to go down Farrow Lane, and the only thing that could possibly be of interest to Gresham down there is Beth Smallwood's house.'

Paget brought his gaze down off the ceiling. 'Or Beth herself,' he said.

Tregalles frowned. 'But she was dead.'

Paget nodded. 'Exactly. Perhaps Gresham *is* telling us the truth.'

'There is no way that man was telling the truth,' Tregalles growled. 'Look at what he did to that poor woman. Look at how he fell apart in there. He's as guilty as sin!'

'I agree. Guilty of abusing Beth Smallwood – but is he guilty of *killing* her? We would like to think he is because of what he did to her, but is he? The evidence against Beecham is far more convincing.'

Tregalles shook his head stubbornly. 'He must have left something behind,' he said. 'Prints, hair, fibres from his clothing. He couldn't just come and go without leaving a trace.'

'I went over everything last night,' said Paget, 'and there was nothing there that I could ...' He stopped abruptly. 'Or was there?' he said softly. He reached for the folder on his desk and began flipping through the pages. 'Prints,' he muttered as he searched. 'Prints and fibres. Yes, here it is.' He quickly scanned the page and marked it.

He picked up the phone and punched in Starkie's number.

'Reg. Paget,' he said when the pathologist answered. 'Tell me again about the fibres you found caught in Beth Smallwood's nails. I have the analysis from the lab, but I want you to tell me exactly what you saw when you first examined the body.'

Paget had just put the phone down and was about to leave the office with Tregalles when it rang insistently. He paused, half inclined to leave it, but turned back and snatched it up.

'Paget,' he said brusquely.

'PC Toogood here, sir,' said a voice that smacked of rural Shropshire. 'Sorry to trouble you, sir, but we have a domestic situation here. Woman beat up by her boyfriend, and she refuses to talk to anyone but you, sir. Says she has something important to say about that killing in the church last week. Name of Fairmont. A Miss Rachel Fairmont.'

'Is Miss Fairmont all right?'

'She'll have a bit of a shiner, but no bones broken or anything like that.'

'You're ringing from her flat?'

'Yes, sir.'

'Do you have a WPC there?'

'Yes, sir. Sergeant Radcliffe – he's my sergeant – sent one along straightaway. WPC Cooper.'

'Right. I'm on my way. Be there in ten minutes.'

Rachel Fairmont sat huddled in a chair, her long legs tucked under her. She held a cold compress to her face, lifting the cloth just long enough for Paget to inspect the fast-closing eye beneath.

'Gresham?' he asked.

She nodded and winced. 'He's gone mad,' she said. 'He burst in here shouting and swearing. He wouldn't give me a chance to explain. Just kept screaming at me and shoving me across the room until I was backed up against the wall. Then he hit me.'

Rachel put the cloth back in place and closed her eyes. 'It was him, wasn't it?' she whispered, choking back a sob. 'I didn't want to believe it. He swore to me that he had nothing to do with it, but he was so frightened when he left here that night. Beth had told me she was going to the church, and I'd mentioned it to Arthur. He must have gone straight over there to talk to her, and . . .' Her voice broke and she buried her face in her hands. 'I'm sure he didn't mean it,' she sobbed. 'It must have been an accident.'

Paget glanced at Tregalles who was scribbling furiously in his notebook. He pulled up a chair and sat down facing Rachel.

'You knew what happened in Gresham's office that afternoon, didn't you, Miss Fairmont?' he said quietly.

Rachel lifted her head but she wouldn't look at him. 'That's what you and Gresham were arguing about that night when Beth rang, wasn't it? Gresham told us that you kept going on and on at him until he couldn't stand it any longer and he left. You must have known for some time that Gresham was turning his attention to Beth Smallwood – even the tellers knew he'd been pursuing her – and when Beth came out of that office, you knew exactly what had taken place. You tackled him about it that evening. And then when Beth rang and spoke of going to the police the following morning, you thought she meant to tell them about what had happened in Gresham's office. And that's what you told Gresham. But that was wrong. Because of her swollen tongue, her words were garbled, and you misunderstood. What Beth wanted to talk to the police about was her son, Lenny, who had just beaten her up, and to tell them that she'd lied for him in court.

'Arthur Gresham was getting tired of you, wasn't he? He liked to play the field. He never did intend to marry you; he had too much to lose. He has no money of his own; his wife has it all, and he wasn't going to jeopardize that!'

Rachel was shaking her head vigorously. 'That's not true!' she protested. 'He *was* going to marry me. He was! He swore to me that night that it was me he loved, and he begged me to forgive him.' Her face darkened. 'It was Beth. She led him on. It wasn't his fault. He loves me, and he'll need me more than ever now.'

Rachel saw the look in Paget's eyes as he regarded her swollen face. 'Arthur didn't mean to hurt me,' she said defiantly. 'He was angry. He thought that I'd betrayed him.' She shivered and tugged the loose sweater she was wearing closer to her. 'If only he'd told me,' she ended miserably.

'That's a very nice sweater,' Paget observed. 'I noticed it last Sunday. You were wearing it then.' From the corner of his eye he saw Tregalles look up, obviously puzzled by the seemingly unrelated question.

'It's Arthur's, actually...' Rachel stopped. 'But what has that to do with...'

'And you were wearing it the night Beth Smallwood died,' Paget continued as if she hadn't spoken.

'Yes, but...'

'It's wool, isn't it? Vicuña wool?'

The woman remained silent.

'I can have the constable check the label.'

Rachel's lips set in a thin line. 'So it's vicuña,' she flared. 'But what that has to do with anything I don't know.'

'Don't you?' asked Paget softly. 'Then let me explain, Miss Fairmont. Let me tell you what *I* think happened a week ago Monday when Beth Smallwood was called into Arthur Gresham's office. In fact, let's go back further than that, to when Arthur Gresham had to decide how best to cut his staff to satisfy the dictates of head office – and himself.

'He'd begun to take an interest in Beth Smallwood recently, but Beth was doing her best to stay out of his way. But Gresham knew, as most of you did at the bank, that Beth was living virtually hand-to-mouth. She would do almost anything to keep her job, and she'd jump at the chance of a promotion, no matter what the cost to her personally. Which was what Gresham was counting on. In fact, she was even more desperate than he suspected, because Lenny was bleeding her dry and she had turned to embezzlement to try to keep the boy out of trouble.

'By getting rid of Harry Beecham, Gresham would save the bank a senior man's salary and perks, thereby enhancing his own image as a manager. He would then make Beth Smallwood an offer she couldn't refuse, and she would have no choice but to submit to his demands.'

Rachel put her hands to her ears. 'I'm not going to listen to this,' she whispered fiercely. 'You're wrong! Absolutely wrong!'

Paget continued as if she hadn't spoken. 'But Gresham got carried away that afternoon, and he raped Beth in his office, didn't he, Miss Fairmont? You were sitting there outside his door. You *knew* what had gone on behind that door, didn't you? You *knew* that it was Beth he wanted, not you, and that's what you were arguing about that night when Beth made that very unfortunate call to you. She didn't want to talk to Gresham, not after what he'd done to her, so she called you instead. She said she was going to the police, but her words were garbled because of her swollen tongue, and you thought she was about to turn Gresham in.'

Rachel's face crumpled. 'I shouldn't have told Arthur,' she whispered. 'He was terrified. He could lose everything. He said Beth had to be stopped, but I never dreamed he meant . . .'

Paget was shaking his head. 'Oh, no, Miss Fairmont,' he said softly. 'It wasn't Arthur Gresham who went to the church that night. It was you!'

The woman became very still.

'Gresham had a lot to lose, but he was confident that he could buy Beth off with money. Which was why he set out early next morning to see her at home. He had no idea that she was dead. He was trying to get down Farrow Lane to see her, but was stopped by the police.

'But you, Miss Fairmont, you had set your heart on marrying Gresham, and if Beth went to the police and charged him with rape, you'd lose everything. Your affair with Gresham was bound to come out; your hope of marriage would be gone, and where would that leave you?'

Rachel had dropped the compress and was shaking her head violently back and forth. 'It's not true!' she cried desperately. 'None of this is true. It was Arthur. He's the one who said she had to be stopped. He's the one who raped her, for God's sake!'

Paget nodded slowly. 'Yes,' he said quietly, 'he raped her and you knew it. You tackled him about it the moment he arrived here that night. And when he left, you got into your car, drove over to the church, and confronted Beth. You didn't even give her a chance to explain, did you? Why should you? You were so sure you knew why she was going to the police, and you wanted her out of the way. Permanently. As long as she was around she was a threat. Knowing Gresham as you did, you thought he might even talk her round and take *her* as his mistress.'

Rachel squeezed her eyes tightly shut as if by doing so she could shut him out, but Paget continued on relentlessly.

'You confronted Beth, grabbed the candlestick and hit her. She tried to defend herself, so you hit her again. But in going down Beth grabbed your sweater, the one you have on, and fibres from it were caught in her nails. I doubt if you even noticed.

'Then, of course, you had to try to make it look as if it was a random killing for money. You decided to make it look as if Beth was taken unawares while kneeling at the chancel steps, and try to hide the murder weapon at the same time. So you pulled the Cellophane wrapper off the new candles, wiped the holders clean, then set them back on the altar and lit them.

'You wiped everything you'd touched, or thought you had, but you forgot the Cellophane wrapper on the floor. I doubt if it occurred to you that prints could be taken from it in its crumpled state, but they can. And you forgot one other thing: that you'd handled some of the items in Beth's handbag when you helped her pick them up earlier in the afternoon.

'Forensic have a match. The irony of it is that if you hadn't told me you had helped Beth put things back in her handbag that day, we wouldn't have had any reason to ask you for your prints, and chances are they would have gone unidentified. As it was, the connection almost slipped past them, and it wasn't until today that I was able to get confirmation.'

Rachel Fairmont looked very small and vulnerable as she huddled in the chair. She raised a tear-stained face to Paget.

'I don't know anything about any Cellophane,' she said, 'but you have to believe me. It was Arthur. When I came round to see you yesterday, I thought by telling the truth I would be helping him. I had no idea until he stormed in here today that it was he who had killed Beth.'

Rachel buried her face in her hands. 'I thought he was going to kill me,' she whispered hoarsely. 'I've never been so frightened in my life.'

She unfolded her long legs and sat up straight. 'As for the sweater, I told you it was Arthur's originally, and he was the one who was wearing it when he left here that night.'

'You told me *you* were wearing it that night.'

'I was, but...' Rachel hesitated and lowered her eyes. 'Arthur liked me to be wearing it when he came to me. I – I don't wear anything underneath, you see, and he liked to take it off me when we made love. When Beth rang, I slipped on my housecoat to answer the phone, and Arthur put on the sweater when he got out of bed.'

'Are you trying to tell me that you made love that night?' asked Paget sceptically. 'I find that very hard to believe, Miss Fairmont.'

Rachel lifted her head and looked directly at him. 'We were in bed when Beth rang,' she said simply. 'But Arthur was in such a state when he left that he simply forgot to take the sweater off. He

220

brought it back the following night and picked up his own sweater. That's the truth, Chief Inspector.'

'The truth?' Paget sighed. 'We shall see,' he said quietly. He motioned to WPC Cooper, who had been standing unobtrusively in the background all this time. 'Help Miss Fairmont get properly dressed,' he told her. 'And she's not to wear that sweater. We will need it for evidence. I'm charging her with murder.'

'They're both down there now,' said Paget, 'each accusing the other of killing Beth Smallwood.' He sat across the desk from Alcott in the superintendent's office.

'It was a good thing Rachel wasn't in the room when we read him extracts from her statement. As it was he had to be restrained. When he calmed down, he told us he'd been trying to break off with her for weeks, but she wouldn't have it. He claims that she flew at him that night; accused him of raping Beth – which of course he did but is still trying to deny – and of trying to break his promise of marriage to her. Which, incidentally, he denies ever making. As for the sweater, he swears that it was she who was wearing it when he left that night.

'As far as I'm concerned,' he continued, 'they can argue all they like about who was wearing the sweater, but it will be the fingerprint that will clinch it. Rachel couldn't help but know what had happened in Gresham's office that afternoon, and when Beth rang that night and talked of going to the police, Rachel saw a way to get rid of Beth and – she hoped – make Gresham grateful to her for saving his skin. But Gresham wanted to be rid of her, and when Rachel realized she couldn't hold him, she turned on him. I think she came here quite deliberately yesterday afternoon to throw suspicion on him while pretending to defend him.'

'What did Trent say Gresham was wearing when they met?' Alcott asked.

'Trent *thinks* he was wearing a turtleneck beneath his jacket, but he can't be certain.'

'So it all comes down to a fingerprint,' Alcott mused. 'They both had motive.'

'That's right, sir, but I think we'll find that Rachel Fairmont is the more determined of the two, and she had more to lose – at least she thought she had. Regardless of what we may think of Gresham, I think she really loved him, and when she saw him slipping away from her, she was prepared to do anything to get him back. So, when it looked as if Beth was going to have Gresham charged, she took matters into her own hands.'

Alcott shook his head. 'I really thought it was Beecham,' he said almost wistfully, 'especially when his prints were found in the church.'

'So did I at first,' said Paget, 'but Beth was dead when he arrived. Which explains why Rudge heard nothing before Beecham ran out. Beecham came storming into the church, probably at least a little drunk, and banged the door. Rudge heard it, but by the time he got to the bottom of the stairs, Beecham had discovered Beth's body. No doubt that sobered him up in a hurry, and all he wanted to do was get out of there as fast as possible.'

Alcott scowled and drew deeply on his cigarette. 'She's liable to get away with it, you know,' he said. 'A good brief will use Beecham as a red herring and create so much doubt in the minds of jurors that she could get off, despite the fingerprint. Juries are so bloody unpredictable. You never know what they'll do.' The superintendent rose from his seat and stretched.

'Let's hope they get it right this time,' said Paget as he, too, got to his feet.

They left the office together. 'Mr Brock wants us both in his office first thing tomorrow morning,' Alcott said. 'He'll need a full briefing before he talks to the media.'

Paget suppressed a smile. Trust Brock to step in at the last minute and take the credit.

As they came out of the building, Alcott nodded in the direction of the pub across the street and glanced at his watch. 'Still time for a quick one,' he observed, 'and young what's-is-name will be disappointed if we don't stop in for at least one.'

Paget looked at him blankly.

'Maltby. Wife had a boy this morning. Everybody's invited to wet the baby's head. You *are* coming, aren't you, Paget? I mean, it's not as if you have anybody waiting for you at home, is it? Come on. We can't disappoint the lad.'

Paget hesitated only for a moment. He had thought of stopping in at the hospital. Just on the off-chance that Andrea might be there. Still, even if she were there, she'd probably be busy. She had phoned him to thank him for the flowers, but it would be foolish to read too much into that. Anyone would have done the same.

He became aware that Alcott was waiting for a reply.

'Why not?' he said. 'As you say, it's not as if there is anyone waiting for me at home.'

He was home by ten o'clock, having slipped away from the party as soon as he decently could. Paget had all but forgotten how noisy a pub full of boisterous young coppers could be, and his ears were still ringing as he climbed the stairs. The acrid smell of smoke and stale beer clung to his clothes, and he undressed quickly before stepping into the shower. Hot water poured over him, and he turned his face to it, luxuriating in its warm embrace.

His mind began to drift back to the day's events. There were still many things to do as far as the case was concerned, of course, but they would be dealt with in the days to come. As far as he was concerned, the case was closed.

There was no doubt in his mind that Rachel was the one who had gone to the church that night. The fingerprint on the candle wrapper proved beyond a doubt that she was there, and since it was on the *inside* of the wrapper, it had to have been put there after Mrs Turvey saw the candles sealed in their wrapper when they slipped out of Beth Smallwood's bag. Paget had rung Mrs Turvey himself to check on that very point.

But enough of that, he told himself firmly as he stepped out of the shower and got ready for bed. He stifled a yawn and thought of young Maltby and his friends back at the pub, and wondered how many of them would make it into work next morning – and how they would feel if they did.

His eyes fell on Jill's picture on the bedside table as he slid beneath the covers, and memories of other evenings, of other celebrations, came flooding in. Memories of the days when he and Jill were together. Memories that would remain no matter what.

But he was beginning to realize that *memories* of the past and *living* in the past were two very different things. It had taken him a long time to recognize that. It would probably take even longer for him to accept it, but it was a start, he told himself. It was a start.

He turned out the light and lay there staring into the darkness. He must phone Patrick in the morning. Tell him he'd be there in

London to meet him and Louise when they arrived next month. And, painful as it would be, he must find the words to break the news of Jill's death to his old friend. An old friend he'd long suspected of being in love with Jill himself.

DATE